Dead Long Enough

James Hawes was born in 1960. His first two novels, *A White Merc with Fins* and *Rancid Aluminium*, were both bestsellers; both are currently being filmed. He lives in Cardiff.

Dead Long Enough

James Hawes

JONATHAN CAPE
LONDON

Published by Jonathan Cape 2000

2 4 6 8 10 9 7 5 3 1

First published in Great Britain in 2000 by
Jonathan Cape
Random House, 20 Vauxhall Bridge Road,
London SW1V 2SA

Random House Australia (Pty) Limited
20 Alfred Street, Milsons Point, Sydney,
New South Wales 2061, Australia

Random House New Zealand Limited
18 Poland Road, Glenfield,
Auckland 10, New Zealand

Random House (Pty) Limited
Endulini, 5A Jubilee Road, Parktown 2193, South Africa

The Random House Group Limited Reg. No. 954009

A CIP catalogue record for this book
is available from the British Library

ISBN 0 224 04468 0

Papers used by The Random House Group Limited are natural,
recyclable products made from wood grown in sustainable forests;
the manufacturing processes conform to the environmental
regulations of the country of origin

Printed and bound in Great Britain by
Mackays of Chatham PLC

For the avoidance of doubt or worse, the fatal incident described in this story is in no way a comment on any real event.

One way or another, this book is indebted to Tara Fitzgerald, Miranda Knight, Marega Palser, Hilary Hodgson, Debbie Ballin, Phil David, Kieran O'Conor, Jeremy Knight FSA, Prof. Martin Swales, Eamon O'Ciosain, Paul O'Doherty, Garda H.G., Matt Fitzpatrick and all at Dunboyne, Jon Sheaf, Flo Paul, Greg Cullen, Allie Saunders, Fr Brendan Devlin SJ – and the two large gentlemen from Notting Hill CID who knocked me up at 6 a.m. sometime in the mid–'8os.

Special thanks to Ed Thomas, Rhys Ifans, Peter Thompson and Teresa Pritchard for certain lines directly lifted, to my sister Annie for writerly company when it mattered and to Liliosa Makurah.

Dead Long Enough

Eternity and Suchlike

Maybe it all happened because when Harry met Shnade again, he was (though he would never have admitted it) kind of on the rebound in a certain way. Or maybe because when Shnade met Harry again, she was (though she would never have admitted it) kind of on the rebound in a different way. Or maybe because all of us over thirty, Harry and Shnade included, are (though we will never admit it) kind of on the rebound from Eden one way or another: our guard is always halfway down, our chins and our hearts are just hanging out there, asking to be taken. Particularly when we are far from home and the lights are dim and we have done a toot or two too many.

(She isn't really called *Shnade*, of course. When I first heard her name I remember wondering if it was *Sihneahd* or *Scineagdh* or something like that. But I didn't have *The Observer's Book of Crap Celtic Groupie Names* with me, despite that being the type of pub it was, and *Shnade* was what I heard, and is what I called her, and is what she is, to me at any rate, every time I think of her. Which is, frankly, a little too often for Peckham and my own logical good.)

Picture this: when Shnade swung round, just after Harry and her met for the first time in fifteen years, I saw her dress flick, along with the movement of her hips, and brush Harry's thigh. It was a small, shortish, flimsy dress of reddish cotton; she wore it over some kind of black, shiny, strappy, swimsuitish thing. This dress let you see almost the whole of her big tattoo: a lizard, a dark-blue lizard, that snaked from her right shoulder blade down to her left wrist. Harry was looking at this tattoo with a sort of quiet, astonished concentration: like it was something he had never seen before, and would never see again, a total eclipse or a moonlight rainbow, an event whole generations might long in vain to witness; something that he wanted to engrave into his mind, to make absolutely sure he would remember this one conjunction of moment and object for as long as he remembered his own name.

I was watching Harry looking at it, and wondering what that look meant, when Shnade turned back towards him. As she did so, that light little dress swished quickly across the thigh of his jeans. And I could see in his eyes that it felt like it was made of chain mail.

I suppose I should have seen right then that Harry was fucked. The only question is why. Which is the problem. I mean, what if it was not *because* of anything? What if cause and effect is all crap; what if it was just fate? Fate? What good is that? Who wants to know about *Fate*? Not me, not you and not anyone this side of the River Euphrates. Fate is for the birds, and for low-GDP folk who wander about eating rice; we burger-stuffing, protein-addled Westerners want to know about freedom and choices, and so the only question concerning Harry (and indeed, concerning all of us who will ever be fucked, which is to say: pretty well all of us) is exactly whether, and when, he could have avoided it. The precise moment when the last points were switched, after which all anyone could do was watch the edge of the cliff coming hurtling up.

And so, as a logical man, I sit here now, alone in my little house, and look out across my housing estate (it is

4

dark and the snow is lying orange in the sodium lights, unmelted on our award-winningly insulated roofs) and reel forwards and backwards over that night, to see if there were not, in fact, little hints we missed. Little tip-offs.

There must have been. We should have heard them, surely? Logically, we should have had the sense to pick them up. Sense, or insight, or wisdom, or whatever the fuck it is you are supposed to have attained by the time thirty is merely a fond and wistful memory.

I mean, shit, if getting older is anything more than simple, brutal, biological decay, if there really is this thing called Maturity and Experience, which we supposedly get in exchange for the loss of our beautiful Youth and Innocence, then we should at least have heard *some* sort of jangling from our early-warning systems well before the guy got squashed with the van and the cops took hold of us.

After all, Harry's Official Thirty-Ninth False Birthday began a little, just a little weirdly, when he called me up as I was walking to the pub. I hunched my ear to the mobile, exposed my brain to the microwave field and drifted myself into a gloomy doorway, out of the rain and the rumble of London; I straddled a fat dosser in his pile of rags, without even seeing him; I stuck my middle finger in my other ear:

—Harry. Happy False Birthday. Forty! Fuck, eh?

—Ben: fire it, forget it, and write it off. Turn round and go home, lovelyboy.

—OK, Harry: your party, your call. Um: why?

—I can't come out, Ben. I am emotionally fucking devastated. I have just seen what my skull's going to look like in a thousand years. I have looked eternity in the bastard face, and it's horrible.

5

—I know your face is horrible, Harry, but why your skull? Harry? Lost you. Harry?

But did I go home? Course not. I grinned. I chuckled. I thought, *Oho, Harry's on good form tonight.*

Because, of course, Harry said all that in his trade-mark way, you know, the way he always used to say that kind of stuff, the way everyone used to like him saying that kind of stuff on the telly, as he juggled ironically with his skulls and mouthed his crap one-liners about eternity and suchlike: like he meant it, but didn't *really* mean it. Like it was true, yes, but not *true* true, not true for him and us. As if seeing it could mean it was disarmed and defused; as if saying it out loud could magically produce a get-out clause; as if knowing it made it all different.

Good old Harry; such a twat.

I mean, *knowing it* didn't do much good for Adam and Eve, did it?

So instead of worrying, I merrily tipped a quid to the tramp, who said *God bless ye, boy* and trotted off more swiftly, even more swiftly, towards the pub, full of happy expectation. I mean, after all, Harry was well used to skulls, skulls are meat and drink to Harry, he is on the telly practically every other day, arseing about in his horrible, allegedly youthful way, with some poor sod or other's skull. I had no idea what the hell he was on about, but *No big deal for Harry, a skull*, I thought.

Well, maybe I should have thought about it more. If I had, maybe I would have realised that poncing about with someone else's skull, under the hot, white camera lights, surrounded by respectful continuity girls, patient directing folk and grinning techies, is not the same thing, not by a long chalk, as looking into the mirror, in the grey, cold fluorescence of your own little bathroom, and seeing your very own skull-to-be.

And thinking maybe you really are fucked.

Among the Dead, Live

Mind you, in fairness to me and to my powers of observation, if you had been sitting near us, *us* being Jan and me and The Wop, in the Museum Tavern across from the museum, the British Museum I mean, some twelve hours earlier, when Harry walked in to meet us, you would have been highly unlikely to have thought he was a candidate for being fucked in the immediate and looming future.

On the contrary, you would have probably thought, assuming you had recognised him, *Oh, that's that bloke off the telly.* And then, given our insane worship of anyone who makes it on to the box, as if being on the box were some sort of moral quality in itself, you would probably, instinctively, have thought that there were very few people currently strolling the globe who were less visibly due to be fucked than Harry. You would probably have thought, *If that is someone who is booked to be fucked, where's mine?*

Yes, Harry MacDonald himself, the presenter of *Among The Dead, Live,* that arse-clenchingly trendy archaeological programme which seems, judging by its slot and style, to be aimed at teenagers who actually would like to go to college so long as their parents don't know it, and parents who are desperate to persuade their teenagers that there are other possible role models than bad black rap artistes and suicidal white-trash rockers. Each week guaranteed to contain at least one shocking juxtaposition of High Culture and drug abuse/sexual deviance. And all filmed in front of various sexy digging locations.

I mean, who had dared, before Harry (or before Harry's producers, rather), to say, live and on prime-time, pre-watershed telly, that Romans *got shitfaced* in their bathhouses *before shagging themselves stupid with whatever they fancied*; that Samuel Pepys had, according to his diary, *a quick Sherman during the sermon while off his tits on sherry* in the very Wren church we were now standing in; or that the beautiful Muse in this classical fresco was *the opposite of a wet dream to wino Greek poets*. Live, prime-time, pre-watershed. Suicide. But then, no one had ever got such great ratings for talking about stuff like Roman Bathhouses and English Restoration Church Architecture and Muses; and if a TV Exec is going to put himself and his balls on the line for anything, it will be for something that combines proven ratings and alleged heavyweight learning. So they did. And, as you may recall, the first series was, one way or another, such a scandalous success (what other kind of success is there, these days?) that, even before it ended, it was being mocked in some crap *Private Eye* cartoon strip and taken the piss out of in other telly progs, which is the one sure definition of Fame.

Remember the opening shot?

Harry in the flesh, in his baggy, black designer jeans with their stupid overgrown turn-ups, in his big-heeled boots and his Indiana Jones rip-off battered leather coat, sitting there, trowel stuck Freudianly through his belt, dramatically half lit in his poshy university office, with his tossily clever PostModern collection of artefacts behind him:

Egyptian scrolls of the dead, bug-eyed Peruvian carvings, gilded plastic mosques that

9

sing Allah Akhbar, swooning Madonnas and Sacred Hearts, giant-dicked Iron Age gods, Roman lead cursing-scrolls from sacred wells, faded needlework portraits of Lenin and Stalin, Buddhas in various forms, aboriginal offering pots, elephant gods, a rebuilt Stone Age bowl full of baked hazelnuts that still rattle after five thousand years, an artfully half-burnt portrait of Hitler and a Union Jack that supposedly once flew over Mafeking . . .

Harry's collection; Harry's backdrop. The icons that the long-lost dead pinned their feeble, fearful hopes on, all now arranged nicely so that Harry MacDonald can piss ironically about with them in that disarming way he has; that way that allows him to say things that would normally outrage the average viewer, but somehow don't when *he* says them, as he intros his latest flying visit to the world of populist archaeology.

Yes, him.

Him with that seriously tragic ponytail hairdo effort. Yes, that one. That Scotto-Welsh git on the telly that goes around digging up ancient stuff. Our Harry.

Ours meaning that we are Harry's oldest friends. Which is why it is *us* who have been meeting Harry here on his Official False Birthdays for fifteen years.

The Last Bastion

The plan on Harry's False Birthdays is always the same, and his recent fame has changed nothing. Each year, on this particular day, we change out of our suits and stuff at work (any embarrassment this causes is, naturally, part of the deal), stick our toothbrushes in our jeans pockets, check we have the necessary cash float and charged-up plastic, pocket the mobiles just in case we need to lie to anyone en route, and trot along down, baggage-free and light of heart, to the Museum Tavern. We have a couple here, then jump on a train to somewhere Harry has thought of; somewhere he *knows* we can't get back from that night.

When we get on to the train, we quickly sneak off, proud of our own devilment, to the lav: there we each take one line of charlie from the little half-gramme envelope that Harry procures for us annually. We sit and drink cans and listen to Harry reading the tourist brochures he has always picked up about wherever place it is, and telling us (in an imitation of whichever local accent) how utterly hopeless and godforsaken this place we are going to actually is. Then, just before we arrive at wherever it is, we sidle off toilet-wards again to do the second line. Having thus knocked the coke ration on the head, we stroll around the centre of whatever city we have ended up in, looking at the alleged tourist heritage gear while crawling pubs, with Harry pointing out how crap and bogus everything is.

Harry is very good at doing this: he makes us feel like he makes his telly audience feel, I suppose, as if we were part of some privileged group of people equipped with the necessary brains or X-ray specs to see all the bullshit of the world for what it is. Then, having reduced the evening to our clever selves alone, we find some nondescript, quietish place to just get shitfaced on drink until the last bar or nightclub closes. After this, we all crash in some cheapish hotel, wherever Harry has found through the local Tourist Helpline, and thus get a couple of hours' kip before decanting ourselves hideously onto the first morning train, the workers' cattle-truck express, back to London.

Over the past fifteen years we have done Edinburgh, Glasgow, Newcastle, Manchester, Cardiff, Leeds, Sheffield, Exeter, Bristol, the lot. Some of them twice. Anywhere except the countryside, of course, because any bit of the countryside that you can get to from London after work in time for a drink is just hell on wheels: *Britland*, Harry calls it with Cymro-Hibernian scorn:

—Countryside? You call that shagging countryside? It's just a fucking stretched-out suburbia, except there are no UCIs, no Safeways and no decent pubs, and the population consists in approximately equal measure of fat pink cunts in Jags and inbred nutters in dodgy trucks.

OK, so no countryside. Anywhere else, though. Anywhere we can be sure of finding somewhere or other to keep us going until we collapse. Anywhere Harry thinks he can build us up to make us feel we are doing something really stupid again.

Stupid, that's the point. Just being stupid. Because if it is a weekend the next day, we vow to cope with the kids and a vile comedown, and if it is a workday, which it naturally is five times out of seven, like this time, *we still have to turn up to work next day*, get changed back, and get on with embracing our careers. (There was only one exception to this, and that was two years ago, on the False Birthday that fell just after Harry landed his telly job and the cheque to match: Harry took us all to New York for one night. Said he wanted to see the Capital of the Twentieth Century just once before it ended.)

Do you see? Lurking under the whole False Birthday business is this big idea: if you cannot hack your life, the life you yourself have chosen freely and made for yourself, after just one pathetic little old-fashioned night on the batter, you should not be doing it at all: you are on the rocks and you better change tack fast. Or else admit you are old and give it all up. All of it. Pipe and slippers time. Shed time. Bye-bye time.

Which is, of course, the kind of thing that is OK to say when you are young, when you are dull, and when your CV and your liver are still fresh and unhardened-up. Not so easy now. But that is the whole point: Harry's False Birthdays are, secretly, so secretly that none of us has ever openly mentioned it, *nothing to do with fun*. They are a private, once-a-year ceremony in memory of our youth and wastable strength. Proof we have something left in the tank. A way of showing, or at least of convincing ourselves, that we have chosen our lives: *chosen* them, freely, not just fallen into them through fear, cowardice or just plain old exhaustion. That we can still get ourselves up for it if the occasion demands.

It is only a bloody silly night once a year, of course, and each of us has a million excuses to drop it, and if one of us did, the others would gratefully follow suit. But we have been doing it for so long now that to stop it would feel like some unpleasantly significant watershed in our lives had been reached. If we decided one year that this simply had to be the last False Birthday, because our lives were now too serious and responsible and all that, well, it would feel like some distant relation of births and deaths and marriages. And we don't want that. Nope. We do not want unnecessary reminders of how fast and vast the universe is ticking.

So we keep up our little private tradition, for the same reason anyone keeps up any kind of tradition: to disguise the ceaseless passing of our own little individual lives. And Harry always calls us all up the day after, to make sure we really are either at work or looking after the kids, or whatever: to make sure none of us has betrayed this last bastion of our free will.

Then we have knocked the False Birthday on the head for another year, and we can relax again, secure in the knowledge that we are not yet hopeless old gits. Yes, it will come: but it has not come yet. Not yet!

Men Who Have Not Had Sex for Too Long

Harry wasn't there yet when I arrived. No surprise: Harry was always last to arrive at his False Birthday gatherings, but this was a prerogative of it being his birthday (theoretically), not of his fame, and it had always been like that, just in case you were thinking we are kind of Harry groupies. No way.

I, on the contrary, was always first. Always have been, ever since our college days. I do it on purpose. Because for me, to be sitting quietly in a bar, thinking of nothing worth talking about and just waiting for old friends I know are going to turn up, with the certain prospect of soon being off my face and embarked on some little adventure or other with them, has always been pretty close to being the best part of the whole thing.

I don't mean because I don't actually enjoy seeing them. I do. But it's just that I love those little times of secure anticipation. You know? When you can just sit and relax and let it all spin quietly about you. At such moments of rare peace, I sit and conjure up pleasant images of tranquillity and security. Sometimes, for example, I imagine I am standing in front of a great big wall, a tall, wide, whitewashed stone-built studio wall maybe, and on it I have put up a vast map of the world.

Imagine it: the colossal wall-map of your own life, on some cunning geographical projection designed to artificially inflate the places of particular importance to you yourself. See it? OK, then. Imagine:

Into this map you have stuck little coloured-topped pins, which you have joined with wool (red wool, say) to mark the planless unwinding of your life. In fact, right now, here as we speak, you have just been busy adding the latest little stretch of red wool; you have just marked off the newest leg of your secret journey. (The big ball of wool is hidden in a cardboard box on the floor, by the way. The red yarn hangs down loose from your last marker, and disappears into it, so you cannot see how much is left; on the lid of the box lies a pair of old garden shears, and on the side you have painted, in rough, red letters, the words: *Not Yet!*) There. And now you are just standing quietly in front of your lifeline map, nice long drink in hand, fine dinner roasting away safely and scentingly in the Aga in the house across the yard, wine uncorked and ready, beds made and aired, kids away for the weekend, friends already on their way, a late-summer moon just coming over the woods and the swallows over the house about to turn into bats. There you stand, as calm and as happy and as inexplicably solemn as someone waiting for a loved and loving lover, just following your thread from pin to pin along the plot of your existence; seeing where your life crossed and rebounded with other people; looking at the faded little passport shots that you have hung on the red wool here and there along the way. All those faces, all those places, all those names and eyes and lips. And now you are stepping back and, just for once in this speedy little world, trying to see the whole thing at one time, in one focus, to see if any sense will jump out at you: some insight into what you have been, and are, and might be . . .

To be honest though, it wasn't quite working tonight. The magic of waiting was not delivering this evening. But I don't mean that I felt some mystic portent of doom. No, it was much simpler than that. It was just waiting *in a pub* which was the minor downer.

This was surprising to me. Slightly more than surprising: mildly worrying. I mean, I had spent most of my adult Rest and Recreation time in pubs, one way or another. I had arrived at the Museum Tavern mentally rubbing my hands at the prospect of my first real, free, uncapped night in a West End pub for several months. Childcare and work and suburbia, and, well, you know the way it is and the way the calendar zooms on. *Yumyum,* I had thought, *here we go again, about time too, let us enter the Neutral Zone again, the public arena in the Big Bad West End World where anyone can walk in and, at least theoretically, anything can happen.* Not that I wanted anything to happen, I mean, nothing had swum up in my mind; but at least the possibility existed here: the possibility of a possibility. Yes, even as I strode to the bar and ordered my pint, if someone had tapped me on the shoulder and said that this would be my last ever visit to a pub, that the State had decided to ban me from every pub for ever, or that every pub in the country had been nuked, I would have looked at the future with something like startled horror. Even as I sat down, if you had asked me if I liked pubs, I would have said: *Love them.*

But for some reason, tonight, it was like everything had changed focus. Instead of being a place where anything was possible, the pub felt like some anteroom to utter stasis. More specifically, it felt like it was too full of men who had not had sex for too long.

So pretty soon, to my surprise, as I said, to my slight worry indeed, I found myself wishing I was not in a pub. Here I was, married, employed, kid and all, my friends sure to be here soon, and yet, tonight, the very pub-ness of the pub made me start to think: *What if me sitting here alone was for real? What if this pub was all I had? What if I was sitting here, with no friends coming, a wife I had left and no kid? What if I was going on forty* (which I was, but I still thought of it as some ghastly 'what if') *and truly, really, here alone? What could happen? Nothing.* The pub suddenly felt like a great big lie, a false haven, a home for people with no home. Not the door of possibility, but the graveyard of all hope.

Before I was halfway through my pint, I was wishing heartily that we had broken the tradition, abandoned our seventies bloody fantasy of pub culture, moved with the times and decided to meet in one of those modern bars in Soho. Much nicer.

But on the other hand, as soon as I thought concretely about this, as soon as I set up this bright, design-led, airy place of my dreams, I had a curious flash of intimation: if I really had been sitting there alone, surrounded by the kind of people those bars are full of, I would not have felt comfortable. I would have been feeling the need to make certain small checks on and adjustments to my posture, my body language and my general demeanour, in order to avoid any chance of being confused, myself, by the kind of women who would be in that kind of bar, with one of the men who had not had sex for too long.

Strange times, and no guide book.

I swigged beer and made myself smile. Stupid. I was

not an old toss. I was not even forty, I had a wife and kid and a decent job and I was sitting here waiting for my friends, my oldest friends, one of whom was pretty bloody famous. Like I said, I am a logical man, and these clear and present truths soon put me right.

I sipped calmly. I refused to allow myself to fall into the ridiculous superstition of looking at the door every thirty seconds to see if the others had come in, as if I could speed up their arrival simply by wanting it.

The only piss-off now was that having vetoed facing the door, I was having to work quite hard to avoid any eye contact with one of the old boozers at the bar who seemed to have fixed upon me in the unnerving way they have.

He was an old, shrivelled-looking bloke, his drink-beaten face exploded definitively a good decade ago, by the looks. A ruin of a man; a man who radiated the carelessness of despair in everything except his clothing. His tweed suit and shirt and tie were obviously the last outposts of his self-respect, the fading echoes of a life which, something told you, had once commanded a degree at least of power and respect. And now he would certainly never shag again unless he paid for it. Nothing in common with me, mate; so why the looks at me? Stupid old git.

No, let's avoid his strangely unsettling gaze, and take the chance to restore some solidity to all this by gazing studiously into my pint and telling you, and reminding myself, who I am to be telling you all this.

Ben, or: The Maths

My right to tell you this story is simply my, and its, normality. Look, I am not some nutter who keeps dicks in pickle-jars under his bed, and I am not remotely interested in bollocks about people who like skinning women alive while discoursing about Greek philosophy or any crap that like. So if its abnormality you're after, better tell the landlord your pint's off, demand your money back, and leave right now. But for normality, I am your man.

My looks are normal, my wife, Anna, is normal, our child, Hugh, is normal and my job is normal. (Well, what else is there? You want to hang out with tree-hugging twats who think *mankind is the skin-disease of the earth*? Dedicate your life to delaying roads or rescuing cats? What else is anyone supposed to do, these days? The park bench and a *Big Issue* franchise if we are lucky? You tell me.)

So there you are and here is me: a normal bloke in a normal job, knocking on forty, living in a little house in Peckham with a nice wife and kid who he occasionally looks at twice and thinks how lucky he was to get, but mostly takes for granted. No, not for *granted*. Just for *natural*. Who, if he was asked did he love his wife and kid, would say, *Of course*, without thinking about it (without thinking that you can never say *Of course* about love. Yes, is all you can say, hard and sure and glad: *Yes*. Or else *My God. No. I don't, do I?*). And who, just sometimes, when he is, for whatever reason, here at home alone, wonders about life and love and all that, and about how the hell he himself (who he still thinks of unconsciously as about twenty-five) ended up like this.

And the answer, if you are young and therefore still do not, indeed cannot, know it, is not that I became a boring old toss by dint of some weakness or moral flab. It is just the maths.

You see, I would never have imagined myself having this kind of life when I was twenty and swanning about on campuses and suchlike. No one does. No: when you and I were twenty, you and I would have laughed at my life. We would have thought it naff and vaguely absurd. We would have despised me. Because when you are young, you think about getting old and boring in the same way that born-and-bred Rich Folks think about being poor: you simply cannot imagine *how these people can live like this.* It is unnatural, inexplicable, unimaginable; at best pathetic, at worst immoral. You, if you are young, would quite literally rather live in a tent in Somerset than an Executive Unit in Peckham; if someone forced you at bayonet-point to live alone in an Executive Unit in Peckham, you would simply walk up the bayonet, guts dragging out behind you, rather than let them shut the door and leave you here alone. Like those rich folk who somehow assume that people who are poor *could have* done something else, you think that all these ancient tossers over twenty-five have some-how *chosen* their copped-out lives, and hence pretty well deserve (a) your righteous scorn and (b) to be woken up by your thudding bass whenever you feel like it.

Wrong. They didn't choose anything. And nor will you, if you are still young now, when it is your turn, in a couple of years. All that happened was: *the maths got them*.

You see, Anna and I have Hugh, a lovely boy of nearly three, and are considering pretty actively whether, so actively that it is almost *when*, in fact, we should have another sprog.

Yes. And one Friday night, I am rattling home early on my train (what with the kid, and the mortgage on the kid-pod, no way I can afford to go blowing twenty-five, post-tax, non-deductable quid on a cab every bloody weekend, even if I could get one to come out this far), I looked at all the endless lights of London, as they spilled and blurred up into that strange orange haze we call night, and thought that all these squillion bricks and tiles, these uncounted overdrafts and jobs and pawned-off lives, are there for one simple reason: *for the kids*. Look at it all, lying quiet under the cold sky: all just a vast machine for keeping children warm and dry and fed.

Yes. The maths of kids. It works like this.

You got a kid, right? Right. Lucky you, because now you have got whatever immortality is going. So now you need to make several basic decisions. Such as: you swap your two-seater or whatever playwagon you own for something responsible, because everyone knows that the world is full of wideboys in GTis who appear not to care if they die (for the good evolutionary reason, says Harry, that it actually *doesn't* matter if young, dull, single men die) and vengeful white-collar sales slaves who take all their various forms of impotence out on their fellow road-users. So you want, quite rationally, to improve the odds that if you meet one of these laddos or saddos coming round the right-hand side of a bend, it is you and little muggins who will be eating grapes in the noisy hospital ward while Young Disposable Twat or Mr Alleged Executive are mainlining formaldehyde in the quiet, dark basement. Which means you end up driving something like me, something like a distinctly pre-owned Volvo estate. Sexy it is not.

Or: you want a place with a little garden, because kids needs gardens to stop them going psychotic. Right. So you get a place, a place at the end of the world, with a little garden. And you have a little lawn for your kid to play on. But once you got the lawn, you got to mow it. So one day, you find yourself, to your own surprise, down the local B&Q and Homebase, comparing lawn-mowers, because, after all, who is thick enough or rich enough to go chucking their money away on lawn-mowers without looking about *a little bit* first. Not you.

So now you can mow your lawn, so your kid can play on it. And so now you find that when you mow your lawn, you get cat-shit on your shoes, and bits of cat-shit in the cuttings, and cat-shit on your hand when emptying out the grass box. The very grass, remember, which you only wanted so your kid could play on it. And now, it might make him blind or whatever cat-shit does to kids. So now you start hating cats. So next Sunday, before you cut the grass again (when else can you do it?), you walk about on your poxy little lawn, getting rid of all the cat-shit; then dig a place in the garden where you hope the fucking cats will shit instead; then after your dutiful mowing, you cover your little lawn with pepper-dust to keep the cats off . . .

. . . and then you wake up and find that you, as in *you yourself you*, are standing there, holding this can of pepper-dust, with your legs, naturally, covered in pepper-dust, and thinking, I mean *actually thinking*, about putting up a big trellis fence on your little garden wall, to keep the bloody cats out: impossibly, inexplicably, undeniably, you have now officially become that little boring bloke you always laughed at. You look around, at your little house and garden somewhere miles from anywhere and anyone you have anything to do with, and it all looks like someone else's, and you know:

the maths has got you.

The funny thing is: you simply cannot, *cannot* work out exactly where you first went wrong. Like a spider in a big white bath. Like that shipload of Vikings on one of Harry's shows, that went to Greenland and found it wasn't green and ended up without enough wood to build a boat to get home, and so lived on seals until they all died out a couple of hundred miserable, pointless years later. You just took a wrong turn somewhere, and here you are, stuck for ever, indubitably fucked.

Which, as I said, leaves me with one consolation as I gaze across my estate when everything is quiet, at night: *we all do it.* And why? Because it is all for the kids, who are, after all, what it is all about.

Yes: we, who run our lives down in keeping it all up, grafting away, unpraised and without sexiness, on the permanent edge of exhaustion; who live, unfavoured by the taxman, unsupported by the State, with the stench of debt kept barely at bay by our real and metaphorical air-fresheners; who spend troubled hours calculating exactly how short our Endowment Mortgages are going to fall of whatever the bloody salesman had suggested it would *almost certainly be*; who wall up our lives alive, for the sake of our kids, while others cavort weightlessly, heirlessly and happily round W1, disposing their income in snacking and flirting; we, we who do it all so that those kids, those little packages of human future, can have the safety and security and proper families and little gardens that kids need: we, we, *we* are the true unsung heroes, the real martyrs and saints of the modern world.

Hi.

So that's me. Ben.

Fuck.

The Maths (II): On the Other Hand

That's all you need to know, really.

The thing is, I am the least interesting person of us four. Five, counting Shnade, as I suppose I must. In fact, I am the least interesting person pretty well everywhere I go. Which is why I am the one telling it now, I guess. It's obvious, really: if I were more interesting, if I were a gorgeous rent boy or debonair movie director, a mad explorer or distinguished wit, if my diary and life were jam-packed with events, if my wipe-off boards and white goods were covered in invitations (held up by bright, ironic magnets) and little yellow sticky notes reminding me of unmissable parties, powerful meetings and vital occasions which I might otherwise overlook due to my life being sooooo fabulous, well, if I was Harry, say, then I would hardly be sitting here in a small brick-sheathed, breeze-block box in Peckham writing this, alone with my sleeping child, as the evening falls. Would I?

No: I would be out there flirting and chattering.

Don't get me wrong. Yes, I *was there* when it all happened (you can't tell a story unless you have really *been there*, even if just for a moment of clear intimation) but *being present* and *doing it* are not the same thing. Really, almost my only part in the whole shambles, at least until near the end, was to happen to be there: to watch, listen and remember. Which anyone could have done. So much for me.

On the other hand, let me just say this: if no one did the remembering, what good would it all have done for Achilles or Cleopatra or King Arthur or Cu Cullen (or *Cugh Cuhmllaighn* or however the hell you spell it)? Someone has to watch, and listen, and remember, just to ward off the dust. A sad activity it may seem indeed, compared to running about in a bandanna, shagging and surfing, but you never know, you never know:

Maybe, if you just sit there softly, doing what you were put here to do, sticking in there, unobtrusively buying your round, gently letting it all in, it, *life* I mean, might, just might, one day happen to look back over its tattooed shoulder, while lost in thought, as it's walking out the door, unaccountably bored tonight, with the bandanna guys. And then, if you are lucky, so lucky that *lucky* is not even in the right league, as lucky as a man whose 'chute has failed but rips through thick pines into deep snow, ridiculously, impossibly lucky, it, *life* I mean, may suddenly see you are still hanging quietly in there, doing what you do just because that is what you do, and look at you as if for the first time, and stop, and consider, and, incredibly, frown in a strange and sphinxy way as it, *she* I mean, holds out a hand.

Well, shit, we've all got to *dream* that there is more to it all than the maths . . .

A Long Game

Jan came into the Museum Tavern next, thankfully interrupting my curious and, no doubt, morally doubtful reverie.

She first popped her head through the door of the pub to make sure I was there, so she would not have to hang about alone, exposed to the sneaky attentions of the men who had not had sex for too long. Then, reassured, she swept boldly through the bar in her distinctly underaged baggy combats and yoof-fully platformed clogs, with her glittery top shining out from under her retro-seventies herringbone coat, plonked herself next to me with the usual hug, and unleashed her rather good red hair from its beret.

—How are you, Ben?

—Steady. You?

—Hate work, hate London, hate myself.

—Love the gear. Sexy.

—I think it's foul. But it's too late now. Like being born, I suppose. I'm not sure about your shirt. Still, I suppose it'll do for Hartlepool or wherever Harry's dragging us.

—Anna bought it. She said it made me look nice.

—Well, if you're sure you want to look *nice*.

—You mean as opposed to *sexy*?

—I suppose so. My God, Ben, that's giving myself away a bit, isn't it?

—A touch. So you think my shirt might be a plot of Anna's to make me look nice and therefore unsexy?

—Well, I seem to recall that in my long-lost days as a

steady partner, if my steady partner had been going out for a potentially wild night, my dress advice would have been secretly plotted to make it clear to everyone that he was somebody's steady partner. So yes, probably. It's just instinct.

—Oh, well, nice I can live with, so long as it doesn't make me look old.

—Younger than last time I saw you, if anything.

—Wow, she never said it was a *magic* shirt.

—Very good, Ben.

—Thank you.

Whenever I see Jan after a long time (which is every time I see her, these days: sad but true), I find myself thinking of a certain moment way back when, as if that is the key I need to unlock this someone again for me. You know, when you meet an old and trusted friend and then, to your slight distress, find that it has been so long that you need reminding who this allegedly intimate person actually *is*, who they are *to you*, even though they are sitting down next to you and already chatting away. You need a point of focus, a souvenir of their reality.

So here is my secret key, my private continuity clip of Jan, my oldest female friend.

It was on her twentieth birthday, we were at college, I went round to see her and found her lying in bed. All I could see of her in the fuggy gloom of her student pad was this head: Jan, newly twenty, punky and kohled, glaring balefully out at a world in which Maggie Thatch was the most unpopular PM in history but no one could think what to have instead of her. They had burned Toxteth a few nights before, as I recall.

—Happy birthday, old Jan. Twenty winters! Into the third decade! Fuck, eh?

—Hello, teenage Ben.

—What's up? I mean, apart from you being over the hill and next stop thirty and all that?

—I am crap and I want to die.

—No change there, then.

—I am still what I am.

—That's reassuring. I thought maybe that all kind of stopped when you got old.

—Not when you get birthday cards, it doesn't.

—Birthday cards? As in bad ones?

—As in one from Dad.

—It happens, on birthdays. Parents write them. They fill them with money, usually.

—Not this kind.

—What, no dough? Bastard. I thought he was loaded.

—Oh, there was plenty of money in it.

—Right. Well, that's OK then. Job done, surely? Um. Pub?

—Ben, he spelled my name wrong.

—How can you spell *Jan* wrong?

—Good question, young Ben.

—Perhaps he's going senile. He must be nearly sixty, after all.

—Let's not grasp at straws. It is *possible* to spell my name wrong, after all. Germans spell it *Dschan*. And I once had a French boyfriend who spelled it *Yann*.

—I thought your dad was English.

—Mmmm. So he hasn't really got much of an excuse, has he? I mean, apart from the fact he hardly ever saw us. Which is an excuse, I suppose. But not much help. I suppose excuses never are, really, are they? Much help, I mean? If you have to start making excuses, it must be too late, mustn't it? Because if it wasn't, you wouldn't have done whatever it is you're making excuses for, would you? So I wonder why we bother spending so much time making them. Sometimes, Ben, I think . . .

—Jan?

—Yes, Ben?

—What did your dad *actually* write?

—Are you sure you want to know?

—I suspect you want to tell.

—A fair cop. OK. He wrote *Happy birthday to my darling Jane.*

—Ouch.

—But I mean, when you think about it, it's not *very many* letters off, and it does *include* my name, correctly spelled. Not *that much* of a misspelling, really . . .

—No, absolutely. Hardly at all. Um. Let's go to the pub. Harry's there already, we . . .

—Ben. Look me in the eye.

—Oh, God, all right.

—Would you really call that a spelling mistake?

—It would be hard.

—Oh it *is*, I assure you.

—Very good, Jan!

—Thank you. So: what would you call it?

—Um, the wrong name?

—Mmmm. That's what I was thinking. Hoping not, but thinking.

—Look . . .

—Bye-bye, Ben.

—Do you want me to go?

—Do you really want to take the whole emotional weight of a fucked-up twenty-odd life on your teenage shoulders?

—A leading question, m'lud. See you down the pub later, then?

—Sooner, I should think.

And then she hid her head under the blankets again,

so I went. And of course, Jan did come down the pub quite soon and we all had a great laugh about this and many other things, because we were all about twenty and at college, and anyone who is not truly fucked beyond all hope and saving can laugh at pretty well anything when they are about twenty and at college and still happily gift-wrapped in Nature's Own Kevlar: youth.

Jan these days, as she, like all of us, knocks on forty, is the walking proof that there is such a thing as a long game. She has become much better looking over the years. Comparatively, I mean, of course. You see, Jan was always difficult, brainy, tall and skinny: but *Difficult, Brainy, Tall and Skinny*, as a come-on in the virtual Personal Columns of life, appreciates over the years in the same way that *Simple, Daft, Cuddly and Curvy* depreciates. Being difficult and brainy and tall and skinny is simply *worth much more* at thirty-eight than it is at twenty, when it is worth very little indeed. Whereas being simple and daft and cuddly and curvy is going to make you many, many friends at twenty, but at thirty-eight it is going to put you perilously close to the trash unless you have a very clever make-up artiste and/or a serious private income.

Jan, when she was twenty, wanted to be a theatre director, but did not have enough sheer trust in herself to go it alone, nor enough low cunning to flatter her way in. And, even in those days before anyone straight had ever *heard* of AIDS, i.e., in that forgotten early part of the eighties which was still really the late seventies (everything was slowly getting crappier and crappier, the inner cities were riot zones, Ulster was off the scale and we all assumed, just vaguely *assumed*, that the big nuke-fest was on its way sooner or later, but at least you could still *shag* without dying), she tended to regard shagging as a rather intimate act to be reserved for very good friends. So all the flop-haired rich boys at college who ran the DramSoc and spent their summers at Jacques Le Dique's mime school in Paris and that shit, kind of condescendingly offered Jan stage-management jobs and stuff. Jan shut up and took the crap jobs and, like some young Stalin-ess, ended up quietly and unobtrusively running the Uni.DramSoc from the wings while allowing Rupert and Daniella to collect the flowers up front. She went into boring Local Authority Arts Admin at twenty-one, in 1983 or thereabouts, at that very time of life when everyone else was bounding like posh little spaniels out of college, utterly sure they would end up running Channel 4 or the *Guardian* or the RSC in five years and generally be the next Tarkovsky or Ken Branagh, and *no fucking way, darling* would they go into horrible boring Arts Admin. In Peterborough! Might as well be *accountants*, ho ho ho.

But they reckoned without the Real Eighties and the triumph of all forms of accountancy. And so now Jan more or less controls several million quid of the Arts Council's (i.e., your and my) money; and now Rupert and Daniella, pushing forty, looking somewhat sandblasted by too much sun and drugs, and with the trust fund now via-ed on to their own offspring, queue up at her door, at the door of this tall, skinny, brainy and difficult woman they once condescended to horribly, begging for a few poxy grand to do their next laughably crap Community Show, enthusiastically jumping through whatever politically correct hoops Jan has set up for them to negotiate. She is woman enough to admit she loves it.

On the other hand, she is also prone to write the whole thing off as a load of old cobblers after a few drinks, and propose the following theorem: that the higher the proportion of Arts Council funding in any given project, the crappier that project is likely to be. Because the Arts Council *has* to fund crap: if the stuff it funded turned out to be viable anyway, without subsidies, then the Arts Council would have no reason to exist, would it? Nope. And so its many committees and officers would have done themselves idiotically out of jobs which are, as far as I can see, still among the nearest thing in this tough day and age to money for old rope. So: unpopular crap they fund.

Nice to be able to laugh at your job when you are with your friends in the pub, isn't it? I do too. On principle. I always think it suggests a certain ironic distance, a certain distinction.

On the other hand, if we Brits *are* really simply what we are hired to *do*, what then? If you think, in your secretest thoughts, that what you *do* is actually quite probably a pile of lies, crap and evasions, at best an entertaining farce and at worst a ghastly satire starring you as yourself, it is likely, is it not, that after a while, without even noticing it, you will start, in your innermost halls of internal judgement, in the silent places that you only go to when you cannot sleep at three a.m., to think that maybe you yourself too *are* nothing but a pile of lies, crap and evasions.

And it is a lot harder to laugh about it at three a.m. when you cannot sleep than it is in the pub with your friends. When it is three a.m. and you cannot sleep, when your plumbing creaks and your wiring hums and every slamming car door is a gunshot, a certain ironic distance and a certain supposed distinction are not really much of a consolation.

Jan has a kid too now. For some years, blinded by the

34

relentless barrage of smiling mums and babies in every mag in the world, she conceived the notion that having a kid would make her happy, or at least content. She thought maybe her view of life was too black, too self-indulgently tragic, and that maybe the problem was actually that she should be a grandmother by now, *would* be a grandmother by now in any society but the decadent modern West, and that the Voice of Nature was calling to her on a bad line, and *this* was what was making her drink too much and powder her schnoz too regularly. She believed, in short, that Life could still be sorted. Her Man, however, doubted this. So she ditched him, made sure that for several months the only acid she took was folic, cut right down on the red wine, and spent a long weekend, the *right* long weekend, according to her little white electric detector device, in the back of some surfie campervan, shagging a good-looking posh young trustafarian juggling crustyboy she'd met at some Arts Festival she was running. And got a hole in one. And so now she has baby Oliver, who is adored and cared for by surf-boy's grateful parents in Notting Hill much of the time, when he is not being looked after in the Arts Council crèche or by upmarket baby-minders. And so, according to her theory, Jan should be happy. Or at least content.

Guess what?

—How's surf-boy junior, Jan?

—Remember the neutron bomb? Designed to annihi-late all human life?

—Fuck, yeah, that. We all thought it was the end of the world. Wrong again.

—Well, Oliver really is. Don't you think one of us should go off and discover whichever gene it is that makes *some* of them sleep through right from the start? If we could patent it, and offer it on the open market, we'd be Bill Gates's neighbours overnight. Roll on genetic engineering. Why does he have to scream and wake up? He's First World, white, upper-middle class for God's sake. Doesn't he realise he's one of the luckiest hundredth of a per cent of babies in the world? Ungrateful little bugger.

—He cries because of the lions, Harry says. In case you leave him too far from the campfire.

—Well, now we have technologically wiped out the lions and campfires, don't you think it's about time we knocked out those outdated genes too? My God, I wish he'd hurry up and go to college. Hmmm: I wonder if my parents thought that too? Do you think they did? That's rather scary, isn't it? I mean, what if it's a self-replicating cycle of abuse and despair? I have two questions for you, Ben.

—Fire away.

—One: how did it all go wrong?

—Um. Someone ate an apple?

—I mean, really.

—Pass.

—OK, and two: what's the point of it all? Kids and families and things, I mean?

—Definitely pass. Either you give your kids hell and they hate you, or you give them a beautiful paradise and then they're fucked up by having to leave it.

—So what do we do with them, Ben?

—Pass again.

—It's insane. Suicidal. We live for fifteen adult years, worshipping our individual liberty to do whatever the hell we want when we want, then we decide to have kids, without realising that kids are exactly the opposite of individual liberty. No wonder we're all so mad. Christ, sometimes I find myself thinking the unthinkable, Ben.

—And saying it?

—OK. Sometimes I think that a yashmak, a bloke with a big beard, and no bloody choice in the matter might be quite restful, after all.

—Yep: maybe we should never have given up on God and lullabies.

—No more babies, no dilations or lullabies, no tongs or snipping. Less babies, more beer, or I am out of here, rapped The Wop, having sneaked up behind us in his pimpy chromed-leather jacket, white T-shirt and black cords: —I tell you, mates, *l'enfer, c'est les enfants des autres.*

—Yeah? said I, who am well known to speak nothing but English.

—Hell ain't other people, mate, it's other people's children. Here, what you reckon? My trilats developed since last year? Bloody better have.

We gave each other a pathetic imitation of a high-five, Jan and he gave each other a clunky imitation of a Mediterranean peck (what is wrong with us Brits? Do we think that if we actually *touch* we might all immediately start shagging each other indiscriminately?) and he plonked his proud, Continental-style arse on the chair beside us.

A Practical Philosophy for the Twenty-First Century

The Wop loves his weights. His definition of personal development is the right curve in the equation of muscle over bodyweight.

The Wop is not actually a wop as such at all, but just a dark-haired, squat, hairyish individual from Streatham, who was an eighties man before they existed and used to pretend he was French to get off with women. It was he who introduced us all, at eighteen, at college, to such delights as the Stan Smith tennis shoe, that long-forgotten artefact whose evolutionary importance lies in its being the Late Seventies Ancestral Stock of all those ridiculously big-tongued, overpadded and generally bulked-up training shoes that came to dominate the known world for years.

The Wop also had his proto-eighties, quasi-Darwinian philosophy to go with his pre-eighties trainers. It was this: we (Harry, The Wop and me) were the Salt Of The Earth because we were from state schools but had gone to Ye Olde Poshe College, thus proving our evolutionary superiority to all the thick bastards from home. Now we had to prove that we could shag more, and more attractive, women than the Posh Public School Wankers, in order to show that their social position was a mere anomaly, a blip that would be wiped out by any true, evolutionarily accurate meritocracy.

Soccer, lager, weights, blokes, biology and French cinema: The Wop was doing it all back in 1979. He should have been a millionaire, really, because he was that vital year or three ahead of everyone else. He should have founded the first crap men's mag or something. Instead, he has ended up teaching and hitched to a girl called Angela who he met in his gym. Everyone, including me, fancies her immediately because she has a very flat stomach, which she shows at every possible opportunity, and red lipstick. Which is a bloody stupid reason to fancy anyone, when you think about it, but since when was fancying anything to do with thinking? And the fact that she is thick does not stop you fancying her, either: it just makes you wish that you were thick too, so you could sit with her and merrily admit that you fancy the pants off her and no harm meant luv.

To The Wop, Angela, and more especially this effect she has on other men, are the living and irrefutable proof that he has escaped the horrible fate of being A Wristy Intellectual. Angela has a kid already, a girl of nearly ten, by some previous boyfriend; The Wop plays little or no part in her upbringing:

—What, catch me managing some other bloke's gene pool for him? Yeah, really.

—Well, so you going to have one of your own? If you believe in gene pools and stuff, you must want to.

—Look, mate, I can't, it'd ruin my looks.

—*Your* looks?

—Squire, I have got about five years left in play if I am lucky. I can't sodding afford to have three years of sleepness nights. I'd be buggered. Irretrievably lined and old. I am waiting until there's no hope left for my body before I allow it to reproduce itself.

—What about Angela?

—Who's in a hurry to lose their pelvic floor all over again? shrugs The Wop.

I once saw a few scraps of paper in his flat, entitled 'A Practical Philosophy for the Twenty-First Century', which began something like this: *Look, mate, you really think you are going to find Her, I mean, The One, down the tennis club?* but he always denies that this essay, or note, or whatever it was, ever existed. I hardly ever see The Wop these days, either.

Here is my key moment for The Wop, for you. Now, The Wop always despised almost everyone at college, either because they were Wristy Specky Swots or because they were Posh Dickless Twats. He was, on principle, always late for any meeting you arranged with him. I never minded this, but you already know about that: many of my happiest hours at college were spent waiting for The Wop. Anyway, this one night I got inescapably held up, and was very late indeed, so I rushed into one of the chief student-lifestyle pubs of the neighbourhood to find The Wop alone, having clearly been waiting for the length of a pint and a half. I approached at speed, arms already half out, ready to apologise, only to find him hissing at me, without moving his face from its trademark calm smile:

—Don't! Don't you dare let all these nightmare little tossers see that I've been waiting for someone! Make out it's an accident.

—Oh, um, yeah, er OK: Hi, Wop, hey! What you doing here?

—Passing the time, Bensta, passing the time. You staying for one, mate?

—Yeah, why not. Yeah. I'll get them.

—News.

That was him.

God's Original Number Nought

So there we all were, all together again and eyeing the demands of the coming night with that mixture of anticipation and vague, inexplicable unease that signals all the best things in life. We had not seen each other all together since the last False Birthday, and things were, to be honest, a bit slow to gel while we waited for Harry.

However, by lucky chance, Machiavellian calculation or fine subconscious skills, Jan broke the ice by mixing up the lagers on the way back from the bar. We had all ordered different stuff, you see, and were now tasting each pint to work out whose was which. A pregnant silence fell. We all tried to keep looking serious.

—This one is mine, growled The Wop, brooking no chance of being wrong.

—Look, I said, —you're so sure, you choose, Wop. I'll take whichever one no one else wants.

—You'll take whichever one no one wants? said Jan.

—Hey, I must have said that once, when they were handing out lives.

We were thus now satisfactorily re-established in double-quick time as the ourselves we knew from back at college, discussing the choices facing third-millennium mankind as we allowed our bodies and minds to relax into the certain knowledge that the evening would not be some hideous mistake, that we would all get happily pissed up tonight, more or less as we expected, planned, needed, without any danger of unnerving personal revelations from any of us. Instead, we were talking ironic bollocks. To be precise, we had just finished discussing the phenomenon of those Tintin shops (gay men and Tintin? Why? Are gay men just recreating the pre-women's lib male world, only more so?) and we were now wondering about whether we order our beer, our clothes, our loves and our lives on the basis of just whatever we happen to be used to, or do we make our selections just because some crap designer has stuck his label on whatever it is? Do we, in short, really *choose* at all, and if so, on what basis? Is there any authenticity of feeling left in a world where bushmen goggle at *Baywatch*, and every man in the halfway developed world has been systematically bombarded with pictures of half a dozen more or less identical blondes wearing nothing but little pants and underwired bras? And if there is no such thing as real, authentic feeling, how can there be anything worth calling Freedom?

You know. One of those crap thirty-something-going-on-twenty chats. Great fun.

Then:

—Look on my skull, ye childless, and despair! shouted Harry, bursting through the door with finely judged apparent carelessness. —What you all drinking?

—We don't know, said Jan. —Fuck, Harry, you look like a queer.

—Stella, said The Wop. —Harry, you look like a cunt.

—Whatever you're having, I said. —Happy birthday, Harry; you look like an old git.

—An old git who's going to have to crawl bigtime to his bastard producer tomorrow, said Harry. —Thank Christ I signed the contract for the next series before I had this done. I don't *think* they've got a tonsorial get-out clause . . .

Of course, he made sure all this was pitched not only at us, but at the gallery. That was Harry being our Harry, too. Always has been a twat like that. And so we forgave him for being such a plonker, because he knew and we knew and we knew he knew we knew that this was what Our Harry was supposed to be like. Anything but serious.

Anyway, he looked so truly gutted, standing there with God's original number nought shaven head glowing pink in the light, that you couldn't take him seriously if you wanted.

Our Harry.

Pickled Cabbage and Parma Ham

Harry had collected his pint and was about to join us when:

—Ah, Mr MacDonald, they do allow you off the television, then? said a reedy, poshy old voice from beside him at the bar. Harry jumped like he'd just been stung, turned, and stared. It was the ghastly old soak whose eyes I had been avoiding earlier. He was looking at Harry with every sign of amused indulgence. And vice versa.

—Still boozing, Stoney? asked Harry.

—Indeed. After all, there is little point in anyone, including me, telling me to make something of my life: it has so clearly run its course. And you are still leading archaeology into your brave new populist world, Mr MacDonald. Yours, not mine, I am pleased to say.

—Ah well, got to please the little twats in combats and daps, Stoney. You too, Stoney, if you were still in the game.

—*Daps?* I asked, as Harry sat down with us.

—*Trainers* to you, you Saxon gobshite, said Harry, giving me a thump in the ribs.

—Who's the human still? asked Jan.

—Stoney, said Harry, —Professor Stoney, God save us, the old git who got my Ph.D. turned down the first time. The disgusting old bastard who cost me an extra year of my fucking twenties. Boys, I tell you: when I lead my pincer movement on London, down the M1 and the M4, he's on the list. Number fucking one.

—Talking of which, what does Sarah think about the haircut? asked Jan.

Instinct, I guess; or just the wish to change the subject; or maybe the insight of someone who has seen Harry's eyes from shagging distance.

—Well, she hasn't seen it yet, said Harry evenly. His voice carried no identifiable hint of meaning, but we all heard the silent fall of the little stone into the deep well; we all knew it had still not hit bottom yet.

—So: you just had the haircut today? asked Jan, subtly.

—Yes. So she won't see it for a few days.

—A few days?

—What, you moved out? demanded The Wop.

—Thank you, Einstein, said Harry.

—Cut to the chase then, said The Wop.

—Well, Wop, you see: one of the many things Sarah and I agree on is that little Hannah, being little and innocent and all that, deserves to be brought up in an atmosphere of love, or at least considerate behaviour. And since our relationship has now developed to the point at which it seems to consist mainly of a competition to see who is having the worse time with the childcare and work and stuff, we're splitting up. I am currently passing the time with one of my sisters.

I quite distinctly recall a shiver passing round the three of us. A grave-walking, fate-sounding shudder, like when you are in your twenties and the second of your gang says he or she is getting hitched. The first is still a joke: they are the odd one out. But the second time someone says it, everyone quite suddenly starts to wonder who of them will be the last still single, left begging for company, alone and headed for a sad, bad end. Or when the first of your mates has kids. In the beginning, you are amazed at the lunacy of the first people to do it, to voluntarily destroy their lives: you look at this couple of your transformed former friends; you consider that when a single-celled creature, an amoeba or whatever, parts and multiplies, it also dies, in a sense; and you wonder light-heartedly if it is not the same for somewhat more advanced creatures like us: to breed is to cease living. Except that, just like with marriage, in a couple of years you find yourself looking over your shoulder to check that you are not the only sprogless wonder left on the block, that you have not somehow missed the boat of vicarious immortality by devoting yourself blindly, for one year too many, to partying and holidays and work.

Maybe divorce is becoming the next marker in an allegedly normal progression of life. Perhaps we will all soon feel weird and outsiders if we do not have a divorce under our generous belts. Even as we all looked at Harry with that strange mixture of shock and fascination, I think all of us were wondering: right, so Jan pulled the plug on her long-time guy a year before, and now Harry has unshackled himself. Who next?

Or indeed, what next? When you know that your so-called career is bollocks, and that you are never going to get The Job that you vaguely half-dreamed of without ever quite getting a clear outline of what it was? When settling down and sprogging seems the only possible thing to do, but then fails to deliver that still, serene, self-sufficient Life you dreamed of one day when it all seemed too meaningless? What? Do we end up full circle and alone again, at forty, starting it all over once more, except this time without that unde-fined trust and hope in the world that we had at

46

twenty? Is that it? Is that all? And if it is, just what the fuck are we going to put in our Lonely Hearts ads?

There was a brief moment of silence as we let this particular stone fall into the deep well. Me especially, maybe, because I have always rather liked Sarah. Another moment, perhaps, when we should have decided to pull our horns in for that particular night.

If we had, I might still be married myself, who knows.

—What? said Jan, before she quite had time to take an unconscious and quite scary grin off her face. —You actually getting divorced?
—Well, not yet, said Harry. —The plan is to get a quickie before they close the doors on them. Which means I have to confess either to shagging someone or knocking Sarah about.
—And? I asked, seeing that Harry was waiting for a cue.
—Well, by the time Hannah is big enough to want to look up the records, if she ever does, it will be even more acceptable to shag around than now and even less acceptable to knock women about. So I think I'll admit to sex with a Person Unknown in Macedonia.
—Macedonia? roared Jan. —God, Harry, you old drama queen.
—Actually, it did happen, said Harry, gloating openly at her. —When we were doing that thing about Alexander the Great's dad. Effect, though, not Cause.
—WoWoWo! said Jan as a cheerleader.
—Well, said Harry, —I reckon marriage and monogamy are like pickled cabbage or Parma ham: something our ancestors invented to get them through the hard,

dark days without dying out. And now we've forgotten why we had to get to like it.

—Hooray for Mr MacDonald! came a ghastly cackle from the old drunk. Harry chewed his lip and looked at his nails.

—So now you definitely have to go down the gym, gloated The Wop. —News!

—Sod that. What? And be condescended to by the kind of bastards I used to avoid in the playground. No thanks.

—Back in play now, Harry. Got no choice.

—Balls. My body is only a life-support system for my brain.

—Yeah? So get fat, mate, and lose your telly show.

—I'm not bloody fat!

—Good job, said Jan, treacherously. —Bald, four-eyed and fat: the three things that make any casting director think: Comedy Character. Speaking as a woman, Harry, the way I do, you can have any one of them no prob, if you have the spark. Fat *or* bald *or* specky. Maybe you can get away with two of them, if you've really got pizzazz. But all three? Now that is going to be a problem out in the vicious world of singles.

—Why do you think he wears contacts? I chipped in.

—Listen, you bunch of bastards, I can still return the first serve of any bastard round this table without my contacts in and I am not fucking fat. There's hundreds of blokes in my gym that . . .

—In your *what*? demanded The Wop.

—OK, yeah, so I swim a few times a week. Just to stop me getting a bad back.

—News news news! Harry's down the gym, boys. Victory is ours!

—Not yours, Wop: mortality's. Here's to it.

—Hooray for Mr MacDonald! screeched the drunken academic.

—OK, Mr Existential Fitness, let's celebrate mortality, said Harry. —Let's see who's still standing at three a.m.

We threw back our drinks, shoved back our chairs, and surveyed each other happily. Yes indeed: as long as you are fighting your set-piece battles with your old friends, you know they are still friends, not just old.

OK, so that was our first chance gone: we didn't run at the mere sight of Harry's skull-to-be, or at the news that he was splitting up. Hardly surprising. No one would have. Well, maybe some stupid, superstitious Third-Worlder. Who, in this case, would have been right, of course. But we don't run at that kind of thing. How can we? If I refused to get on a plane every time I have a totally concrete, technicolour vision that this particular flight is cursed to go down in a fireball shortly after take-off, I would never get on a plane. Of course I get on. But I always buy extra insurance at the last minute, just as a message to whoever is listening that I am at least receiving their warning, and am reacting to it somehow, even if I am not really acting upon it, so can I maybe be given the benefit of the doubt? Please? Which, come to think about it, means I am acting like some stupid superstitious Third-Worlder.

So much for Socrates.

The Lions

I want to freeze us for a second, Harry spieling away and all of us grinning like teenagers. Secure like teenagers together around our little pub table. Do you know that feeling? I think we all do.

Sometimes, when I put little Hugh to bed, he asks me to stay and sleep on the floor beside him because the lions might come. Nothing to do with real lions, of course: it just seems to be whatever that primate instinct is that says there are things with claws and teeth that might roar in from the dark outside, beyond the campfire, and gobble him up. I lie down, and see him looking at me as if I could hold back all the lions in the world. I am there; nothing can hurt him. He is asleep almost immediately; my heart surges with love, pride and longing as I watch him a while.

So much for instinct. Because one of me, or one of any man alive, or one of some proto-human half-gorilla with a stone club, would, in fact, of course, be no good against the mangiest of the lions. But that is nothing to do with it. The only biology that matters to us is human. We are simply machines for bouncing off each other, and everything else we do with ourselves is secondary. When Hugh goes to sleep with me there, his learned experience of me (not instinct, because some dads come like lions in the night) tells him, and quite rightly, that here beside him is someone who would lay down his life for him. It is no logical calculation of the odds in any match of myself versus a lion that settles his brain to Go Away Somewhere Else (that is what he calls his dreams) but simply a fact: *someone who would die for him is settling down to sleep beside him*, and that alone makes everything all right.

Maybe it is just another word for love. You can see it plainly in soldiers and actors: they live through months of wildly intense togetherness, and afterwards they can never give up on the bear-hugs and kisses. And weren't we all like that when we were young? And haven't we all lost it somewhere along the way? And isn't it that loss, that yawning gap, that haunts us when we lie awake in the property-safes we call our homes, our hearts beating for dread of something that we can now only call Nothingness, but which we once called the lions?

And isn't that what made us hang close together, smiling idiotically at nothing other than the sense of our togetherness?

Christ, to be walking free with your real friends again! To be with the people again who once, at least, would instinctively have backed you against anyone: your old, good friends, the sort of friends you simply cannot make after about twenty-five, it seems: people from your own private Lost World, from that time, that time that will always seem like the only really Real Time to you, for ever; free for the night, suddenly off on Adventures again, suddenly feeling that strange rush of expectation that comes when, just for a change, you *don't* know what is going to happen next again except that it is going to happen again with your irrational, misfit, unbreakable group of friends. Together again, in that strange and wonderful presence of ourselves as our gang, that thing which is more than each of us and yet makes us each feel as if we are ourself again, that self which we still believe, still long to believe, is our self for ever: the Wild Bunch reincarnated, lion-hunters burning with the longing to find things we had never seen or felt. Mow my lawn? Not me, mate, count me out. We haven't stopped making hay and memories yet: we have not yet finished carving the patterns of our brains.

Laughing now in the Museum Tavern at all the boring couples planning boring evenings at boring restaurants or boring shows to put off the crushing boredom of the rest of their boring fucking lives. Which we knew were so boring because they were our lives too.

But not tonight. Tonight, just this one night, let it be as if we were crazed and confused and yet somehow pure again; as if we were daring and careless of our health and our bones, fearless of admitting our love and our need for each other again; as if, dear God, we were young again.

Young!

Harry, or: The Supposed Day of the Mince

Young.

That's what they always call Harry. The *Young* TV Archaeologist.

Yes, while us other poor over-the-halfway-line sods of whatever sex have to pull in our guts, tuck up our arses and thrust our pelvises subtly forward, heave up our spines, raise our chins, look bravely in the mirror and lie straight into our own conniving eyes, to convince ourselves that we can still pass for young on a good night in a low-lit club, Harry only has to read the papers, watch the box and flip happily through the lifestyle mags. Young, he is declared.

And who is to argue? If the papers and the telly say someone is beautiful, or desirable, or posh, or famous or whatever, we believe them. We have to, because we have nothing else to go on: the verdict of the media is final. And so as long as the TV guides keep on informing Harry that he is Young, in a way he really *is* young, the lucky sod.

Christ, the other digging-folk must hate his guts when he descends from the clouds with his TV crew to wander about their excavations for a day or two. Why (they must ask), given that there are x thousand sad, devoted, overeducated crusties in the country whose idea of a fun day out is squatting all day in mud while toothbrushing out the eye sockets of some poor Bronze Age bastard who thought he was safely dead and forgotten a long, long time ago, should Harry bloody

MacDonald, of all people, the most superficial, cod-Celtic twat who ever walked the earth, be the one they have to crawl to if they want publicity? The one that makes sure he gets all the good lines? The one that trousers the wedge from the suits that run the telly and gets eternal, press-fed Youth into the bargain? Why him?

Good question, and here's the good answer. Harry MacDonald, as known to the world, is one of the by-products of the bizarreness of your modern TV programming. He is a creation brought to us by the same Mysterious Telly People who decided, sometime back in the early eighties, that from now on, and for no comprehensible reason, all programmes aimed at the under-sixes had by law to be presented by yelling, grinning, nineteen-year-old coke-head tarts and rent boys. Well, it certainly wasn't the five-year-olds who demanded it. I mean, sorry, but have you ever heard a five-year-old complain that some nice uncle-like presenter in a cardigan wasn't trendy enough? I think not.

The thing about Harry's job is this: you or I or anyone with approximately the right number of chromosomes could read everything that is actually said in those allegedly upmarket telly progs about history and archaeology and the like in ten minutes flat. And surprise surprise, you usually *can*, that weekend, in one or other of the Sunday supplements. None of it ever gets much above GCSE, because if it did, Eric Public would zap back to the game shows. Well, and so: all in all you don't just *not need* some tweedy old boring prof to spout the crap on air, you don't *want* one.

No, what you really need is an energetic twat who looks nice on the camera and talks good. Not too posh, natch, because that's a turn-off for your Mass Audience.

But it can't just be one of the tarts and rent boys: this person also has to have a kosher Professional Title and Job Description so that it isn't too bloody obvious that the telly bosses are actually just taking the piss while trying to show they have Quality Programming Concepts.

Not so easy to find the right person, when you think about it. Lively without being a kiddies' TV speed-freak type? Acceptable to the Mass Audience yoof yet also to the critics? A genuine professor but one without the usual stoop and Clarks' pastie shoes? Enter stage left Harry MacDonald (at this point still sandily hirsute) armed with many useful qualifications.

These were: (i) a crazed, synthetic, classless accent which, though basically a ghastly Taff-oid sing-song, slides madly in and out of Scots, Oirish and mockney as the fancy takes him. A typical Harry sentence on the box would be something like *By Christ, here we are then, boys, down in this wee dismal dungeon, where it is, as you can see, as black as Newgate's bloody knocker*; (ii) a disarming ability to say *fuck* and suchlike with an engaging smile that reassures the audience he means nothing bad by it; (iii) the surprisingly rare ability to walk about without falling over things while talking to a camera in a relaxed and sociable manner; (iv) the requisite Ph.D. parchment plus kosher university job in archaeology; and (v) an ambition so strong that ambition is not the right word; a hunger, a need, a desperation to make it if it kills you, more like. And if he never (vi) gave a blow job to some old telly queen to land the part (which he swears he didn't), it will only have been because he knew what every kind of tart knows: that you are hotter while fancied than when fucked.

That's Harry.

Now, everyone knows (thanks to his many interviews in the *Radio Times* and *Hello!* and suchlike) the story about Harry and how he got his Ph.D. But just in case you don't read *Hello!*, the story goes roughly like this:

It was, says Harry, on a certain day, just as the eighties were actually becoming The Eighties of unfond remembrance, just as absurd anecdotes about London house prices began to filter through to pre-boom Ireland and coagulate as the unbelievable but undeniable truth. Young Harry MacDonald, at that time still hanging out in Bogland as an allegedly happy-go-lucky digger of the parish, was obliged on this particular afternoon by sheer, brutal lack of the extra *coppers*, never mind silver, never mind paper money, never mind a credit card, to ask a butcher's boy in Boyle, Co. Roscommon, to take off a couple of ounces from the small heap of Economy Mince that lay greyly on the greasy scale (the colour died from the hashed flesh, said Harry, as the boy slid the tray out from under the cunning, meat-friendly UV light). Because Harry could just, *just*, pay for the four ounces he had shyly ordered, hence (when combining it, back in his tent, with a handful of old spaghetti) eating for the first time that day; but he could not pay for five and a half ounces. He reckoned it must have made the spotty little git's day. The very next day, Harry saw the advert for a London college bursary to do a Ph.D. in archaeology. Sold his horrible crusty drum, his *barong* (or *bowhrohgmn* or however the fuck you write it) to some laughable German hippy and hitched straight home.

Harry always tells this tale to the press, to demonstrate his credentials as a non-poshy boy and the kind of devoted guy who would do something as stupid and pure as start a Ph.D. at a time when Maggie was kicking the unis in the teeth and everyone else was making insane amounts of cash in advertising, in the City or just in plain old accounting.

Actually, of course, it is all lies and bollocks.

Birth of the False Birthdays

I'm not saying Harry never had to buy mince and couldn't afford it. I'm just saying that I always knew that wasn't why he did his Ph.D. and became respectable.

Obviously, I knew Harry had done archaeology at college, but I had never heard him talk about it in the four years since we all finished, apart from as the way he earned his paltry, crusty bread. Wherever we met, what he talked about was festivals, lifts, bullfights, beaches, sex wonderfully great and sex comically crap, drugs, music and witty examples of shoplifting. And here he was, suddenly telling the world that archaeology was the perfect Woppish balance between intellectual activity and physical exertion.

Suspicious.

In fact, we all knew he was lying through his teeth. Because what the big world does not know is that the conditions of the Ph.D. bursary which Harry applied for said you had to be under twenty-six to apply, and Harry had been twenty-six for several months. So what did he do?

Simple. He went for the grand, big lie: he knocked six months off his life, just like that. He expanded each of his digging stints by an easy little month, and, with the connivance of some well-disposed lady digger, he promoted himself from bog-standard Digging Volunteer to official Site Assistant and bumped his d.o.b. six months forward. In short, he lied his way into his bursary and simply bet they wouldn't find out.

—Anyway, he snapped at the time, —so what if they do? What are they going to do about it? They're not the fucking *State* or something!

They didn't twig, natch. Harry got his bursary, which meant he got a nice room in a postgrad house up Swiss Cottage way, cheques every quarter, and a virtually guaranteed job at the end of it provided he kept his head down and his nose clean. And most importantly, if you ask me, he got something he could admit to when anyone asked him, as Brits inevitably do, what it was he did. He got an identity. Salvation!

Salvation: that was what Harry said that first night in the Museum Tavern, when he came rushing in and announced that he was never again going to have to live in a squat, or tell some spotty little twat to remove a bit of his economy fucking mince. And Salvation we toasted. (Talk about premature celebration.)

Then Harry told us about his clever little whitish lies, and we decided in the heat of the beer that no matter how old and crap and married and fucked-up we all got, we would always meet up, in this pub, on Harry's False Birthday, and he would always buy the drink, and we would always cane it decently together. To celebrate salvation through lies.

I shared his relief. Me especially. Because to be honest, Harry had been getting to be a real pain in the arse about money. In fact, the very last time before he made his great Change, Harry had seriously proposed to me that I let him pinch my credit card. All I had to do, he swore nervily, was wait until late next morning to notice, while he went shopping. At ten fifty, Harry would bin the card; at eleven, I would call the bank. The pub could confirm I'd been there all night to the cops. Foolproof, he said, and I saw his eyes burning.

And if he somehow got caught, and if that led somehow to me (though why should it? said Harry), he would take the blame and admit he had abused my friendship to nick my plastic.

Later, I followed him to the lav and said:

—OK then, Harry.

—OK what? he asked, surprised.

—OK, Harry, my chequebook and my card are in the left-hand pocket of my jacket and I'm in here and if you take it now I will never know for sure it was you because I don't intend to look again until tomorrow at eleven. Once. Never again.

He did, too, the bastard. And it worked.

But knowing how bad things had got, I was delighted when he got his bursary. See? Salvation.

The Wop and Jan do not know about this little piece of unwanted financial history. It's a funny old thing, being human and all that, isn't it? I mean, Harry is one of my best and oldest friends, and I know that he knows that at certain times the thought has crossed my brain, of course it has, no more than crossed, but crossed all right, that I could flog this story to the tabloids. And he knows I know that at some time or other it must have crossed, just *crossed* his, that it would be pretty handy if I was to be subtly shoved under an oncoming tube one fine night, just in case things between us ever got nasty.

Really, there are some things you just have to agree to forget.

Kilts and Big Boots

But one thing I have never forgotten is the sheer obsessiveness of Harry's transformation. You have never seen anyone work so hard as Harry did at changing himself. I remember in particular one time when I went to meet him at the British Museum. He worked there every day, treating his Ph.D. like any ordinary nine-to-five, and since I was at that time in my first kosher-ish job, in Bedford Square, we often used to meet for a swift pint after what we both called work. I was early, of course, and was planning to just hang around, waiting happily in my usual way, looking at mummies and statues and the crap in the museum shop and stuff, but on this particular day I thought I'd just take a peek into the Reading Room, since I'd never done so before. They wouldn't let me in because I had no card, but through the door I could see the people, beavering away like monks, tiny under the big dome.

I scanned for Harry among the massed big-heads. I knew what he was doing, logically, of course. But it had never quite occurred to me that these people, the vast majority of them males of some indeterminate age between twenty-five and fifty, who generally looked as if they would not worry about not having sex for too long even if they never had sex again, were the very same boys that Harry was up against, head-to-head, when he talked about getting his articles published. Scary.

Snoring. I could hear it quite distinctly: several of the monkish lads were turning and sniffing in the direction of this unseen snoring. Their shufflings added to the disturbance of the great, soft, cathedral hum. They looked around for vengeance, and eventually one of the librarians, a little guy with a tragic moustache, extruded himself from his pod, stood for a second undecided, and then stepped smartly off in the direction of whoever this snoring bastard was.

My adrenalin told me. I ghosted sideways, closer to the barrier, and craned to see between the oaky, blue-leathered desks.

Harry, of course. There he was, sprawled over this big heap of books, with filing cards spreading out from under him and spilling down into the carpet: carefully colour-coded filing cards he had, I had seen them before and been amazed at their unexpected orderliness. His face was squashed up against the pages of one of the books; his specs were shoved upwards and outwards by the weight of his own head; he did not look like a man who had got bored and tired and decided to have a quick, sneaky forty winks, but like someone who had simply been shot in the head, mid-work, by some merciful hitman with a silenced gun up in the gallery.

I had never seen Harry actually working (not surprising: when did you ever see any of your friends actually working? Strange, when you think how much of our lives we spend doing it). I knew that he was, at this time, just starting on the second year of his three-year grant. He had already cunningly had two chapters of his Ph.D. published as articles, and was thus, as far as I knew, well ahead of the game and under no pressure of deadlines or expectations whatever. I had always imagined him swanning hippyishly about the place, idly plucking bits of arcane knowledge from rare volumes he happened across by chance, but here he was: quite literally collapsed in a heap over his work.

As I watched, vaguely aware that the keeper on the door was starting to think I was a nutter rather than some respectful tourist, I tried to imagine Harry in big boots and a kilt, with his hand up a toy ferret's arse.

You heard right. Because, you see, when Harry went for the job as presenter of *Among The Dead, Live*, he had the final trump card, which few academics, however young, could match: he had indeed been one of the tarts and rent boys anyway. By which I mean he had experience as a kiddies' actor. Experience which he eradicated from his CV at the time of his change to a Respectable Lecturer and which he now keeps very quiet indeed.

And who can blame him? I mean, who wants the now-respectful world to know that when they were allegedly a young and dedicated archaeologist, all they were actually doing was digging trenches and filling wheelbarrows for the real excavators, while being more truly engaged in poncing about in a kilt and big boots with their hand up a toy ferret's arse, singing horrible crap to six-year-old kids at summer festivals, bashing shamelessly on one of those wanky Irish drums and swilling Guinness round the campfires with big-arsed digging chicks of an evening? Not Harry.

Yep, Harry always wanted to be a thesp, really. According to Harry, he gave up after he was offered his Equity card (which you still needed in those days to have any chance of working as an actor) in exchange for a shag. He didn't do it, and so he didn't get the job, so the old boy and Harry agreed that Harry did not really want to be an actor that badly.

—Nope, said Harry, —I will not have a dick up my

bum. Not me. I got standards. My arse stays virgin. Instead, I plan to sit on it for three years in a library growing piles to get a steady job. But I will not let a dick up it. How pure can you get?

Good old Harry, such a twat.

And such a fucking liar.

I was just thinking this, and trying without much success to superimpose that Harry on this slumped, book-bound Harry, when one of the librarians came up and shoved him awake with surprising roughness. Harry came to, looking stunned and shocked to find himself still alive and here, and began to apologise (it was like watching a mime show): watching him explaining himself to the snooty little bod, I caught the quite distinct sense that Mr Quiet Librarian had only dared to be so brusque with Harry because this appalling breach of British Museum regulations had happened more than once before.

Then Harry saw me, caught my eye, and laughed. The laugh shot round the dome of the library, the hundred bookish heads turned anew, and Harry looked like he was having to grovel pretty sharpish, all over again, to avoid being banned for life.

I never told Harry how long I had watched him that day, but ever since then, I had known that his manic change, and all his subsequent success, had happened because of more than just a lump of bloody mince. For years I kind of gently waited for him to spill the beans, but eventually we accept anything as natural, and by now I had more or less given up hope of ever being vouchsafed some big insight about what was really motoring away in Harry's head. And who cared? I was content to just enjoy the False Birthdays as a given thing, and be bloody glad we still did them.

Glad that we have got something a little dodgy left in our lives; something that still holds out just a little, tiny suggestion, a hint, that maybe the stories have not quite stopped; that we are not yet doomed to simply revisit the land of Wild Tales in our old, worn stories, like restless ghosts of our own lives. A promise that something might still happen, that the world is still fresh and all the doors, in the world and in our heads, are there to be kicked open still.

Of course, you might say that it is truly pathetic to keep clinging on to this with Forty just around the corner, and no doubt you would be right. But what does being right have to do with it? You think that life is like some sodding pub quiz? You think there is some big prize, someday, somewhere, for being *right*? You want a gold star for being *right*?

I don't. I just want to breathe a bit. Christ, who doesn't want to have his cake and eat it? And we didn't even ask to *eat* the bloody cake: just to be allowed to take it out of the secret, glass-walled cupboard where we locked it safely away all those years ago, and just sniff it, just maybe taste the cake again, on the tips of our tongues, just once a year. Is that so bloody wrong?

Enough, enough: Let's unzap the pause button and get back up to speed.

Now you know about us all, here we are again, finishing our drinks in the Museum Tavern and ready to rumble.

Rameses the Second on a Bad Day

By now, we were on our third drink, and we all knew that any moment now Harry would up and propel us all towards whatever unknown crappery we were booked for tonight. Expectation buzzed between us. Meanwhile we had discovered, to our great delight, that each of us had, in some way or other, had a Ghastly Revelation of sorts in the last few days.

The Wop had had this favourite student of his, a young man of whom he expected great things, a youth who appeared to combine physical fitness and intellectual honesty in the doses The Wop desired, come bounding out of his A levels and proudly tell The Wop, sure of his teacherly approval, that *he had not bottled out* in the face of pressure from a hypocritical society because he had just deliberately failed his exams.

Jan, fresh from a recent triumph in which she forced some theatre or other to change its lav signs from *Ladies and Gents* to *Men and Women* or lose their grant, had been gunning for an even hotter slot on the Arts Council, only to discover that the only other candidate was an Asian lesbian. She had withdrawn rather than face certain and public defeat.

As for me, it was nothing so dramatic. It was simply that we had all just been handed out our *next* year's office wall-planners that week, in order that we could plot out our lives a whole eighteen months ahead. Coloured stars, bars, dots and all. Nothing unusual in that; it happens every year. Except this year, I looked at next year and realised that I could now, if I wished, put

66

a little red sticky dot on my fortieth birthday; that I could now, would now *have* to, watch the days counting away; that I could now tell exactly which training group I would be team-leading, in which room in our office, in fifteen months' time, on my fortieth birthday. Which left me with a feeling I find hard to describe, except to say that it was, for one second, uncomfortably close to lift cables suddenly giving way.

As for Harry, he had, of course, just lost his horrible ponytail.

—It's so fucking unfair! he cried. —I thought it was OK, I thought the bastard gays had covered it for us all. You know, no gay man wants to think about getting old, getting old for gays just means getting nearer the day no one wants to shag you any more.

—What, unlike us happy straights? demanded Jan.

—Yeah, really.

—At least we have structures to hide it. They don't. They can't have kids and grandkids, so that knocks Births and Marriages off the list. The next big life event is going to be Death, however long they put it off.

—News! Harry the Homophobe!

—Not at all. I am astonished by their suicidal bravery. And I copy their hairstyle. I think they have this tactful plot, see, between the young gays and the old gays. Everyone agrees to shave their heads so that the old gays can pretend it's just a fashion statement. The young gays know that when it's their turn to recede, they'll get the payback.

—Well! And to think I thought it was all about misogyny and testosterone!

—Whatever, Jan, I thought they'd won that one for all of us. Job done, I thought: thanks boys, I thought. I thought I could trust the power of Pink. Have it cut short, and fool the world, I says to myself. Fuck, but look at me: it's horrible. I swear I could feel the bastard clippers tracing the outline of my skull-to-be, boys; I could follow the archaeological fucking plates of bone. Shag my granny pink, I look like the mummy of Rameses the fucking Second on a bad day! And you know what I saw today? In the university?

—No, I replied, as needed.

—One of my *colleagues* had clipped this page from some horrible local rag; it was a photo of him and another *colleague*, right, standing at some crap conference holding oh-so-fucking-daring Pints Of Beer, darling, two twats with beards and stupid grins and Pints Of Beer, and the git had written underneath it, in big bloody felt pen: *'Would you buy a used degree from this dodgy duo?'* I could feel my shoes turning into grey leather squeaky things as I stood there. My colleagues; my life. Right, so we're all fucked, one way or another, and one day they can stick us all in some Long Barrow, with this epitaph carved in ogham script:

> On Earth they always made, then failed
> The last Selection Board
> On Judgment Day they heard their fate:
> Short-listed by the Lord.

OK, boys, let's rock and roll, the cab'll be here now.

—What cab? I asked happily, hitting my cue again as soon as my throat was free of beer.

—Ask not lest ye be told, said Harry. —Come on.

We had all forgotten in the meantime that we had travelled light from work, and found ourselves instinctively looking down and patting pockets to see what we had left behind. Then we all saw what we were doing and laughed again.

—My God, said Jan. —We are *not* weighed down with crap for once!

—Free and lost, said The Wop.

And so we all sauntered to the door, as if being unencumbered by files, briefcases, bags, overcoats and newspapers was a sure and visible sign of wildness and danger. Yes, we had become so used to trundling about with armfuls of everyday rubbish that just being able to hop up like that and leave a pub without gathering up armfuls of shit felt like a sort of wicked liberation.

—Good luck, Mr MacDonald. —And congratulations on your tonsure.

—Actually, said Harry at the door, striking a pose. — Actually, despite your efforts, the name is *Doctor*, arsehole.

—Ah, changed your surname as well?

Harry looked at him, knocked for six. Then he burst out laughing.

—Dr Arsehole leads the way!

—Um, Harry, said Jan, taking Harry's arm as we made it on to the street.

—Yes?

—Just let me get one thing clear.

—Fine.

—Are you actually getting divorced yet?

—Oh, well, we haven't *actually* gone to the lawyers yet.

—Not, then.

—Not yet. But it's clearly the only logical thing to do.

—So you are going to do it? I asked.

—Obviously, shrugged Harry.

—Cop-out! cackled The Wop.

—But of course, said Harry.

So we proceeded out to the street and the light and the real world, where a black cab was indeed waiting, hearse-like, in the fuming rain.

—Luton Airport, said Harry. —Quick as you can.

—You what? said The Wop.

—You heard, said Harry.

—You didn't say anything about passports! yelled Jan. —You stupid sod. I haven't got mine! We'll have to go via my place, we . . .

—Aha. Let me guess, I said. —You don't need a passport for Ireland, right, Harry?

Harry looked closely and privately at me, as if unsure whether I had caught him out or just made a lucky hit.

—Ben, man, what makes you think that?

—Dunno. I was just thinking about it earlier. Mince and ferrets and stuff.

—Well, well. There we are. Always watch out for the quiet ones.

—And?

—Give that quiet man a Nobel Prize.

I should've guessed right then that this was more than just another False Birthday jaunt. Really, I should. I think maybe I had, half.

As Skinny as Fuck Again

—Right, said Harry. —Ireland it is. We're in central Dublin by half eight. Room's booked. We get the eight a.m. flight back on GoganAir, in work by ten. (Harry was already talking on his mobile, even as he fished four of those pre-mixed G&Ts out of his pockets and handed them round.) —Hello, this is Dr MacDonald (Harry tried not to giggle) for the 19.10 flight to Dublin. Yes. My party may be a little tight checking in, I've had an emergency patient . . . Yes, hand-luggage only. Oh, good. Thanks a million. Right, boys, that's us doomed.

—Doomed to Dublin? I retorted, more or less as expected.

—Yeah, cried Harry. —Doomed to Dublin. Look, boys, this is going to be *such* a heap of crap. And an investigation. We can try to work out why the hell millions of idiots go to Dublin every year. I mean, why the bastard hell should anyone believe they are going to experience anything unforgettable, some earth-shaking sodding insight or renewal of the wanked-out soul, in a place a few miles due west of Liverpool? With the same horrible weather, the same shite food, the same grey buildings, almost the same bastard fucking horrible accent and everything costing half as much again? OK, so they resprayed the postboxes green seventy years ago. Great. And they have a few squares of allegedly Georgian but actually mostly early Victorian buildings, and pictures of James Joyce everywhere you look. Wow. Give me Amsterdam any day. Or France. Why *Ireland* for Christ's sake? And we're going on some horrible old licence-built BAC 111 they bought off shagging Ceaucescu when it was too crap even for Romanians. Doomed!

—Go, Dr Arsehole! crowed Jan.

—I worked for that title, said Harry.

—And he's got the stoop to prove it, I said.

—Fuck off, said Harry, pulling himself straighter.

—Listen to him, cried The Wop (as he usually did round about this time). —This isn't a question of fitness, it's a nightmare. Stop the cab.

—And what about the ... Colombian Marching Powder, shouted, then hissed Jan, suddenly remembering we were in a cab. —We can't bring Salvador Dali through airport security. What? Don't tell me you haven't ... ?

—Today, we do without.

—What, till three in the morning? Like hell. Stop the cab.

—The music'll keep you up, laughed Harry.

—Music? scowled The Wop. —If you are talking bagpipes ...

—Well, Ben? said Harry.

—I can do without the clown and I can even live with bagpipes, so long as they have Guinness and the crack, or the *craieck* or whatever it's called, is really as crap as they say it is.

—It most certainly is, said Harry. —The *c-r-a-i-c*, which is in fact how you spell it, is just a load of semi-Brits getting off their faces and making a load of noise about it in pubs you can hardly breathe in or move in. It's fucking A1 dismal.

—Fine, said I.

—But then, what isn't? It's a laugh if you take it right. And what isn't?

—Hark at Existential Bloke already going native, *sure and what isn't bejasus*? Let me out the cab!

—Sell it, Dr Arsehole!

—Right, you bunch of Saxon bastards, cried Harry.

This (as we knew very well) was a sign that Harry had now hit his full-on Celtic Twat mode and was thus, as we all knew, unstoppable for the next fifteen minutes at least.

—People people people, we are all closing rapidly on forty, and when I say forty I refer both to our ages and to our Levi's waist measurements, quite ignoring the fact that only sad old fucks like us wear Levi's any more anyway. 34 . . . 36 . . . 38 . . . Where will it end? On the day we think *Hey, great, I'm thin again, I can wear 34-inch Levi's again*, then realise that we have put the belt under our beer gut? Not even then. Not ended then, not by far, all the defeats and degradation. No, I'll tell you where it ends, boys: shite and potties again, then skulls and bones, that's where. Take it from me: we are all doomed to be skinny as fuck again one day, however much we stuff ourselves in the here and bloody now. Well, boys and Jan, I am getting divorced, I have today declared the unequal battle with my hairline officially lost, and, if you will excuse me mixing my fucking metaphors, I intend to face the firing squad with all guns blazing. I am going to Dublin to have a laugh at its crapness and hence my own crapness for going there. If you're not up for it, go fuck yourself, cash in your ticket and we'll meet one day for a stiff Horlicks in the Retirement Home, and talk bowels. Well? Are we still alive? Ben? Wop? Jan?

Why *did* we go, just like that? Because it was what we secretly wanted. You know: you spend so much of your life checking your timetable, arranging your payments, flicking through your diaries (manual or electronic) and working out your actual or psychological mileage allowances, that it is sometimes, just once in a while, such a bloody, bloody *joy* to have someone else take over: to *not* know exactly what is going to happen next. To know that because you have just said Yes to something, things which you cannot possibly predict are now bound to happen. To feel the wheels rolling again. Just a little taste of that freedom again. Within reason, naturally.

What could we have said? No? Yes, we could have said No. You always can. Christ, all it takes is enough Conviction, and you can say No even when the guys in black have the electrodes ready, never mind when some twat like Harry offers you a stupid dare. But I suppose the secret truth was: we had none. Conviction, I mean. We had, in various ways, all been saying No a lot in the last few years (even if we would never have admitted it). We had all been doing a lot of things because they were supposedly the right things to do, and not a lot of things that we actually wanted to do. But every time you do something because you tell yourself *it's the right thing, the sensible thing, the only sane thing to do*, that means you are saying No to something else; and if it wasn't something you wanted, or at least half wanted, you wouldn't have to tell yourself exactly how right and sensible and sane you were *not* to do it, would you? Somewhere deep down, we had it up to here: our hearts were shouting SAY YES FOR ONCE and as we looked around London, at the milling hordes of people, people like us, struggling home through the rain to their quiet lives, lives like ours, none of us could think of any good reason to say No.

And there was something else. In Harry's eyes, something more than just that stuff about hair and forty

74

and skulls, the usual crap. The bastard was up to something. I thought about that Day of the Mince, and for some reason I guessed – no, I felt it in my guts – that tonight I was going to find out something about Harry, my oldest friend, that I had never known. The gap in his past. The black hole around which his life secretly spun. The curtain was twitching, the lights were going down, and a strange show was about to begin.

Go home now?

Yeah, really.

London

So we sat happily in the cab and crawled through London instead.

London. That's one of the things about Harry's False Birthdays and the Museum Tavern and all that crap. It all happens in London.

Now, we all live in London, but not in *London* London, I mean, not any places you would recognise as London. The kind of places where black cabs are almost as rare as they are in Birmingham. Where people come to live once they have finished with falling in love and all that. Why? Easy: we all fall in love in Zone 1 and then we all live in Zone 3 if we are lucky.

We all used to live in Zone 1. Well, Zone 2, which is nearly the same thing really. We had vile little bedsits to ourselves or hideous, smelly, noise-infested flats shared with nutters in places like Shepherd's Bush and Earls Court and West Ken. You know, the sort of bachelor and girl-about-town gaffs that are nothing to do with homes: they are just base camps for your assault on the big world of work and play, so you don't even notice the horror of them. Then we all hit our thirties, and met people we thought we might actually like to live with, and realised that we were living in shit. Whereupon we all, as we later discovered, spent months pursuing the same insane fantasy: that somewhere, out there, is a last, lost corner of Olde London, circa 1978.

It must be there, somewhere, we all thought: the

76

forgotten island. An oasis in between the impossible places everyone on earth knows from postcards and the inconceivable places no one has ever heard of except the poor sods that live there. It must be there, still, somewhere: nothing flash, not the kind of place where shops selling chromium taps punctuate boulevards of ridiculously-named cafés; just a neighbourhood where ordinary, hardworking, untrustfunded, child-having, educated-ish, interesting-ish people can afford normal, sociable little houses with modest gardens for the kids. With the odd pub where you can take said kids and have a quiet pint and maybe the occasional friendly word with other late-thirties blokes who are trying to read large newspapers and enjoy their pints while likewise minding their kids. With schools where said kids will not be attacked every day because they are not in the Young NF and/or don't know what Gangsta Rappers should wear when they are eight. And neighbours who don't play White Trash Thrash or Devastation Techno and don't kick in your car just for the fuck of it and axe-murder one another on Saturday nights when the gear runs short.

And only half a dozen stops from town.

And you can afford.

The kind of places that used to exist. That surely used to exist?

But since none of us is an oil analyst, corporate lawyer or suchlike, the result, circa the millennium, was: Hahahahaha!

And so now we all live in places way outside the Black Cab Belt, places you can only get to on trains, except for The Wop, who has a truly ghastly little kip somewhere up wherever the hell it is, double-digit NE whatever, you know, some place no one has ever been to and returned, some region beyond all hope, up near where the Central Line, we assume, finally plunges gratefully into the North Sea.

Which, in our defence, makes it, as I'm sure you know, very nice, very nice indeed, just once a year for God's sake, to be hanging out again, baggageless, uncaring about the last tube again, Up West again, here through the dead centre of the undisputed capital of Northern Europe, crawling free and easy in a shiny black car like a gondola on wheels through the dark and the rain and the lights again: back in our old stomping ground. Everyone's old stomping ground. Where every corner has some shred of your own private past and your own lost innocence, still clinging on in the night and the neon and the wind.

Nice to be here again, isn't it? It is, it is. Far too nice for any sensible thoughts to make us stop the cab, and get out, and return alone to our grey, unloved homes at the ends of the world. Far too.

And here we were then, having failed miserably (but, I hope, understandably) to spot the first spidery cracks in normality, hurtling towards the unseen disaster, or rather honking and weaving our way towards Luton and disaster through the traffic. We laughed and wallowed in our mutual revelations: the important word being WE. We had that lovely feeling that someone out there is like us, that we were part of a gang, that our own private anti-lion squad was assembled around us, ready to take whatever sugar or shit was thrown at us as intended for general consumption: all for one and one for all and all that crap. Which just goes to show, perhaps, that you should be careful what you laugh about.

But laughing we were, as we decamped at Luton Airport.

Now who's a boring old near-forty suburban toss then? Ha! Dublin here we come!

Dublin

I have to admit that I had always wanted to go to Ireland. Pathetic, I know, but then again my democratic defence comes in handy here too: me, and millions of others.

Harry explained it all on the plane. I say *explained*, by which I mean a very extended and loud riff. He was, I have to admit, on great form. Loud, git-faced, embarrassing and doing that very weird thing whereby his accent began to change, before our very ears, to Irish. But on great form.

Look, I can see I have to stop a minute here. I have to explain a bit more about Harry just so you can see why it was we were his mates and liked his company even though he was, and had always been, a complete and undoubted twat.

You remember I told you about his accent, the one he uses on TV, the one everyone seems to like because it comes from everywhere and nowhere? Well, wherever Harry is, he slips towards whatever way people talk. It is very useful, no doubt, and does appear to put people at their ease, and he does it so well, or rather, so *unconsciously*, that no one ever seems to notice. But it can be a bit unnerving if you are a close friend of this bloke who seems to be changing sound and body language (because that's what it actually is, mainly) before your eyes.

Unnerving, at *least*. I know many people who ask me and The Wop how the fuck we can stand it. One answer is that he doesn't do it to us. Or maybe he does, a bit, I'm not sure. No, I am pretty sure he does, actually. Or . . .

Christ, it is hard to see our friends clearly. We do not look at them the way we look at other people: we do not really look at them at all, we do not need to, we simply feel their foggy, friendly presence, like images in a night-sight. Which is no doubt why it is often so very weird and unnerving when we introduce two friends who have never met, accomplices from different bubbles of our lives: we mix up the happy lenses of our friendships, and find ourselves looking at one of these people, or worse, both of them, with a sudden, pitiless, hostile sharpness. Harry says that, archaeologically speaking, this is probably because we were designed to operate our whole lives in clans or tribes or whatever of about a couple of hundred people. For ninety-five per cent of all human history, we knew everybody who we needed to know and who was likely to be well-intentioned towards us, and we only really *looked at* strangers, who, in every culture, are regarded first as potential enemies. Hippies are so full of shit, says Harry, because they only know myths, not truths: the truth is that anyone we do not know personally, or can quickly establish some common relation with, would, throughout most of human history, have tried to do us as soon as they had made whatever necessary trade, salt for olives or whatever. The historical model of human history and trade is an armed exchange, says Harry. Kosovo was standard practice, says he, and if you don't believe him, check out the Old Testament to catch the Lord's colourfully detailed instructions as to how to conduct diplomatic relations with your neighbouring strangers, i.e., do the lot of them at the earliest possible opportunity, male sprogs especially. So now, here we are, and we meet so many people that our built-in ape-like defensive watchfulness is in a state of almost constant readiness, and we can, if we are not careful, find ourselves applying to those who are our true friends the same wretched and fearful standards of risk over profit that we spent hundreds of thousands of years applying to the Rest Of The World outside our own little inbred valleys. Hence, says Harry, our relief when we find ourselves in a gang, in any old bloody gang again.

So all in all I think it best not to think too hard about Harry. Why the hell *should* I? He is my friend, part of me for better or worse.

And here's another thing: so my famous mate Harry is arguably, or even certainly, a laughable human windsock. So what? Who isn't? I mean, who of us here in the First World West isn't? Compared to whoever: peasants and desert horsemen or whatever? Why do you think we are all so obsessed with Wordless Cowboys and 4WD-driving blokes who can talk to horses and all that crap? Because we are obsessed with what we *aren't*, that's why. Our stories are simply the evidence of what we are not; of what we would love to be, but aren't, because if we were, we wouldn't be making up stories about it, would we? No. We would be doing it. Which none of us do. There is this gigantic gap between the life we lead and the life we would like to lead, and this black chasm, this yearning great hole in all our hearts, is the place where all those billions of dollars worth of advertising are successfully poured every day. Offer us A Life and we will give you the world.

So my vote on Harry is this: a quintessential twat, yes, a rootless wandering joke, maybe, but no worse than us all, really. He is of us, of his time, and really only plagued by whatever hopelessness we all have buzzing about inside us. And he is my friend.

And anyway, it's the same as with his telly shows: he doesn't even *ask* you to take him seriously, he knows you know he is being a total dick. Mr PostModern Harry knows you know he knows you know he doesn't believe in any of his religious kitschy crap and his guff about the *strong-walled mansions of the dead* and all that. It's just a laugh: stick your tongue out at a dead saint's skull, hell, why not? Play a penny-whistle tune on some pre-Colombian Peruvian king's thigh bone? Sure.

And if you take it like that, so long as you do not expect anything like Truth from Harry, or Seriousness (and who the hell wants saaaad stuff like *that* anyway, these days?), he can be pretty good company.

At any rate, on the flight to Dublin he achieved the respectable feat of persuading us that we were really going somewhere worthwhile-ly, differently, newly crap. He got us up for it, and who can ask more of anyone?

So, for example, he explained what the Germans are looking for in Ireland:

—Easy, says Harry. —They want the opposite of Germany.

They want the Olde Irish Provo Groupie pub of their dreams, he explained, where happy old men drink whiskey, and fiery young men with red beards and fiddles talk to backpacking German girls without seeming to be actually thinking about shagging them later. A place where life is peasanty and rural and Catholic, yet not dodgy and dusty and dark-skinned and Southern European. Poor, but green; backward, but not smelly or dangerous. And where everyone (handily enough) speaks English, like all Germans. Where you can sit round a real, genuine authentic turf fire and sing allegedly ancient songs written twenty years ago, in English, about how vile the English are, and generally wallow in the kind of folksy, indeed volksy, emotions that are now wisely forbidden to Germans. They want to be allowed to come as modern people to a time before the sixties; they long to wander happily through the last traces of the Second World in Northern Europe.

—See? continued Harry. —And that is why they cross the English Channel and the Irish Sea in their camper vans full of German food and beer. Why not stop in Wales, the bastards? Why not go somewhere where people really *do* speak a different language in Marks and Sparks and the NatWest? Because they don't bloody want any reality, that's why. They want a dream they pre-ordered before they left, and they are willing and able to blot out however many miles of be-bungalowed bastard reality it takes to get it. And some of them buy farms no Irishman wants, for stupid money, stick barbed-wire fences up everywhere, and sell organic sausages in Galway market while living off their Mercedes shares. Oh yeah, and Ireland is the only place they never invaded and the Irish prime minister was the only person in the world who sent a telegram of condolence when Hitler topped himself. And now the Germans are paying for all their roads, so they have to put up with them and smile.

—OK, I quickly put in, to keep Harry going, —so what about the Yanks?

—Oh, well, the Yanks want roots, because everyone in Yankland is lost, and they want somewhere without the blacks because that is what they all actually mean by *social problems*. And Dublin happens to be the only sizeable city in the Western World with no blacks to speak of. And they speak English. And unlike the Scots, as I know to my cost, they count anyone who has an Irish name and is a Catholic as a distant cousin, never mind how they talk. Perfect Yankland tourist pitch. Now, I remember one time, I was . . .

Funny.

I mean, I knew that Ireland was important to Harry: he talked about it quite a lot in the old days, and he still had that ridiculous tang in his TV accent, that helpful suggestion of blarney, but I never realised how seriously he was attached to the place. I use the word attached advisedly: you can always tell how much Harry is keen on something by the amount he bad-mouths it.

Well, why not Ireland? No one chooses the places that have meaning to them. *Meaning*, you know. The places that just make you feel alive, important, significant. People or places. Or things, even. I, for example, once went out with a girl who drove a Citroën 2CV, OK? In Basingstoke. I suppose I was young and impressionable; still open to impressions; my brain still available to make impressions in, like clay. For several weeks I used to go round to see her, just on spec. I didn't dare phone her up first, in case she was in and agreed to see me; I had to go round as if I just happened to be passing: I did not have the guts to say to a girl, *Look, would you like to do something with me?* I needed excuses, like *Oh, I was just popping over to the pub and I thought I'd look in to see if* . . . (I still do, actually). Anyway, whenever I rounded the corner, my heart would leap, really leap, if this crap 2CV was in front of the house. I did this for three weeks or more, and occasionally she came out with me, but she never shagged me, and to this day I feel the tiniest, most distant after-echo of yearning and loss every time I see a bloody Citroën 2CV.

Harry would say that in the constellation of my dreams, one of the far-off, feeble but unmoving stars is a Citroën 2CV. So I supposed that this was what Ireland meant for Harry: one of those places where something happened to you when you were young, when a mark in the clay was made that will never completely be smoothed out: one of the places that makes you *you*.

But I had no idea what that event was.

As I watched him spiel away on the plane (it was not, as he promised, some kind of ancient crate: it was a perfectly normal Boeing. Not exactly the latest model, maybe, but one with no definite signs of ever having been leased to a Third-World airline or being more likely than any other normal European plane to kill us all) I felt I was seeing a part of him I had never quite noticed before.

Anyway, once he spotted there were two nuns on board the plane, there was no stopping him: he began explaining to all and sundry, by now in hallucinatory and perfect Oirish, that it was only the nuns being there that was stopping us plunging into the Irish Sea in a ball of well-deserved flames. He told us (or rather, he told anyone within hearing distance) about mad priests he had known in Ireland when he was a young Crusty Digger. He told us about the priest, a professor at Maynooth University, the spit of Ian Paisley, claimed Harry, but the other side, naturally, who explained how come they still had five classics lecturers there for three students, in these days of cuts: *Because, laddie, when the wee accountants come and ask that question, I reply: St Augustine wrote in Latin! End of story!* And then about the officers in the Curragh Barracks who told Harry

86

that we Brits should leave the Provos to them: *We can't afford H-Blocks, Harry, but there are plenty of bullets for the backs of heads!* And about getting a lift with a Fianna Fail MP who was interested in the London colour problem: *Jesus, we have a problem in Dublin too, now. There must be at least ... two or three hundred of them.*

Actually, Harry said TD, not MP, and we had to stop him to ask what he meant. He was really getting into it, by now. So we laughed and drank steadily, while Harry covered our descent to Dublin Airport with an extended mock-Ian Paisley diatribe about *what hope was there for a world where young people thought Primum Mobile was the most expensive time to call your Vodafone?* Say what you will, but even the air hostesses loved him.

We three were thus still buzzing nicely in the cab from the airport, enough to get us past the miles of convincingly Brit-like suburbia without too much loss of morale. Harry now sat quietly, as if emptied out. Jan and The Wop were looking out of the cab windows in the normal False Birthday manner: they were arguing happily about which pub or bar looked like the crappiest and hence the best place to stop for our first call. But Harry was spying ahead like it was all not as it should be.

—What's up, Harry? I asked.

—Nothing, he said. —I almost stayed here, you know.

—Lucky you didn't, by the sound of it.

—Yes, I suppose it was.

And the way he said it, the look I surprised in his eyes, should have made me realise what was going on: buttressed by his fame and fortune, Harry was coming back to knock something on the head once and for all.

Hitler and the Beatles

I should certainly have realised this as we trundled from failure to failure round Dublin.

We extruded ourselves from the taxi, and Harry, pocketing the receipt to put against his tax, boldly led the way to the centre of Dublin in order to show us some truly shite stuff. This area turned out to be full of pubs built in the last few years called O'Gorbal's or whatever, many of them subtitled *Irish Pub*, which is slightly bizarre when you think about it, mostly pumping out hideous sub-techno Eurocrap and all stuffed with Brits on stag nights and office benders.

There is crap and there is crap, but this was just too much. We had to leave the first few bars out of simple shame; the same shame we feel when we happen across our fellow Englanders in Europe; shame, and fear that we might be mistaken for them. In our case, this fear was doubled because, after all, we too were, in fact, looking for a night on the batter away from home. We weren't singing 'Vindaloo Vindaloo' and 'I Will Survive', but we could hardly deny that our evening would be a failure unless we got legless and noisy at some stage too: I mean, underneath our veneer of superior education and culture, we too were just craphead Northern Europeans, incapable of actually enjoying stuff like conversation and eating and wandering about unless we were in the process of boozing ourselves senseless.

I mean, have you ever wondered why we poor

Northern Proddie sods keep our kids out of pubs? Because we secretly think that what we do in pubs is so hideous and disgusting that our kids shouldn't even *see* it? And what if we are right?

By the time we left the second bar after queuing in vain for twenty minutes while dodging slopping lager, Jan was starting to mutter stuff about how the Arts Council might as well abolish itself tomorrow if this was who it was for; The Wop was beginning to stand with his weight planted menacingly forward, in pre-emptive Fight Mode; and I could feel in my head the sniffling nose-end of the dreaded question: Just How The Fuck Did I Come To Be Here.

Harry smiled nastily, strangely content.

Now and then, sidestepping the vomit outside the bars and wilting away from the music as we passed the body-heated doors, we collided with pinky-scrubbed, anxious-looking German or Dutch backpackers who were certainly not looking for this kind of Ireland.

Harry now led us down Grafton Street, and we found several pubs that looked wonderful from the outside, and were impossibly packed with the sort of tourists who looked as if they never usually went to pubs and did not quite know how to stand in them. There was also the odd lost German backpacker again, and slick young Irish business folk in suits drinking mineral water, checking their watches busily, asking *was the body count high enough in Frankfurt yet?* and saying, as they left for their restaurants, mobiles already jammed on ears, that they would *see yous on the ice, my men.*

Then we crossed to the north side of the river, and found massed fast-food takeaways packed to overspill with spotty, pallid teenage girls spending their last winter of chips and kebabs and publess hanging about: next year, they would be lying to their fathers. The few places we found here were free of tourists simply because they were ghastly. Even more smoky and sex-free than British pubs; simple ante-rooms to low-level despair, wife-beating, child abuse and petty, wretched crimes; the kind of pubs you might visit when slumming it as a student, for the simple human pleasure of being called a cunt (or in this case a *cont*); hell-holes that remind you alcohol is a drug and the barman's livelihood (not to mention Lord Guinness's or whatever the hell he's called) is pushing it to anyone who is not actually, visibly, indubitably dying of it before their very eyes.

—Well? said Harry. —Are we agreed? Is Dublin crap?

—Yes, we all said. —Very.

—Fine.

And then something happened which had never happened before. Instead of laughing and stepping out to just find by chance wherever it was we were now going to drink our heads off for the rest of the evening, cured of any dreams of exotic locations, we all stopped and fell quiet. It was Harry: he was radiating some dark light that made us hold still and watch him.

—Harry? said Jan, at last.

We were by now on a little humpbacked wrought-iron bridge across the Liffey, stopped as if by unspoken but unanimous election. Beneath us, the river was doing what rivers do anyway, all the time, and which only seems ridden with dark, human significance at moments like this: flowing, of course, ever onwards, darkly, towards the invisible sea. The moment lasted; the silence between us grew longer and stronger. It began to feel like those dreadful silences towards the ends of failed affairs, the gaps of nothingness that scream *get out of this* inside your head, and which no amount of talk and laughter will ever fully close again.

—Crazy, chuckled Harry softly, —I mean, fuck, it was only ten years ago. Well, fifteen. How come it's all so fucked up? Christ, I can remember going on a demo against cruise missiles right here somewhere, it was really good fun, I was up on this wall, somewhere over there, and . . .

—Harry, said Jan, slowly, —cruise missiles?

—Well, I think so. Or perhaps it was to do with the miners' strike. Or the hunger strike. The Falklands War, maybe. I don't remember. One of them. All I'm saying is . . .

—Cruise? The Falklands? The miners' strike? The hunger strikes? Harry?

—Yeah yeah yeah, OK, so I am crap, did I ever say I wasn't? I admit it. I shout it to the fucking world. I AM CRAP. Yes, yes, I belong to the generation that was wrong about everything.

—Harry . . .

—No, no, let's admit it. Our generation of leftie twats. Fuck. We chucked stones at NATO while the Russians were invading Afghanistan. We thought cruise missiles were inherently eviller than SS-20s. We believed the IRA was all for liberalism and justice. We got ridden at by police horses to keep Arthur fucking Scargill in a job. We dressed in sodding bin-bags. We told everyone East Germany was overtaking Britain. We called the Falklands the Malvinas and said they should be handed over to some general in boots and a big hat. We thought chips were cool because steelmen ate them and we believed our car-workers were leading the revolutionary struggle of the international proletariat by making the crappiest cars in the world. We carried banners about overthrowing capitalism and chucked bricks through shop windows and if anyone got arrested doing it we wrote to the *Guardian* to complain. Christ, would you look at us: the last generation to actually care about *being right*, and we were wrong about everything. No wonder the next lot decided to just find beaches, drop pills and party. Jesus, we . . .

—Time! Time, Harry! yelled Jan.

—What? snapped Harry.

—I'm not talking about right or wrong. Or us, even. I'm talking about time, Harry. Just fucking time.

—What time?

—Harry. The miners, the Falklands, Maggie Maggie Maggie Out Out Out, all that stuff. Time, Harry. The gap between all that stuff and now is as long as the gap between World War Two and the Beatles. Just time, Harry. Just fucking time.

The way Jan said that made us look up at her in the light of the horrible Balearic-Beat dive we had just escaped from. There was a nasty pause. We all did the same brief and disbelieving calculation.

—Fuck, said The Wop. —She's right. Hitler and the Beatles. Or: we have been legally driving, voting, boozing and shagging for longer than the time between World War One and World War Two. New-ew-ews.

—We're Old Gits, I said. —We actually are Old Gits. It's happened. To us. It's for real. It's definitive. It's for ever. The next ceremony is the Grand Opening of the pension book.

Harry said nothing. But he was thinking something all right: whatever it was, it made him suck his tooth like he had a bad molar and shake his head slightly like he was about to start laughing.

Roadkill

So there we stood, on the back of the steep bridge, silently and with something uncomfortably close to dread hovering in the air.

Of course, we had always known it would happen. Logically, I mean. Even when I was twenty (i.e., when I was, being male, still not quite human) I had enough sense to know that if any life assurance company was nuts enough to offer me a bond that would mature wonderfully *if I reached thirty-nine*, I would have ripped it from their idiotic hands. No one did, of course, because they knew as well as I did that I was an actuarial cert to make it. But that's the Adam and Eve thing again, isn't it: we know; so what? Knowing is no preparation: if it was, we would all have accumulated so much learning since Homer that we would all be gods of taste, philosophy and reason by now.

Instead, we learn stuff and learn stuff and learn stuff . . . and then it *happens*, really happens, to us ourselves. We feel it in our own flesh at last, and we cry out with panic, like children lost in the dark. However much we know, it is all news to us: knowing is no protection, and carries no reward.

Look at me now, for example: I know that I am odds-on to get my pension. I know this as a rational fact; I appreciate it as a mathematical proposition. If I did not, after all, why the hell would I continue to pay huge amounts to the spotty little, Polo Sport-smelling, BMW-driving bastards who (I assume in my darker moments) run my pension fund and chortle at my gullibility? But

I believe in it, so I do it. It is a sound, a purely logical decision. But but but. But I cannot truly imagine getting hold of it, this pension.

I have no tactile image of it, any more than I could really intimate, at twenty, what I feel now. *Collect my pension?* What, will these hands, my hands that I now see outlined against the dark River Liffey, with my blood and nerves and memories locked away inside them, will they really ever struggle, blue, shivering and dry, to open those long-planned, long-paid pension envelopes? Yes, they will, you know, and I know it too: mathematically, they will; God and the fags and the stress willing, they will.

And maybe as we open them and nod at the correct, expected figures, we will occasionally wonder: just how the fuck did we come to be here, doing this?

Let's hope it will come on no stronger than that. Maybe we are as incapable now of intimating what we will feel like when we are old, I mean really old, as we were incapable at twenty of guessing how we would feel, *do* feel, *are* feeling, now. Maybe, when we are seventy, we will feel that we knew nothing at thirty-nine; maybe some generous law will arrange things tactfully so that our feelings get slow along with our legs; so that in the end, well before the end, when all we can manage is a short walk in the sun, all we can feel will be a vague, distant regret.

Let's hope so.

Because you tell me: if it doesn't all just fade gently away, what, just *what the fuck* are we all supposed to do these days, when we get old? When our bodies and minds finally give in definitively to the barrage of dioxins, microwaves and plain old brutal time? Become our parents? Buy slippers and dressing-gowns? Look forward to thirty years of terrifying comfort? What is to become of us when we finally have to leave the great Youth party for good?

Look around, next time you are out in a bar in W1 or Islington, look at us: sagging arses, settling guts and stretching tits bravely held at what we fondly imagine to be bay by Lycra and weights, sad bastards fighting our hopeless, heroic little rearguard actions against mortality, crowding the bars and restaurants because we have nothing to stay at home for, frantically acting like twenty-year-olds, *acting* being the word, because that is all we know. We can only *do* young, it is the only part we have ever played and ever want to play.

So now walk boldly to the centre of this nice London bar and pull the plug on the music and cry, in God's own tannoy voice, the fatal question: *Yes, OK, and in five years?*

Suddenly I thought: we are all fucked. By freedom. Freedom has us fucked. The old hippies, the real oldies, at least had the excitement of '68; the feeling they had invented it all. We? We are just the spoiled kids and younger sibs, born holding our invites to the longest, sexiest party in the history of the world, the party everyone who isn't in wants desperately to join. Ask anyone who can't get in, from Beijing to Acapulco, if they'd like to come. And then jump to avoid the stampede.

No wonder we don't want to leave it. No wonder, as the time we unwillingly booked our cab draws near, as the clocks tick towards the time we know we really *should*, sensibly, be off, homewards, at our age, we look around with increasing desperation for another hit, another line, another fucking stupid party game, another crap old film, another topic for talking bollocks, a new fetish or the latest Yank cartoon, anything,

96

anything to put off the long, long, lonely comedown that we know, in our secret hearts, is waiting the other side of dawn.

Christ, look at us here, Harry & Co., stuck in some crap half-foreign city, slightly off our tits, desperate for something, anything to hike us up again to a place we no longer have the natural energies to climb: we, the ambassadors of our generation, the unelected representatives of millions like us, the oldest, most laughable swingers in town, who only get away with it because we are no worse than anyone else and no one wants to blow the whistle on the whole shebang and shaggery.

Everyone was still silent on the little iron bridge. I looked through my fingers at the dark river rushing by and thought:

Suddenly, I want to hide my head for shame, for the sheer crying *shame* of those wasted, blasted, prime-time years; that priceless decade between twenty-five and thirty-five, when we were fully-fledged humans at the height of our powers. That irreplaceable time and freedom which we squandered wretchedly, monstrously away, to the profit and delight of mincing designers, pandering restaurateurs and grinning holiday salesmen.

Maybe I would not have done anything unique. But at least I could have had, should have had, teenagers by now, children I could have brought up when I was young and full of life, instead of poor Hugh, my little, latecome boy, whose daddy is always shagged and who is cared for, so-called cared for, largely by people who only do it because I pay them.

But think what I would have missed: all the wonderful crap designer meals I ate. All the pointless holidays I took. And all those utterly meaningless non-relationships I had.

Sweet fucking Jesus, what will we do when the new Taliban comes? Young men with guns and scorn, swaddled in bullets and righteous outrage? We shall have nothing to hold up against them, nothing to make our barricades with. When we speak of freedom and justice, the Taliban will laugh and hold up to us the undeniable proofs of our lies and hypocrisy. They will despise us because we have partied, just partied and shopped it all, all our time and freedom and youth and strength, appallingly away. And even we ourselves shall breathe a sigh of bitter relief as we feel the cold of the judging gun barrels on our necks.

See what I mean? Not exactly party mode. No, we were tired, depressed, coming down fast and already longing secretly for our lonely, private beds. We had lost Us; our little tribe was running away like water; we were being dragged back into our hopeless selves, towards the little, one-single-person, mental Starter Units to which, somehow, we have allowed ourselves to become condemned.

At the other end of the bridge was an alley, and beyond it you could just see the light from yet another horrible theme pub. We had passed this one earlier on our desperate wanderings. It was Beach Party Nite, said the sign: they had dumped a few bags of sand on the floor, got in a potted palm tree, and heated the place up to suffocation level. It was full of Brits in shorts and swimsuits, filling their guts with beer and screaming at each other over the music. If we went north, we would be back to the land of Abra-kebab-ra, Burger King and the Child Molester's Arms. If we went south, we would get Brit Beach Party Nite or New Young Euro-Ireland. We stood in horrid indecision, and I could feel the seal settling down on the evening.

Suddenly, knowing that it was all crap was not like fun. Like the opposite of fun.

At that moment, yes, I think we really could have escaped; any of us could have called it all off. One word, and we would all have agreed gratefully that we were actually a bit tired today and Dublin was actually not all it was cracked up to be and let's find a nice quiet hotel, and write this one off for once. And we would all have gone early to bed smiling lyingly at each other, knowing in our hearts that we would never do this again, that the book had closed on Harry's False Birthdays.

In which case, it might all never have happened.

But when Harry stopped dead in the middle of the road, it was not to announce the end of the evening. It was to take a deep breath and say this:

—Right then, so now we know. The good days are gone. From now on, the best we can hope for is to get off on a fucking technicality. Yes, when we stand before the pearly poxy gates, the best bastard deal we can hope to cut is for St Peter to look up our entry in his big bloody book, frown, shrug, wink and say: *OK, look, tell you what, I'm in a good mood today, boys, and business is quiet. We'll just say your life never happened, yeah?*

Then he got out his mobile and started dialling.

—Of course, he said, with something like a chuckle, —archaeologically speaking, we have already lived longer than most of the people who have ever died, so we can hardly complain. *Hoi, is that Sean? Sean: it's Harry. Harry MacDonald. Harry the Brit archaeologist? The eejit with the drum, who . . . Right! Fine, and yourself. Ah, stop! Listen, Sean, are Sticks and the boys playing tonight? They are? Great so. No, no message. Oh, Sean, one thing. Tell me this and tell me no more: is the music room still like it was? Is the fire still there and all? Great so. Don't say anything. See you later.* Right. Let's find a cab.

—Where are we going? asked Jan.

—One more piece of crap to see, said Harry. —Out in the country.

—The country? said The Wop, in blank horror.

—Harry . . . , said I.

—It's half an hour in a cab. Less. Come on. The ultimate cunting Irish experience awaits you in all its crapitude. Taxi! Taxi, ya bollix! Good man yourself. You OK for Kilcoggan?

—Twenty-five, said the cabbie.

—How long? demanded Harry.

—Ah, maybe twenty minutes this time of night, with the new roads.

—See? said Harry, triumphantly.

—Not actually the country, then? I asked.

—Well, a sort of suburb nowadays, I suppose, said Harry. —You're on: if you do it in under twenty there's a fiver on top.

—Fair bollix to you. Hop in so.

—Harry, said Jan, —what's this place? Really?

—Well, said Harry, poised halfway into the shiny black car, —it's just a place I used to go. Just

100

somewhere I want to see once more, so I can close it off. So I can stop it being a dream and see it's really shite.

—So this is why we're in Ireland? I said quietly.

—Partly, yes. After all, you don't want dreams rattling about in your head as you approach forty. Do you?

—Best not, nodded Jan.

—This isn't going to be fucking bagpipes and crap, is it? groaned The Wop (but he was already getting into the cab, happy to have something to kick off about properly at last).

—Bagpipes and crap and a lock-in, then we'll hit a club back here so you can chase girls pathetically, job done, bed booked, birthday over, said Harry.

—News, said The Wop.

—Any sexy IRA men? said Jan in her most excruciating Loud Brit Poshy Girl voice.

—Fuck, breathed the cabbie.

—Yeah, one with authentic seventies sideburns, too.

—Oh no, my old mum always told me: *Never shag a man with sideys.*

—You wouldn't want to shag Sticks, anyway.

—Sticks? asked Jan, taking the front seat without a blink of feminist hesitation. —What, as in dynamite? As in baseball bats? As in crutches?

—Y-X, said Harry. —S-T-Y-X. As in the Greek river. The river in Hades.

—Hades? growled The Wop, settling his muscle-bound arse elegantly into the back of the car.

—So why Styx? I asked, following into the car and thus ending up in the lumpy Death Seat, perfect for being fired out through the screen.

—You cross him, you're dead. You cross him, you're roadkill.

—Lovely guy, by the sound, said the cabbie.

—Ah, he is too, said Harry, bumping his arse up against mine and slamming the door.

I looked up quickly and caught Harry's eye as the taxi jumped away. And to my surprise I saw that under his merry voice, Harry was not merry at all. He was nervous.

No, more than nervous. Harry was scared as fuck. Not scared as in *fear*, but as in *trembling*: like when you know that you are about to do something precisely because it is the thing that you have known for fifteen years that, one day, you are going to have to do. You have just got up on to the ledge of the bridge, your ankles are strapped in, the crowd is watching, and now, at last, it's your turn to jump. No escape.

Yes, I think it's fair to say that by now, we should have taken the hint.

A Potentate

But we didn't, we went to Styx Fitzpatrick's pub, and
so now picture this:
   a pub which could be transported straight out to the
set of an ad for horrible Irish beer. The old bar with its
oak top polished by a thousand tweedy sleeves; with its
little letter-racks and hand-painted signs and photos of
forgotten racehorses and faded hurling teams; the turf
in the big grate banked up into a yard-high, red-and-
orange mass; the old boys with dogs; the young, strong-
faced, curly-haired girls calling each other *lads*; everyone smoking happily away as if their Celtic ethnicness
gave them some special relationship with medical
probability; and not a jukebox or fruit machine or telly
around. The only noise in the place, apart from the
riotous babble of human beings having the *criac* (or
however Harry said they spell it), is the unamplified
sound of two violins, two bagpipes, about six guitars
and three *bowrons* (or whatever they are called) being
scraped, squeezed, strummed and battered in the
corner as the male lads belt out a Rebel Song that
everyone here seems to know but you have never heard
in Britain. And none of it new, none of it chain-built, all
of it clearly real and old and true.
   What makes it true beyond all doubt is that one of the
walls is a photographic shrine to Michael Collins and a
load of people who all look like an unnerving conven-
tion of Georgie Best and J.P.R. Williams lookalikes.
Apart from the hand-tinted ones of Michael Collins,
bordered with painted-on shamrocks, the shots are all

from the early seventies (which is what we usually mean when we say the sixties). They show IRA men all frozen eternally, like Besty and J.P.R. are for ever stuffed in curls and sideys. These IRA gunmen are drinking pints, leaning on cars, smoking fags and looking at the camera with the cocky smiles of young men who have just realised that they are the sexy boys in a new world where neither mam nor the priests can stop you fucking. The only English-speaking, English-singing, white, armed Rebels on earth, admired every-where, filmed ceaselessly, interviewed religiously, the revolutionary vanguard in the worldwide war of sideys and curls versus Brylcreem and suits; adored, deferred to and shagged on sight by hippies the Western World over. They guarantee the pub; they authenticate the music; they gift that little touch of hardcore that no adman would dare play with, even today. Something beyond irony: not postcard reprints in some clever shop for students, but hard little shards of truth and time.

It was, in short, the pub that has materialised straight from half the world's idea of heaven.

And now Harry led the way through the incredible fug of tobacco smoke, breasting the wave of heat from turf and bodies, trailing us behind him. The whole set of his body let us know that at this particular moment, none of his radar was on us. He would not have noticed if we had all three been tripped up, kicked in and frogmarched out right behind him. All his scanners were beaming through the smoke and the people ahead of him. I looked over his shoulder to see who or what was the object of his slow, tense approach.

I spotted who it was straight away. This big bastard who still had the sideys and shades that some girl twenty lost years ago, whose name he could probably not even recall, must have told him suited him. He was sat with wide-splayed legs, strumming and strangling a fat, black, plastic-bellied guitar with two vast builder's paws. All my ancient, low, horrible primate instincts immediately read the hundreds of little human, social signals flooding the place, and located him as the main man, the cock of the walk, the king of this particular little hill, Styx Fitzpatrick himself, no doubt about it.

Harry walked up, and shoved his way through until he was standing right behind one of the pipers and thus directly in Styx Fitzpatrick's eyeline. Styx Fitzpatrick did not seem to notice him at all, and played on to the end of his song. It was something merry about how *Vengeance Will Be Ours* or whatever, you know the kind of thing. After the whooping had died away, the attention of the pub firmly focused on Harry. Now Styx Fitzpatrick looked up through his black lenses, a potentate well used to hesitant requests:

—Jesus, now, I'm not some fucking jukebox, you know, he growled good-humouredly. —But sure if you're a friend of Ireland all the way from Germany, or is it Holland, well you promise to stick a fiver in the bucket for the Cause later on, say after me Fuck The Politics, Plug The Brits, and by Christ you can name your tune and . . .

Styx Fitzpatrick fell silent even as the expected laughter and applause began to swell up. It died as he stopped. He stared at Harry with his sightless shades. Harry stood there and spread his arms in one of those ancient human gestures which mix friendship, apology and surrender. Styx Fitzpatrick stayed frozen.

Then at last he easily laid his big guitar down beside him, freeing up his hands for attack or embrace. He plucked his cigar from out of his mouth and parked it in the ashtray. He hoisted his shades and stood, no taller than Harry but with a natural weight in the neck and shoulders that left no doubt about it:

—Well fuck me over a barrel of beer. Harry fucking MacDonald.

Happiness and . . .

—Styx, said Harry.
   —Long fucking time.
   —Fifteen years.
   —The big man on the box now.
   —Any chance of a drum then?
Styx stood poised. Unknowable terabytes of history
and mystery passed between the two of them as they
looked each other in the eye. And then Styx laughed
once, dropped his shades again on to his nose, lifted up
his big arms and spoke again in his public voice:
   —Harry fucking MacDonald, what the fuck have you
done to your head?
   And Harry was embraced.

And now, following Styx's lead, everyone else grins,
mouths hellos and shoves their bums closer together to
make space and way for the shy arse of Harry, who,
having first received the full imprimatur and blessing
of Styx himself (a bear-hug that lasted twenty seconds,
combined with a threatening reference to people not
getting too big for their halos and forgetting their old
friends), is immediately surrounded by people who
seem to remember him. He stands there, frowning,
guessing names, making connections, dredging up bits
of ancient stories, accepting and returning jokes about
his lack of hair and bullshit famousness, glowing with
something more than pinkness and deeper than baldness, something that makes me gasp a little inside,
because I realise that I have not seen Harry like this for

years: years and years. A line-free Harry; a bright-faced Harry; Harry with light and uncalculating eyes; a man with a stupid, thoroughly uncool, chimplike grin cracking right across his face, taking simple pleasure in being here, in being *allowed* to be here again.

Christ, the bastard is happy.

I am looking at Harry now, gazing at Harry's happiness, and feel very left out in the cold. It is not nice. So I allow my intellectual bubble to form fast, insulating me, pulling me back, deadening the sound, like it once deadened the sounds of a hostile playground or unwelcoming school disco, allowing the voice in my head to be heard, asking:

Happy?

Is that it? Just Happy? The second-most overused word of our times. What does it mean? A mild cigar called bollocks? A cuddlesome shag in front of your new real-fire-effect gas flames? The avoidance of fear? A top-performing PEP? A smile from the boss? A line like a baby's arm; a fat pink pill; a clean-filled syringe? A mother's smile? A baby's smile? A fuck-me smile? The light and air on a glenside in spring? A painless dying? A roaring birth? Vengeance and triumph? Laughter and crying? Suffering and desire?

Happiness?

Really, there should be words that are taboo again. Forbidden words that may not be used on greetings cards and ads, to guard their value. So that, after years of feeling that we can safely answer the daily question *Are you happy?* with *Hey, I suppose so*, we might have some word left to describe what I was seeing, which was: someone I knew, transfigured.

The test should be this: consider. If you could be frozen, right now, all your emotions and sensations preserved, right now, in crystal for ever, if this moment, whatever it may be for you, was going to be your changeless eternity, what would you say? Would you say: *What? Christ, not yet?* Or would you whisper: *OK then, go for it.* That is what deserves to be called happiness. And I was looking at it: at someone who was, at that precise and unrepeatable moment in time, exactly where they wanted to be, and with the people they wanted to be with; someone at the point where the distant parallels of thought and action, which haunt us all our lives, meet and converge into a glowing moment.

Harry was, in short, a man who seemed to be doing what he had been put here to do, and in the place he was meant to do it.

And so Harry looked happy.

The change was so clear it almost made me dizzy with this thought: how long since I myself was last happy? *How* long? Christ, have I got that used to things, not *un*happiness as such, maybe, but *lack of* happiness, that I no longer even feel it? Am I just used to living without happiness? Have I written myself off? Why? Did I make a wrong turn, or turn the wrong thing down? Or does our capacity for happiness simply shrink along with our capacity for staying up all night? Is a quiet smile the most we can hope for now?

By the time I had finished thinking this, Harry had introduced us all, and we were made room for at the table next to the sacred table of the musicians, where there had seemed to be no more room. We were in at the second-top table in the pub. Styx growled:

—Can you still beat time? and handed Harry a

horrible old beer-stained hippy drum, whatever they call them.

—Would I be sitting here if I couldn't? said Harry.

—Good man yourself, said Styx. —I've me Armalite out the back; did you bring the ballot box?

—Didn't I fuck that out years ago?

—Gowan yaboy! cried Styx, and bashed Harry across the shoulder. Harry beamed. Then he looked at us, and shrugged. He held my gaze for a second, and I have never seen him look so much like a true friend.

But then he did something I have only ever seen junkies do. He smiled, and then, while he was still looking at me, he just *turned his eyes off.*

Then he leaned towards Styx and began to beat time with his stupid bloody crusty drum as the music started up.

Dry Powder

Well, yes, it was that kind of music. Irish music. By which I mean the sort of thing everyone used to play everywhere in Europe until they stopped everywhere except Ireland: jigs and reels that now count as Irish. Also songs about national sacrifice, doom and vengeance that would go platinum in Belgrade for anyone who could be bothered to translate them word-for-word into Serbian. Big States may be bad, but God save us from Small Nations.

However, I have to confess that as the Guinness kept stacking up as if by osmosis and the fire got warmer and the smiles got broader and everything started to have that nice fuzzy sort of feel, I soon found it quite easy to buy into. I had even started to get hackle-rising feelings when one of the women sang some slow ballad about seals or hills or bloodthirsty redcoats or whatever. I too was starting to believe. I was starting to get waves of Belonging.

I know you know what I mean, because half the crap in the world is sold to us by the lie that it is something to do with belonging, and you do not sell things to people on the basis of what they *have* got, but what they *haven't*.

And now the fire was blazing and the beer was flowing and everyone was smiling and the music just went on and on, diddle-dee-eye. Harry was beating away with what looked to be some degree of skill on his whatever-the-hell-you-call-it. His eyes were glazed

with the beat. Mine were heavy with beer and wallow-
ing sentiment.

A perfect little holiday.

Jan was looking at Harry with annoyance.

—Christ, she said. —Look at him. Thirty-nine going
on fourteen, would you say? Ben, could you clear up
one small but important point for me?

—Shouldn't think so. But fire away.

—What exactly is wrong with men?

—What's your problem? demanded The Wop, on his
male mettle. —He's just hooking up with an old mate.

—Balls. Look at him.

So we all did, trying to see what she might mean. I
also looked quietly at Jan. I realised that here was a
woman who had often shagged this man, and who
prided herself on her insight. Yet she had never seen
him doing this thing that he was so obviously, so
heavily, secretly into, and, worse, had never ever seen
him so obviously deferring to another man. This,
despite all our liberalism and our various advances in
human relationships is still, in my experience, a thing
no woman likes to see in a man she considers in any
way to be hers.

Annoyance and envy and betrayal. I looked at her as
she sulked and drank her pint, and realised that she
had not yet quite written off the possibility that they,
she and Harry, might still in some way be some kind of
number. An occasional number maybe, a number you
did not call for years, perhaps, but a number nonethe-
less. Until today?

Meanwhile, The Wop had discovered that the piper
and violinist on either side of him were not, as he had

suspected, Bearded Wristy Intellectuals, but, respectively, a plumber and a builder who happened to have been brought up to play pipes and violins as well.

—Are the beards compulsory? he asked the piper, with his regulation aggressiveness.

—They pretty well are for touring in Germany, the piper replied, unoffended. —You into this archaeology too?

—No, fuck, replied The Wop, mistakenly aligning himself to the assumed mindset of an English plumber in an English pub.

—No? Oh. Jesus, I think it's great stuff. Always used to love chatting to Harry about it. Nothing like a bit of education to improve the evening.

—Oh, said The Wop. Then he fell silent, hopelessly confused by this representative of a non-anti-intellectual blokedom.

I allowed the music to worm its way into my head, I lay back and yielded to the fantasy of timelessness. I scanned again across the pictures of the seventies IRA men on the wall.

What is our connection to the past? I mean, how can you imagine someone in a purple jacket and a flowery shirt, with big hair and sideys, being a brutal killer? And yet these men had been real, as real as me, and in their day they would have scared the living shit out of me. And the old gits who walk in dwindling numbers on 11 November every year ran forward, yelling their death-yells, against machine-guns and flame-throwers.

I remember seeing a picture in a paper once. It was of Gareth Edwards, the great Welsh rugby player of my youth: there he is, sideys, curls and all, his body parallel with the ground but five feet off it, his legs corkscrewed up behind him, just out of reach of hurtling English players, in a way that makes you think his spine must have snapped the next second, his hands firing off a spin pass. I could never do that. I could never *have* done that. I was never a hero to anyone. He was: a nation worshipped him. And now he is old and fat. Simple. So that's it, that's the story, is it? The best any of us can hope for is that we get a few good years, are respected, maybe loved and admired for a few years, then we get old.

And when you get old, you better not be poor. Not because the health service is crap or anything like that, but because when you're old, you're gone. No one will give a fuck about you unless they have to. So make sure you plan for management before you get old: if you are a dancer, get studying choreography well before your ankles give out; if you are a teacher, get out of the classroom, and if you are a painter, start thinking about a job with the Arts Council. The front line is for the young ones with fast, loose muscles, charged up to kill or be killed; by forty, you better be wearing staff-officers' tabs, in whatever army you are in, because you are not going to be quick enough any more, out there, and when the shrapnel starts flying you will still be in the open, startled, frozen and wondering why your legs will not move. *Poor old toss*, they will say, *he was good once.* As soon as it is gone, none of it counts: yesterday's news, last year's number one, last era's haircut. The most you can hope for, as Youth rushes past on its incomprehensible way, is that one day some condescending little twat in combats and trainers will think that it might be a good career move to go retro and find some godforsaken pub where they still have your face on faded little shreds of newsprint.

Or else, or else: enjoy it while you can and be happy to chuck it all when you have to. Smile, and say goodbye, and go back along the long road that leads from the big neon city back to the quiet place you came from, ready to sit with your grandchildren and cheer with good heart as the next wave of Youth moves jauntily off towards the smoggy, devouring metropolis. And if one or two of them self-consciously jog over to quickly shake the hand of someone who was good once, take it the right way, and thank them for it. Hell, you still got the old boys to have a pint with, and if every man ends up being one of the men who have not had sex for too long, well, not having sex for too long never killed anybody...

—I suppose, said Jan, seeing me entranced by the pictures, —that they only look innocent to me because I'm just old enough to have wished, in the days when I wore toe socks, that I could be fancied by blokes in sideys and flares myself.

—No, they look harmless because they're skinny, said Harry, looking up momentarily from his drumming. —Like those punk bands with no biceps and smooth bellies. Yes, boys, they come from that strange, lost world before Lycra and weights. And well, everything seems innocent once it's part of history...

—No, Harry, it's because we *were* fucking innocent, said Styx suddenly, and then he turned back immediately, flushed with something like anger and some other emotion I could not yet identify.

—Look, sorry..., Harry began, but Styx now turned back, having swallowed or banished whatever he was feeling.

—Ah, you're right, Harryboy. Long fucking time ago.

—Not still keeping your powder dry? You always said you would.

—Ah, I am too, in a way.

115

Styx winked. Harry laughed, but it was the kind of laugh that merely expressed a wish to please and be friends: I saw that he hadn't understood whatever joke Styx was making. Nor did I, for that matter. But yes, Styx was the kind of man you tended to laugh along with.

—Anyway, fuck the Brits and fuck the begrudgers, here's to the boys, and here's to us!

And he started another rollicking, jolly song about happy-go-lucky exiles, famine and war.

Surely Not?

After some time, we decided to leave Harry to it for a bit, and go somewhere we could chat, so we moved away from the music, into the next room. We had hardly been aware of this other area until now: you could see a big double door and were vaguely aware of space and people the other side, but that was all.

It turned out to be a bloody great extension, dwarfing the olde worlde musical bar of the pub, all plush wallpaper and copper-topped tables, filled with quiet, car-coat people who would not have seemed out of place at my own hideous local.

—Let's not show Harry this, I said. —He thinks nothing's changed.

—No, let's, said The Wop. —The truth hurts.

—Would you say this is new? asked Jan. —Would you? Do you think this is some new extension? I don't. Look at the window frames. Look at the Artex. How eighties *is* all that? Am I wrong? Well?

—Check. Fuck, it was always like this, said The Wop, nastily.

—Always as far as Harry's concerned. Don't you think?

—It must have been, I agreed, mathematicising vaguely.

—So it was *never real*, said Jan.

I looked back through the doors into the IRA shrine room beyond and really, it did seem from here as if everyone in there had agreed by ESP to conspire in the notion that this other, much larger bar, the actual pub in economic reality, simply did not exist.

—What a nightmare, moaned The Wop.

—Harry's happy, I said.

—Harry's off his head, said The Wop.

—Exactly, said Jan, draining her pint. —Come on, we're here, so let's go for it.

And so we all gave up fighting, and returned to the music bar, where we just managed to get our seats back after some growling from Styx about Harry's Friends. At the end of one particular song, when there was, for once, a break before the next set, a very pretty and serious-looking German girl took the chance to come up and talk to Harry while he was at the bar:

—Zat vas grand stuff, she said.

—Wasn't it? smiled Harry, absently, engaged in ordering his beer.

—I vas in Galway last year. It vas grand stuff in Galway. You know Galway?

—I wasn't there for fifteen years, said Harry stoutly.

—Which part of Oirland are you from?

—I'm not. I'm just pretending.

—Pretending?

—I'm pretending to be Irish. Ersatz Irish, like you. Like everyone else. Me Brit you German, we all pretend be nice Irish? Isn't that the whole point? It's all just a game, didn't you know that? Grand stuff?

She went very red and could not look Harry in the eye. She stood with a stiff back and went to her friend and said something; they both hoisted their rucksacks and left in search of the Ireland they wanted to find. I think she was near to crying.

—Nice one, Harry, said Jan.

—Oh well, some smooth laddo in Galway is in for a good time.

—God, you're a bastard.

—Oh, so we all just buy into crap and pretence, do we? So everyone feels good?

—Well, what the fuck are you doing sitting there? You fucking love it.

—Ah, but I don't buy it. That's the difference. I know it's all balls. That's the point. Styx, grab these willya? And Harry craned a load of pints over to the musicians, before winking to us and joining them again.

—Cool bloke, really, said The Wop, reluctantly.

—What, you think cool means being horrible to girls? snapped Jan.

—Personally, I would have lied to her, mate.

—Yes, well, maybe lying's best, sometimes.

—Like when? Like when I fancy some bird?

—I just mean, if someone's having a nice time for once, why bother spoiling it?

—Always best to have your eyes open, mate. Especially when shagging.

—Is it?

So then we had a fine argument about whether people who shag with their eyes shut are just escapist fantasists who aren't actually, mentally, with the person they are with (said The Wop), or whether maybe people who shag with their eyes open are visually-fixated narcissists who are really only interested in watching their own actions, like mad spectators of their own lives (said Jan). Which is more real? Touch or sight?

At one point I did attempt to suggest, fairly obviously, it seemed to me, that this argument was a particularly stupid one, even by our standards, since there was no reason you couldn't do both. But when I tried it, I realised to my slightly miffed surprise that neither of them was in the least concerned about what I thought about shagging and eyes. I was suddenly and quite strikingly superfluous.

I looked at them with sudden amazement. Like I said about Styx and Harry, you sometimes find yourself agreeing with someone just as an excuse to declare that you like them. This was like that, only in reverse: Jan and The Wop were arguing just as an excuse to fence and parry each other. Their complete ignoring of me only lasted a second, but that was long enough for me to see, think, and hear the phrase bubbling up inside me: *No, surely not, not these two, not . . . ?*

And, of course, you never think that unless it is true.

I was stunned. Jan and The Wop? After all these years? And then I remembered what I had just thought about Jan and Harry, how she had suddenly looked at Harry differently. She had just written him off. And so now . . .

I shook my head with vertigo at the thought of just how simple and ruthless our choices really are, and how we will do pretty well anything to make sure we get our finishing in first and thus preserve our self-respect against the evidence of our intellect. Jan, quite simply, was dropping Harry: pre-emptively, finally, after all this time. And had thus switched focus.

But my mad insights were drowned because now the music started up again, louder and faster. This time, however, it quickly transformed from a few polkas and reels into stuff like 'Me and Bobby McGee', from whence it then mutated into a bizarre mixture of *Oasis's and REM's Greatest Hits* and the *Gerry Adams Singalong Show*. The audience had, unless I am much mistaken, been waiting for this as the main event of the evening: the shouts and whoopings were now all of a sudden so loud that they made the earlier levels of applause seem merely respectful, and the general air of camaraderie and togetherness was so complete in the jammed, air-free room, that it would have been sonically impossible and socially very hard to do anything except give up and join in.

Fun, actually. A little break from the brain.

Jan and The Wop tapped their feet in time and stood there, not touching.

I watched and listened.

Harry drummed, glowed, and was happy.

We drank and drank.

Time passed at a wild pace and, before we knew it, last orders were upon us. At this point we were advised, or rather ordered, by Styx to get two pints each in so that we could have them quietly *until the strangers fucked off.*

Just that little phrase shot waves of feelgood hormones through me. I secretly checked the faces of Harry, Jan and The Wop too: and I could see they were getting the same hit. *Till the strangers fucked off.* Till the Others went. Till *They*, the poor saps, the non-members, the outsiders, got the hell out of it and left only *Us* ourselves alone. Christ, the temptations of belonging. So I went with The Wop to grab our double round. (Fortunately, Irish and Brits have identical pub manners, apart from that the Irish always hand round their fags, so we knew, without having to take the least hint, that we should include all the musicians too. It was Their Place, we were New Members, and this was our ticket for an all-nighter. So handy to know the rules; comforting, in a way.)

As we waited on our bar stools to receive our two or three gallons of slow-poured Guinness, Jan was away

in the lav, and so I took the opportunity to look at The
Wop quizzically. He bristled:

—What? What you looking at?

—Well, well, well, I said, —surely not?

—Listen, mate . . .

But then he saw something far away behind my left
ear, quickly looked away again, then pricked back his
ears, composed his coolest, most dago-like face, and
pulled in his stomach in that way which for twenty
years has always only ever indicated one thing:

—News at three o'clock! he muttered.

Following the rules, I did not look round for several
seconds.

News and Beauty

The News was a gang of people, coming in from the back door which led out from the modern section of the pub into the large car park. In a second, the whole atmosphere of the pub was transformed, for when I say *people*, I mean women. Young ones. All round the tables and the bar, older men looked shiftily up, younger men instinctively straightened their spines, wives and girl-friends pursed their lips. The Wop flexed his trilats privately and sat tall on his clenched buns.

To me, I have to admit that they were little more than a cloud of coloured hair, black Lycra, big shoes and kohl; to them, I have to acknowledge that I did not even exist except as a nameless, formless, genderless obstacle to their ordering. They marched on through to us in the music bar, miming utter ignorance of the effect they were having, and basking in it.

Frankly, I cannot these days tell the difference between eighteen and twenty; these girls, women, whatever, were simply out of my firing line, the same way I am now simply out of the firing line of Young Bloods looking for a scrap. Yes, yes: even though I can now not even think about talking to the kind of women I could have chatted up happily ten years ago, I can now easily shove my way up to bars where, ten years ago, I would have been taking my life in my hands. Such compensations.

We made way for the girls at the bar, and ferried our ranks of glasses over to the music table in threes. On my first trip, I saw Styx Fitzpatrick nod to Sean the barman and hold up a single big finger: I guessed he was telling Sean to give them a drink, however late it was. I had to shuffle my way sideways through them to pick up the next instalment. They made way happily enough for me: I saw that my stock had risen now that it was clear I was attached in some way to Styx. Or rather, that I had actually started to exist in their world. One of the girls even said *Hoi* vaguely as I hoisted my triple, keystoned-together pints, two-handed, over her head. I hoped my deodorant was still working, and smiled back. Since they had acknowledged my presence, I was, as a fellow primate, now located in their social network and thus allowed to focus on their eyes gently without seeming to be sending out signals of aggressive, indiscriminate lust.

Of course I was glad that they seemed ready to agree that I had at least some *degree* of social viability. I mean, Christ, there was nothing bad about it, and anyway . . .

—Christ, said Jan to me and The Wop, —You could *try* to pretend you didn't fancy them.

—Course I do, mate. And him. Not our fault, is it? Can't fight against biology. Young and slim: It's an evolutionary guarantee of fertility, innit?

—Nope, said Harry, who had appeared between us. —Slim is absolutely bollock-all to do with evolution. Ask the majority of the human race today: they don't think Kate Moss looks sexy, because their six shagging sisters all look like that after a bad harvest. Give them happy and fat.

—Exactly. Thank you. All Western men are half poofs. You only like thin young girls because they look like boys.

—Balls, retorted The Wop.

—Hardly. But little bums and no tits, said Jan.

—Look who's talking.

—Fuck off, she blushed.

—No, no, no, boys, it's easy as pie, said Harry. —See, when we say *slim* we do not really mean anything to do with the abstract desirability of not having a big arse.

—What, you saying you *like* big arses? Balls, mate.

—No I don't. But why not? Big arses were probably a good evolutionary thing, or else women wouldn't have them. Present company excepted.

—Excuse me, Herr bloody Mengele, but I'm not actually infertile. I believe I have proved that.

—Exactly, exactly! See? It's nothing to do with biology any more. When we say slim we just mean: *young-looking*, see? Because being slim means: *aha! probably young.*

—Yeah, right, exactly, so it's like I said, innit: we like them young because young means fertile.

—Wop, you one-man brain-free zone, then why aren't the supermodels young but plump, with big tits and arses?

—Excuse me, this is getting too bloody laddish. You'll be asking each other if you'd swap Naomi Campbell for a Ferrari next. Which is when I will go home.

—No, no, you girls want the same as us, nowadays: the twenty-year-old guy with the six-pack and no bum, just like we want the twenty-year-old girl with square shoulders and no bum. See: evolution, boys, is history, and therefore bunk. Now, we have society, God help us.

—Balls. You just said: we all like young ones now, Jan as well as me. How come we all just *happen* to agree? Easy: 'cos our eggs and sperm are better at nineteen.

—Poor bloody Wop, you don't get it, do you? See that bloke sitting in his poxy little house in Peckham, wondering why the hell he isn't still out there with the wild boys and girls?

—Peckham? Should I take this personally?

—No, Ben, impersonally. That's us, boys. That twat who longs for something called Life. And that's neolithic man, Wop, looking out from his hill fort, seeing the bonfire in the forest and wondering if the boys and girls out there in the wild woods chasing deer and looking for roots and shagging away aren't having a better time than he is, tending goats and hoeing beans. Just like us. And then what happens? Then it starts to rain, is what happens, and Mr Neolithic thinks, *Ah well, sure, dreams is fine, but at least I have a full belly and a warm bed and I can feed me kids on the beans and goat's milk*, and the smug little stunted git goes back to his safe, smelly bed, and his goats, and his neolithic pension fund of laid-up sodding turnips. Like us, Wop, like us. And who wins? The smelly little farmers, every time. The stunted little fuckers bred more and more, and the freedom-loving hunters got wiped out by sheer numbers, and by diseases that came from the goats and sheep. Fair? Nope. But human. Us, Wop.

—London is just a big machine for keeping kids warm, I said quietly.

—Is that yours? asked Harry, with rather insulting surprise.

—Yes, I bristled. —I thought it the other day, on the train. Myself.

—Can I pinch it?

—Can I stop you?

—Doubt it. Knocked that one on the head then, have we, boys?

—No we fucking haven't, you wristy intellectual

tosser. If it's all about security and keeping kids alive, how come we all fancy the young ones?

—Wop, Wop, Wop, it is only we dull Western saps who worship Young. Come on, boys, let us investigate our own bastard superstitions. Look at them again. Come on, Jan, Ben, you too. What are you looking at?

—Young, said Jan, with no bitterness at all. Well, hardly any.

—Youth, I nodded.

—Lies and crap. We're looking at *freedom*. It's nothing to do with bloody breeding. And nothing to do with good sex. Jan: did we have better sex at twenty or at thirty?

—Well . . . Jan was somewhat taken aback.

—Wop? Were you a better shag at twenty or now?

—I was always better than you, mate.

—And you always talked a good game. Ben?

—I don't bloody know. What's *better* mean?

—Bollock all. That's the point. It's not sex, not kids, not anything to do with Wop and his O-level bloody biology. Why do we want to look like we're in our early twenties? Or dress like we're in our early twenties? Or shag with someone who looks like they are in their early twenties? *Because your average early-twenties boy or girl is free*. Free free free free free. That's what we bloody mean. That's what we bloody want. That's the pill-fucking-popping, line-bastard-snorting, behind-the-bike-sheds party we never want to leave. That's all we mean by freedom. Fuck, look at us all: the whole shagging Western and would-be Western World, which means more people than have ever bloody died, obsessed with doing anything we like *because nothing any of us does matters a fuck*. We are sick, boys, sick from a lack of any bloody consequence.

—Yes, well, said Jan, —all I know is I am so bloody

jealous of them. Those girls. Look at them. They have it so much better than I did. I think I have just started to understand why middle-aged men in the sixties hated hippies so much. We're just getting into the sixties, as far as women are concerned. And I've bloody missed it. What did I get? I got you prats in the seventies and eighties and it never occurred to me that I didn't have to put up with you. Christ. Talk about timing.

—Yep, said Harry. —If there's one thing worse than living in the Dark Ages, it's living just when the light is coming up. If only mum and dad could've kept their pants on for another ten years! Of course, archaeologically speaking, we're all only here for five minutes, and if our five minutes happens to coincide with a period of general fucked-upness, well, tough luck. When I sit on a few old stones and say that *Greek society between 350 and 250 BC was marked by a series of mad schemes and general fuck-ups due to the sudden changes caused by blahblahblah,* no one bats a bastard eyelid. So maybe my esteemed media-whore colleagues of the future, assuming there is one, will wander round the ruins of our shopping malls and say:

> *For several generations in the late twentieth and early twenty-first centuries, Western mankind was utterly fucked by the final and definitive separation of erotic desire and procreation. The poor sods wandered about in places like this,* they will say, *filling up their laughable designer carrier bags (here's one we found earlier, the minimalist design clearly dating it to the late 1990s) with pointless crap, because in their heart of hearts they realised that they had lost out on the old Eden of certainty and security, but not yet reached the new Jerusalem of true, meaningful freedom . . .*

Well, let's hope they can raise a laugh, eh?

—Jesus, fair play to you, said a passing Irishman.

—Ahhh, said Harry.

—Go, Harry, I said.

—Shut up, snapped Jan, and there were tears at the edge of her voice, so Harry did. He shrugged, and went back to the musicians' table. Jan walked stiffly to the ladies'.

—More beer, then, said The Wop, —and remember: if it comes to a lock-in or a party with these, the important thing is to still be standing and in there when the party ends. It's all about endurance, really. Hmm. I wonder if endurance is something we are evolutionarily programmed to seek out? . . .

So there I was, surrounded by free-looking, hence beautiful, girls, and being lectured at first by Harry and now by The Wop. Quite fun, actually. Some things never stop being interesting, and I had a quite pleasant vision of us all sitting round some sunny outdoor pub table at sixty: Harry and The Wop still arguing about everything; Harry and Jan still wondering when they were next going to sleep together, and why; Jan and The Wop still deciding if their profound disagreements on everything would ever be resolved between the sheets; and me just sitting in there, swilling my dark ale quietly, patting my dog and adjusting my cap. Maybe we four were all we ever needed, I thought: that and a few grandchildren.

Quietly happy, I delivered my next three beers to the thirsty musicians, and returned to the bar for my last consignment. By now I was a well-known figure to my little gaggle of Beauty and Freedom, which parted nicely as I approached. I grabbed the final pints with a whisker of regret that I would not have any reason to come this way again. The Wop indicated that he was going to stand at the bar a while longer, by which I knew he meant that he would be waiting for some opportunity to manufacture a swift conversation with the girls. I have never been able to do that, but I knew he could, so I left him to it. I turned to take the drinks back to the musical table, my homeland and refuge and status for the night. Halfway there, I looked at Harry again, and almost stopped with surprise.

Something was going on with Harry.

Harry, who had hung on Styx's every word with almost embarrassing devotion for the last two hours, his worldly success offered up entirely at the feet of Styx's sheer physical and social presence, was not listening to Styx at all. Not even pretending to. To Harry MacDonald at that moment, Styx Fitzpatrick could have been just another bore. The thing that had vacuumed up Harry's attention, whatever it was, was something behind me; something or someone that produced in Harry a sheer, shell-shocked force that made me feel the room at my back was sucking me in. He looked like he was sitting in a private wind tunnel, and I could feel that inexplicable wind stir my own hackles.

I froze, still with my threesome of beers, and was about to turn round when several of the Beauty Through Freedom gang's voices called out, at once:

—Hoi, Shnade, what're you having?!

Like I said, that is what it sounded like. *Shnade*. I looked at Harry's eyes looking past me and I listened to the voices behind me shouting, and I thought, I remember thinking, very clearly: *Shnade*?

Shnade, or: Fucked by Romance

I turned to see who it was but, as I did, something happened which would have warmed the cockles of Slobodan Milosevic's heart: the band struck up the Irish National Anthem. How did I know it was the Irish National Anthem? Because the whole pub stood suddenly, drunkenly, unnervingly, to a shambling semblance of military attention, and proceeded to roar along with pride and passion in a language that not one in ten of them sounded like they spoke with anything like fluency and many appeared simply to be parroting, that's how.

As this forest of bodies large and small sprung patriotically up, whoever Shnade was, she was hidden from my view. All I got was a glimpse of a red dress, an arm, a lizard's head on a tanned wrist, and a strong hand with painted, broken nails. Immediately, I knew (I remember the strangest mix of emotions: surprise, and a curious, inexplicable exultation) that whoever owned this hand and arm and tattoo *was not a young girl*.

I swung back to look at Harry again through the scrum of sweating enthusiasm, but I could not see him. At first I thought he had legged it or just disappeared or something. Then I realised that the reason Harry was not to be seen was because the only person in the entire pub not standing up was Harry.

I was surprised at this; gobsmacked, to a degree. I mean, nothing against Harry, but he is hardly the sort of man who makes his name by standing up (or in this case sitting down) to be counted. Fitting in is more Harry's line; going with the flow; walking in the general way. But like I said: nothing against Harry, because we all do that, don't we? We all tend to obey that deep, old voice that says: *If everyone else is doing it, well, it can't be so bad, can it?* And anyone who doesn't can be comfortably called a nutter.

And now Harry, who a few minutes ago had been the very soul of assimilation, a man shamelessly enjoying an entirely false communality, was sitting alone in this sea of blood-warm emotion. I stood on tiptoe and could just see him: he was staring ahead of himself with a look I had never seen on him before.

It was not fear, at least, not the fear of any pain or suffering or loss. Nothing to do with running, or crying out in terror, or sweating. Dread. It was dread: the dread that comes when someone knows that that thudding in their heart is the sound of their fate, their unavoidable, inevitable fate, knocking at the door to remind them that it has not gone away, no matter how fast and how long they have been running. He switched focus and caught my eye.

I knew, knew, even then: all Harry's look was really saying was *Goodbye, Ben.* It was the kind of look a friend in a horrible dream might give, as your hand slips out of his and he plunges from the skyscraper, a look without accusation or hope: simply goodbye. It came straight out of Siberia.

I know now that what I was seeing was this: the absolute, utter, cosmic difference between happiness and desire.

Then someone shoved me strongly aside, saying, in a deep, fag-wrecked alto:

—Sorry, sorry.

I turned back again, but I had to arc my pint up over the head of an old farmer beside me, to avoid sloshing him in the face, and my own arm blocked my view as Shnade (I already knew it was her, I felt that buzz of destiny that is never totally wrong) wormed past, so I still did not see her face. But now I got the whole tattoo, from the point where the lizard's tail grew from nothing on her right shoulder blade, through twisting body and curling legs, down to the head with green eyes and the red tongue that led right out on to her hand. I smelled her fresh, hot sweat.

The anthem ended among general rejoicing, but Shnade (like I said, I knew it was her) still pushed through. I followed instinctively, without her knowing it. She reached a space in front of the table where Harry was still sitting.

He was looking at her with pure disbelief and absolute longing. He had not moved a muscle as she approached, but it was as if all his armour-plating, that mobile steel we carry around with us to ward off other people, had fallen, plate by plate, silently as rust, to the ground. He was completely there for the taking.

It was so obvious that, as Shnade stood in front of him, I had the most bizarre feeling that the music room of the pub was actually on a very slight rise, and coated with ice, and that Harry, pint, table and all, was going to start sliding, slowly but unstoppably, towards her.

And in fact, he was already standing up, shoving the table aside and moving past it like a sleepwalker. He was already standing in front of her.

—Shnade. Fuck.

—Harry fucking MacDonald. Glad to see you still sitting down to that shite, Harry.

—I still have my thresholds.

—What the fuck have you done to your hair?

—It wasn't me, Shnade. It was the man in the sky with the big shears. Yours is great.

—What was it like before?

—You don't remember?

—Harry, mate, I can't even remember what my natural colour is. Was it kinda punky?

—Yeah. White. Short.

—Fuck. Yeah, I remember: I thought I can't do this any more, everyone'll think I'm a dyke. We kinda invented dykes in Ireland about 1987, you know. After your time, Harry. Nothing against dykes, but you don't want to go sending out confusing signals, do you? So what the fuck you doing here?

—Just . . . just a trip. We're just on a break. This is Ben.

—Hoi, Ben.

—Hi, Shnade. (She shook my hand like a man: her hand was as big as mine, and harder.)

Was she beautiful? Is she?

I would say so. If I knew what people meant, I would say so. It is hard to say, these days. Is it possible to escape the bombardment, to avoid the radiation, *not* to think automatically that when someone says beautiful they mean young, tall, thin, blonde, rich? (And even if you are going out with someone who is young and tall and thin and blonde and rich, can she ever be young and tall and thin and blonde and rich *enough*? How can you ever be thin enough? Or muscly enough? You can't. Once you have let the whisper into your head, once you have started to believe that you are not thin enough or muscly enough, you never will be. Kate Moss diets for Christ's sake, and the guys on the covers of the body-building mags can simply *never* stop working it. Everyone in this big, security-guarded shopping mall we call the Western World has fallen for a fatal rumour, a story, a fairy tale that has been put about: that somewhere just over the rainbow is an impossible heaven of ultimate desirability and desire, where we will love ourselves without limit and be endlessly loved, where the infinite mirrors of our narcissism open up, at last, to reveal our dream lover.)

Well, I suppose you could ask: so what if she was? What? Does she *have* to be beautiful? Beautiful? Full of beauty? So what does that mean? What is Beauty? Nothing, a surface, a passing cloud, a mock of time, a painted face, a mosaic of a thousand fashion shots?

But it is everything, too. Since Helen of Troy's face launched her thousand ships, every cheap song and every old story has simply said: *because she was beautiful*. Today, when we are sitting in our dark cinema seats, our pews in the great multi-screen temple to Longing, we watch the actress walk through the pine forest towards the camera. And when the actress, forty feet tall now, lit in that way that makes the light seem to flow like liquid warmth out of the trees and the grass and her face, raises her eyes to the camera, to our eyes, when the actress stops before us, and waits, and does that amazing pupil-dilating thing with her eyes, we do not ask for one second whether she is clever or wise or good or genuine or brave or funny or warm or honest or bright or bubbly or understanding or unconventional or fun or easygoing or adventurous or chatty or assured or enthusiastic or articulate or tactile or affable or vibrant or eclectic or wild or enquiring or non-judgemental or independent or unpretentious or relaxed or genuine or gentle or challenging or unique or intuitive or thoughtful or sociable or affectionate or ironic or

135

spontaneous or creative or amiable or enthusiastic or extrovert or vivacious or curvaceous or caring or sophisticated or erudite or artistic or outgoing or generous or expressive or companionable or romantic or kind or good or happy or likes us for Christ's sake or any of the other desperate lonely-heart attempts to believe that people want anything else. She may be all of them, or she may be none, it simply does not matter. Because she is beautiful and beautiful and beautiful.

And yet, and yet: we may worship at the altar of mass beauty at the flicks, but Shnade would not look beautiful on the screen. But yes, she is beautiful. She was not as tall as you are supposed to be, and her face was not as cheekboned as a modelling agency would require; her teeth were by no means perfect; her arms were strong and covered in little blonde hairs, and the hairs of her armpits showed out from her little red dress. She was thin, though, as thin as you are supposed to be, as thin as you could reasonably be without thin being your whole career. Skinny, almost, but with muscles. She had small lines under her eyes. Her fingernails were chewed and snagged. Her hennaed dreads were not clean. She stood at ten-to-two in her flat shoes. She had hardly any breasts to speak of, and her voice said twenty a day at least.

I thought she was beautiful straight away.

So maybe there is hope. Maybe, deep down under the neon and lights that burn into our heads every waking, ad-fed, media-soaked moment of our lives, there is still, somewhere, untouched, unpolluted, a dark, strong river that knows the fault lines and secret waterways of our ossified hearts, and can call to us over all the jangling airwaves: *beautiful, for you.* And mean that this someone can make you smile and sigh, and want to touch her hand.

After the first hit, fear comes.

What the fuck was I doing? For a terrifying moment I imagined Anna beside me, seeing me staring, throwing her drink in my face and walking rightfully out of the door, for ever. Leaving me alone with my mad fantasy about a woman whose name I had only just heard across a pub and could not even pronounce with anything like certainty; a woman who quite surely lived a life I could hardly imagine.

I shook my head internally, cleared my mind and looked up coolly again. And got it again, straight between the eyes. Like what? Like the noise of a thunderous wind in your head, is like what. Like a sudden wild zoom that shoots you across a crowded room and right into her pupils, is what.

Like love at first sight, for Christ's sake, is what.

I looked at her again, and tried to look beyond her skin and tattoo and jangling beads and all the rest of her bright young crusty courting plumage. I tried to look at her the way you might look at some interesting, skilful, striking piece of a film: when you rewind and look again and ask yourself what is it, after the initial wave of surprised delight, that makes it work? What was it about her? I stayed cool, and watched. I thought, at length: she looked like she did not give a fuck, but did. Not about anything most people do, but for something. I didn't know what. But something. No, it was not that she did not give a fuck; but she was fucked if she was going to show it. She gave off the signals that said Young and Free and other, deeper ones that said: not.

Serious, that was all I could think of.

She looked serious as fuck. I don't mean serious as in solemn or depressed or up her own arse or whatever. She was none of these. She stood there so solid, it

137

looked like she would stand in front of tanks, so long as she knew why these tanks seriously needed standing in front of. She had weight. She possessed the space she was in. I don't know, I don't know, I don't know what to say: she looked like she was happy in her own skin, she seemed to have no gap between what she was doing and what she was thinking, she . . .

Shit, I don't know. Maybe it was just because I thought she was beautiful? Maybe I was just making ridiculous, laughable allowances, the way we all do, for beauty? Maybe she was mildly stoned? Or maybe she really had something, something like that strange touch of sadness, of wistfulness maybe, that everyone who has truly felt anything has. But also hope and trust in the future. Someone who had taken it before and knew they still could?

I don't know, what am I supposed to say? As a logical man, I know I should be able to pin it down. But I also know I can't.

All I know is that I saw Harry falling hopelessly for her, all over again, even as I watched: and as I looked at her I totally agreed. I could not keep the cool focus, it was lies and bullshit.

Maybe it was because Harry fancied her so blatantly? I mean, our friends get into our heads, we choose our clothes and where we live and even, I sometimes think, what we believe, because of what our friends do (you may know, at first, that you are shifting your ideas because of new friends, but your pride will not allow you to think that for very long: no, a few weeks after you start hanging around with them, pride will have trumped memory easily, and when you say to yourself that what you now believe in was what you *really always thought*, you will persuade yourself no sweat, so little sweat indeed that you could pass a lie detector with flying colours). So if your good friend maintains that, and, more importantly, acts as if, *she is beautiful*, you are unlikely to be completely insulated.

But this is what I think:

You know that way you meet people, I mean, just people generally, in offices and parties and horrible lunches? Well, you know (having reached our advanced and clever age) pretty well where they are coming from as soon as you swap three words with them. You know, with something approaching a despairing certainty, pretty well how they vote and where they shop and what paper they read and what books they buy and where they go on hols and what they would do with the lottery if they won it and *what they are going to say next*, for Christ's sake. When was the last time you found yourself looking at someone after they just said or did something at some party or office or horrible dinner and thinking: *Well, bugger me*?

And now here was this person who mocked all my knowledge. Christ, I didn't even know her name. I mean, I knew it was *Shnade*, I could call to her or chat with her, but I knew that was not really her name, even though I also knew right then that this particular pattern of letters, S-h-n-a-d-e, was already locked into my brain for always, however wrong I knew it was. When I looked at her, I saw only what I saw, what the whole world saw. I got nowhere. My deeper radar just flowed round her and never bounced back; it registered nothing, all my years of quietly sitting and watching were worth zero. She was a map without names or poles or scale, a starless night at sea, a strange, bright landscape without perspective.

When I looked at her, I simply had no conception of her life: yet here she was, living.

So much for understanding.

I thought of Anna, back home.

I mean shit, you can't go around leaving a pub every time you see someone you fancy. Or calling up your partner every time you have a treacherous little hint of a thought, can you? Well, I suppose you can, actually.

(I sometimes wish I had. When I am standing here alone in Peckham, staring out of my window, absent-mindedly tapping my ash into Harry's little hazelnut pot, I wonder what would have happened. Whether, if I had said all this to Anna, it might have sent us spinning off into some fresh new dimension? But I didn't.)

It was so easy not to, because we are all trained to lie. We are so used to being pummelled with bright things we cannot afford and lives we can never have and beautiful people we can never touch, that our whole lives have become, have had to become, one vast exercise in lying to ourselves. Medieval peasants may have looked up at the bright lights in the castle and told themselves it was all nothing to do with them. But medieval peasants did not see their godlike betters poncing about in *Hello!* magazine every week. We all dig this deep, dark ditch between what we want and what we dare admit to wanting. So there was nothing easier than for me to shut the door and say *no, not my type really. Not for me.*

And even to believe it myself.

—You still live out here? asked Harry.
—Fuck no! I'm only here to see Styx. Here he is so. Hiya, Styxy.
—Shnade, how's about this then? The return of the fucking prodigal, or what?

Styx embraced the pair of them, an action which

entailed putting one big paw on Shnade's little bum quite happily. She did not seem to notice. I did. Styx drew them both close. I pretended to have my eyes and ears far away, but everything I could muster was focused secretly on his hand on her bum, and his voice in their ears.

—You staying, so, Shnade?

—Ah, no. Just need a chat with the former General Secretary of the United Nations, Styx, know what I mean? Got to get back to town, party at my place. Hey, fuck, Harry, what are yous all doing tonight?

—Well, we . . . I mean, we were going to stay. But we have to get back for the morning plane, so . . .

—Harry, said Styx, —would you ever put a stopper on the shite and go along with her. You know you want to. Good to see ya, but off you go. Do you want any takeaways?

—Sure, sure, um, give us a load of tins and a bottle of vodka.

—That all you want?

—Well, yeah, some whiskey as well?

—Yeah. Good man yourself, Harry. Sean, sort Harry out to go, willya. Back in five.

Styx and Shnade turned and disappeared through the thinning crowd of drinkers (everyone seemed quite clear about who could stay and who had to get out sharpish) into the back of the pub.

—Earth to Harry, come in please, I said.

—What's this party in Dublin? said The Wop, eyeing the Beauty Posse openly.

—Who the hell's the Cro-Magnon pin-up? asked Jan.

—Nightmare, said The Wop. —Nice trilats, though, for a girl.

—Nice nails, too, said Jan.

—She's called Shnade, said Harry. He pronounced it unerringly, exactly as the girls had done: his version gave no clue as to where the name might fit into our world.

—Harry, you have got a fucking cheek bringing us all this way for that, snapped Jan.

—I didn't know she'd be here! You heard me phoning. I haven't seen her for . . .

—Will there be bagpipes and crap at this party too? demanded The Wop.

—Great, said Jan, —so we're invited to an At Home with last millennium's Miss Ageing Crusty.

—Look, OK, OK, we can stay here, said Harry feebly.

—No way, I can't take any more fucking bagpipes! cried The Wop, and, spotting that the Young Beauties had turned slightly, thus admitting that his outburst had got through to their ring-fenced chit-chat, he went for the tiny gap he had created and in two steps he was over with them, arms outspread and innocent garlicky smile all over his chops. —Girls, excuse me, but I gotta know: will there be any bagpipes at your party?

—Bagpipes? Fuck, no. Jesus!

—Ne-ews!

—Don't you like the pipes, sure? said one of the girls, mocking the pipes, not The Wop.

—I bloody hate them. Oh, any of you into community theatre and stuff?

—Cleaner is. Hey, Cleaner . . .

Cleaner?

—No, no, said The Wop (now he had got past first-smile base, he cunningly undercut his blatant muscles and generally sexist demeanour by dragging Jan over, thus establishing that he had friends with two Y chromosomes. Cute operator, The Wop). —It's her. She runs half that stuff in London. Always scouting, eh, Jan?

—Shit, muttered Jan, and for a moment I thought she was going to break away from The Wop's handhold, ruining his act. But several of the young/beautiful/thin girls were already looking at her with interest, and Jan was already lying, even as she swore. Her face tinged with that little giveaway blush that you see on quiet people who have spent long years plotting their status, and who can never really get enough of acknowledgement. They've had the delay up to here; now it's time for the sodding gratification, however much they try to hide it. Already, Jan was feeling better. The Wop grinned triumphantly.

—Do yous know Shnade so? one of the girls asked me. I detected disbelief, and caught myself vowing to do some shopping for clothes soon, after all.

—Well, I said . . .

—And Styx, nodded Harry.

—Fuck, wait a minute, are you that guy on the telly? Yeah, yeah, that one goes around excavations and that?

—Yes, actually.

—Guaranteed no bagpipes, girls?

—Well, I don't think Skagga does pipes. I mean, if you got them with you he might sample them and mess about a bit . . .

Skagga?

—No, no, no pipes.

—Shnade said she knew him. You, I mean. Like, wow. Cool. Er, is that kinda ponytail yoke a wig so?

—Neev, c'm here, meet Jane.

Neev?

—It's Jan, actually.

—Oh, Jesus, sorry.

143

—Don't worry. Happens to a lot of people. I just *look* like a Jane, I suppose.

—I suppose pipes could work in the chill-out room. If you're really keen.

—No! No bagpipes. No pipes of any description. Pipes are generically bad news.

—Jorldeen and me were thinking of bringing a show over to London next month, actually.

Jorldeen? This is getting ridiculous. Not only all young and/or thin and/or beautiful, but aliens.

—Did Shnade say that about me? I'll kill the cow!

—She always watches your shows. Laughs her tights off.

—Great. No, that's great. So, what's she doing these days?

—Shnade? Doing? Jesus, you know the way she is. She's kinda, you know, hanging out, chilling ... She makes stuff sometimes.

—Oh, you mean you're coming to the Islington London Irish Festival?

—Yeah. Do you know Mary Bourke so?

—Yeah, actually, I saw her the other day ...

—And not too much horrible banging townie techno, girls?

—Ah, none of that. Well, a few minutes when Skagga thinks it right, maybe. He's more into deep rare grooves and trip-hop, you know.

Into *what*?

—What stuff does she make?

—Ah, you know, kinda, picture things like. Dolls and

144

crosses and beads and feathers and fuck knows what. Really cool.

—Sorted, said Shnade, bouncing back in from Styx's office. —Shall we go then? See ya tomorrow, Styxy.

—You do. Harry, if ye're still here tomorrow, come to the session so.

—We've got a morning flight.

—Well to fuck then, you old Brit you. Come back soon. Don't be a stranger now we've made up. Good man yourself! Now get out the lot of yous! Harry: don't get sentifuckingmental on me now. A quick visit is a good visit. Out.

A Box of Matches

So we all piled out into this horrible great van that belonged to Shnade. It looked like she bloody *lived* in it (which, as it turned out, was because she did). Us and the Beautiful Youth. Jan was well away by now, chatting to her admiring sisters with all the confidence she had never had at twenty, taking advantage of the way Youth accepts you as you *are*, without wondering how exactly you *came to be* it: what did they know about her years of quiet working and vengeful planning? No more than Harry's young and idiotic audience knows about his years of Ph.D.-ing in libraries. But then, so what? Why should they care? And is it only the young and dull who work like that? Don't we all? What does biography matter to us? We are not philosophers for God's sake, and there is no one up there handing out Heavenly Oscars at the end of it all for the most logical and correct storyline. We are just the audience of our own lives: if someone is crap and makes it all seem boring, then all the explanations in the world will not make us stay with them; but if someone is fun and makes us feel like getting another round in fast before the long night falls, well, all the accusations on earth will simply bounce off them. No one gives a fuck about the backstory, so long as what is going on is worth doing and watching.

I watched Jan, and saw her coming to life in their eyes. With this gang of twenty-year-olds, she was simply becoming what she should have been at twenty. As I looked at her, I felt this strange mixture of relief and mourning: relief that she was here at last; mourning for all those wasted years.

Or perhaps not? Perhaps it doesn't matter how long it takes, so long as you get there.

The Wop was like a pig in shit: happily squashed between youthful limbs, secure in the knowledge that his long years in the gym were at last fully employed in serving their purpose, which was to counterfeit biological youth and unreflective physicality. Wherever these girls squashed him, body or mind, they would find no flab and no sign of excessive thought, and that was enough for him to feel utterly confident in their society. And as I watched him, my brain flashed with knowledge about him too (no, not *knowledge*, I had always known these things, so it was not knowledge: it was that sudden snap of focus, that new conjunction, that happens when our barren, old knowledge gets promoted to sudden, new insight): The Wop had had a perfect, unsullied, unquestioning London Grammar School Wide Boy youth. He had suffered what everybody suffers: fights, unfair teachers, teenage bitternesses, brushes with cops ... but no more. He had never known strangeness. He had been at home until he went to college.

Yes: Jan spent her years trying to rewind time so that she could have another crack at being young; but The Wop's patient hours of weights were all simply an attempt to get back there. In their different ways they were both asking and fighting for something very simple, and, for them now, very, very impossible: to be happy and young.

So, I thought, *it doesn't make much difference, does it?* You have a perfect youth and you spend your whole life trying absurdly to keep it kicking, or you have a crap youth and you spend your whole life absurdly trying to have another crack at it. Either way, absurd is what you get. Yes: for us, who can look forward to no scarfs and shawls and black suits and caps and rocking chairs in the sun, who can expect no respect for our superannuated wisdom ('Now, in *my* day, 120 Beats Per Minute was considered very adequate') and can hope for no seats of consequence at whatever celebrations are to come, ageing is just biological decay. And all our attempts to hold it back can only take us through ascending degrees of the absurd in the inevitable direction of the grotesque.

Picture this: a box of matches. And each one of those matches represents a full-on Saturday night. Approximately 52 per box. Scritchhhh, whoosh!

How many boxes have you got left? Really? How many real proper, right-through the night, ready-for-romance Saturday bashes do you expect to have this month? This year? Look at the boxes, arranged on your bedroom shelf. Not long ago, not more than a couple of years ago, you had so many that you never even thought about counting them. And now, and now: a slim pile. How will you feel when you start on the last one, and know it is all for real? And don't even think about trying to save them up for later, because it's a damp old world we live in, and if you wait too long you might easily find that when you take out your long-hoarded little box of Saturday nights, all dressed up and thinking *at last at last at last, now I am the person I always planned to be, here comes the pay-off, now I can get out there and* ... you find that all you can do is scrape your saved-up time pathetically away, with scarcely a feeble flare.

You use it, you lose it; you don't use it, you lose it. Who said anything about fair?

It occurred to me, as I sat there quietly, that this would, in all probability, be the very last time I would ever sit in a ghastly camper van, surrounded by young people who seemed, if not exactly warm (and why on earth should they be?), at any rate perfectly ready to accept me as some honorary day member of their tribe. And I thought: that's all I want, really. I do not crave distinction, just a place round the campfire; just a seat in the van; a place accepted as mine by right, where I can watch and listen.

Watch Harry especially, and Shnade.

Shnade was driving. The van must have weighed three and a half tonnes if it weighed an ounce, and she looked small behind the wheel. Small, but in place, if you know what I mean. The muscles on her arms flexed and moved as she wrestled the van round bumping corners. She was as absorbed in this as any ten-year-old boy sitting with burning eyes and reddening face at his killing-machine PC joystick, yet seemed completely relaxed and quite able to chat away at the same time. I watched, fascinated, as she rolled a cigarette with one hand while on a brief straight. Her tattoo looked black on her arm now, when it caught the oncoming head-lights.

Harry was sitting next to her but one. There was some other bloke, a big crusty in a bandanna, sitting in between him and Shnade. I had not noticed this bloke before. The three of them sat up front and watched the road. And then I realised why the whole scene seemed so bizarre. Very bizarre for Harry, anyway, or maybe just very bizarre for a close friend of Harry's to see, because who knows what even our closest friends do when we are not there? Maybe Harry was always like this when I wasn't there?

What Harry was doing was: nothing.

Harry was still, he was quiet, and in the occasional wash of light from an approaching car he too looked completely serious. It was like watching a close friend sleeping: when you realise that all this time you have known them, you have never actually seen *them*.

And then the guy in the bandanna asked if anyone needed sorting, and Harry said yes.

Boutros Boutros and Tina Turners

So: maybe Harry wasn't actually fucked from the day he was born. Maybe it was just the drugs. Later, when he was about to take his third line, I did my friendly duty and pointed out to Harry that he, Harry, had always said that junkies were just very unhappy people who would be addicted to something else if they were not junkies: did that not mean that he, Harry, being about to hit the booster and go finally to Escape Velocity, must logically be deeply unhappy? And if he was, at this time, for whatever reason, so deeply unhappy as to want to whack his frontal lobes through the top of his skull with charlie on top of E, maybe it would be better to knock it on the head right now and come for a walk home with me, his old and trusted friend?

He looked at me and said:

—Do you want a line or not?

So maybe this is not a story of inescapable destiny but a simple morality tale whose point is that it would never have happened if not for the drugs. Or maybe that if you are going to do drugs, you should do them rather longer before your fortieth birthday, and somewhat closer to your own home turf.

So let's assume, for the time being, that we could have turned the drugs down and escaped. It would have been easy for me, at any rate. Honestly, I haven't touched drugs for years, except on Harry's False

Birthdays, for three very simple reasons: (a) I don't need them, (b) I can't afford them and (c) I never come across them now. The bubble I live in never even bumps up against the bubble of the people for whom drugs are just part of Friday night. I'd never dropped an E in my life, actually. Too old to have. Or the wrong place? The wrong bubble? I mean, I had been mid-twenties, single, slim and fit, earning pretty good money, with relatively large amounts of free time and living in Zone 2 ... and I had never even bloody *heard* of the supposedly earth-shaking Summer of Love until I read about it in the papers the year afterwards. I suppose it was probably like that with most people in 1968, too.

We did coke sometimes, back then, but rarely, because it was bloody expensive. Even then I always thought charlie has only three social functions: one is to make you want to shag everyone while talking about yourself, two is to make you want more charlie and three is to make everything else seem ridiculously cheap. I mean *why on earth not* pay hundreds of quid for some crap designer jumper, darling, if you confidently expect to put that much up your nose over the coming week or two? Why not have a Porsche? It's only a kilo, for Christ's sake. The ultimate consumer label. And since I never bought labels of any kind these days (I didn't shop any more, I went to M&S) I didn't long for this one either. Seriously, I had not even thought about drugs for years.

And yet, and yet: even as I saw Harry pay off Mr Bandanna and palm a teeny envelope and four little pink pills, even before he reached over and handed me three of them, without a word, I could feel cold waves of change rippling up and down my body in expectation, as if I was one of those kids' transforming robots.

It couldn't have been physical addiction, so what was it? What was I addicted to?

All addiction is mental. No, not mental: social. It is *people* we are addicted to, hopelessly: the crap that we think we need, that carries the signs of our addiction, is just whatever particular brand of crap we associate with the people we have met and liked and now need. If they are into old cars, we will start helplessly ogling glossy magazines in order to store up facts about vintage Aston Martins we can never own; if tennis is where we found them, we shall start to obsess about racquets which are infinitely, comically better than we are; if movies are what we talk about, we shall become film buffs, just to be able to talk to them. And if they happen to be coke fiends or smackheads, or E-chicks, then we shall cultivate a semi-addiction just to make sure that when we sit with them, with these people we like to sit with, we are never short of a subject for a chat. A sure subject for a chat: that is all we want, and we will pay whatever price we have to pay to get it. Whether it is your poshy Soho cokehead club or some horrible ten-pound-bag party in a council flat that rears above the station in Sheffield, it is always the same: we do it because the people we are with do it.

So we chat, about philosophy or fitness, French lit. or soft furnishings, just to keep hearing the sound of the voices we like. We don't care what we chat about, because in the half-lit depths of our heads, all we see are their lips moving, their eyes looking, and the soft, unsynched, meaningless sound of their presence with us. Which is why people become smackheads or coke fiends: what security! When you find your smackhead or coke-fiend pals in your bar, be it marbled swankery or some dive one step up from the park bench, you know instantly what to say the moment your arse touches the still-warm seat left by whoever just got up. And there you sit: secure as any born-again in his chapel, snug as a bug in a rug.

Snug as a Brit bumping along in a van in Ireland, surrounded by nice young folks, secure in his position as the proud and public possessor of one of the little pink pills they all have too. I looked at Jan and The Wop.

—Well, said Jan, eyeing her pill and her new young friends, —at the risk of revealing myself to be hopelessly old, I have to confess I never did one of these.

—Oh, these Crowns beat Mizzis anytime! said Neev.

Jan looked at me, and I raised an eyebrow to see if she would actually tell them that what she meant was she had never taken an E at all. But there are limits to everyone's honesty. So instead, she nodded wisely to Neev, and, copying her young guide while cunningly appearing not to do so, like some very skilful social climber aping poshy manners off the cuff, she snapped her pill neatly in two and necked half of it, then accepted a drink from a pre-owned and refilled water bottle as if she had been fully expecting this. I caught her eye and wanted to giggle: it was like when I was fourteen, and first taking joints with the ancient, original hippies I then worshipped. Except now the gurus could have been our kids.

Jan met my eye, with our positions now reversed. Now she was the one challenging me. I wasn't going to say no now, was I? What, and risk breaking the magic circle of our presence? Raise questions? Open up cans of worms? Not me, my friend. Like I said: I am Nature's middle-of-the-road man, the Man Who Loves To Say Yes. So I snapped and swallowed mine too, and took the water from her.

—I don't suppose we'll die, I said quietly to Jan, covered by the rattling van.

—They don't seem to be dead. And tonight, Ben, I have this very strange but very strong desire to be like them. Don't you? Just for once?

—Right, I said.

I looked at her in the dark, next to me, and for the first time in fifteen years I felt a strange desire to kiss her and hug her. It was nothing to do with drugs, and everything to do with when an old friend suddenly shifts focus: when you realise how little we know about each other, and how much, how much too much, we are all alone. Now, suddenly, I knew what it was she was thinking about when she sat and watched the thesps queueing up outside her office for their grants, what she had always thought about them: are people who can just sit and look pretty and giggle and rap away about utter bollocks for hours on end without an apparent care in the world just brainless pains in the arse? Or superhumans?

And what, if anything, is the consolation for being self-conscious? Is the human brain an evolutionary dead end? Why not just knock it on the head? Why not just take the pill?

Then we both looked at The Wop. He glared back. But he was sussed by his own philosophy. I mean, since his entire belief system comes down to arguing that all his training is not just about an idiotic and passing fashion for abs and tight buns, but actually makes him somehow Biologically Fit For Life, then obviously, if he is so bloody fit, he should be able more efficiently to metabolise the occasional bit of crap than some desk-bound wristjob like Harry or me or Jan, shouldn't he? If not, his life is a wasted lie.

(It has to be said that one could, if one wanted,

undermine The Wop's entire religion by asking the simple question: well, Mr Wop, *what exactly is* this amazing existential-cum-physical challenge that is going, one day, to make full use of, to use, to *need*, all this overblown musculature? Will it save you from Global Warming or Microwave Cancer? Will it ward off the lions? On the other hand, *he* could ask *me* back what exactly it is that I hope to gain, in the end, at the bottom-most line of lines, by all my mortgages and PEPs and investments and, well, my work. And I would have no sane or rational answer either. Why do I do it? The Japanese economy and George Soros willing, my various schemes should guarantee me a comfortable last decade on earth, yes. Yes: I can say with some mathematical confidence that I do not expect to want for cardigans in my old age. But then, when you think about it, it is only marginally sane, if that, to argue that a good way of spending the majority of your one and only shot at Life On Earth is to devote it to making sure that the last, crappiest, tiredest bit of it is nice and cosy. So I don't ask him my question, and he doesn't ask me his.)

—Oh well, I said. —Everyone's at it these days, Wop.

—Just because everyone else is a wanker doesn't mean I am, growled The Wop.

I love The Wop when he is like that: it is so obvious to everyone except The Wop himself that he is lying through his teeth. He is like Bogey in some film, with his voice-over telling you how he didn't give a damn while we are seeing big eyes looking up at the girl's window through the rain. I mean, look at The Wop: spends all his time doing something, his weights and training, which is clearly intended, when you think about it, to impress people, any people, all people, anyone who sees him at a hundred yards, in the most basic, blatant, open way, and yet he pretends to scorn the opinion of the world. His carapace of not caring what people think about him is so obviously an inside-out version of the fact that he cares what *everyone* thinks about him, what the most wretched spotty little barman or fat little waitress might possibly be thinking about him. He lives in a world of unceasing judgements, that drive him to his ascetic manias of alleged Fitness.

I saw him once through a window, pounding his running machine, when I was going to meet him after his session at his club. Him and a whole row of other types: the fat sweating ones labouring along, mottled and near death, at hardly more than walking pace; the troubled, normalish lot desperately fighting a heroic but hopeless reargard action against mortality on the ground of mortality's own choosing; and the others, The Wop and a couple of stringbean, muscled girls, hammering away at the rolling rubber floor, high on their modern sainthood, consulting their little fitness plans between machines, like new converts reading *How To Pray The Rosary* with flushed devotion. For a second, I imagined a fat Cuban, in uniform, at the end of this line of strivers, cigar in gob and Kalashnikov on lap, swigging tequila and laughing as he roared *More! More! Generate more electricity for the Workers' Palace of Pleasure, you sons and whores of the wretched bourgeoisie! Ha ha ha!* I mean, shit, what kind of world is it where we work to get money to buy labour-saving devices that stop us having to walk, bend, lift, wring, pull or whatever, and then go and pay more of our money so we dress up in ridiculously overpriced crap and go on stupid little machines, doing exactly the kind of things we have just saved ourselves from having to do at home or at work? You call that sane?

—I could take six, if I wanted, mate. But my body is a fucking temple to fags and lager! Oh, sod it, come on then.

Exactly: Oh, sod it, come on then.

Like I said: give me one good reason to say no.

Looking Down on Clouds, Waiting
and Hoping

The house was dark. Netting, festooned with little red lights, covered the walls of the hall and up the stairs; car-repair lanterns were clamped on to banisters and door frames, giving soft yellow light that reminded me of somewhere I had once seen. Something to do with horses. I could not think where the memory came from.

It was what they call a party, these days. Very confusing. Like: when they say *a record* they mean (I think) a CD, or else they look at your old actual *record* record collection and go, *Wow, vinyl, excellent behaviour!* like it was some fashion decision you cunningly made twenty years ahead of the game. When they say *a song* they mean a series of beats and tweetings and electronic whooshes, while a *tune* seems to mean a two-bar bass line which is looped for ten minutes and a *club* means any old place they set up the decks. And now everything is, amazingly enough, *cool*, which in my own, primordial teenagehood was something only the mockable old hippies used to say. And they don't seem to realise that the seventies was utterly naff the first time round, and that the only saving grace of flares was political: in the early seventies, you really *could* get into trouble at school or work for wearing them. My own comprehensive school headmaster used to measure our trousers to make sure they didn't count as flares. Talk about another country.

Of course, the whole point is that the Yoof choose what they like, music and clothes, mainly on the basis that us old folk consider it absurd and inexplicable and will hence stay well away, leaving the repulsive Yoof in its own pimply ghetto. This all seems so natural to us now that we have to pinch ourselves with pliers to make ourselves remember that no one in the history of the world had ever thought of it until about 1959.

But that means nothing. The other day I was in a plane with Hugh, my son, OK, nearly three years old now. He was quite happily looking out of the window, down on to clouds, without even noticing it. And I had this sudden whirling feeling when I thought: Christ, ever since some unusually brainy chimp, off its tits on fermenting mangoes, walked away from all the other proto-hominids snoring happily in their caves, and looked up at the sky, and reeled as it saw gods in the stars, we have dreamed of flying above the clouds. A hundred thousand dead generations of us. And now, here is my son, the fifth or sixth generation, no more, since flying became possible, and the second or third since it was anything but a wild adventure for heroes, sucking a lollipop cast in the shape of Mickey fucking Mouse and looking down on clouds like it is the most natural, boring thing in the world. Nothing I can do will make it seem more interesting to him than this lollipop, and he will never in his life think of looking down on clouds as anything other than a banal and utterly natural part of life. Change? We must be genetically designed for it.

But it's still hard to take the pace of it in this, our one and only shot at living. So I stood quite still in the House Of Yoof and waited for my head to turn down my aural sensitivity in response to the new level of sound, and wondered what was supposed to happen from this pill.

As I drank slowly, I was vaguely reassured that this

DJ Skagga (or *Schieageach* or whatever he was actually called) was definitely even older than me. I supposed that at some point DJ Skagga's like-age pals would appear and we would all play Clash records (actual record records, I mean) or whatever.

Jan's thinness was serving her well, I noted: in the dry ice and low-laid lamps, it really was difficult to say if she was much older than everyone else. Ditto The Wop's well-defined muscles. And I had already seen how Harry's fame, like Skagga's decks, seemed to have officially knocked years off him, thus allowing him to spout ghastly crap like *How good is this house* and *What are they like* as he entered, close in Shnade's wake, chattering away without seeming to attract the least mockery. Also, many of the young male folk were still hanging on to shaven or cropped headstyles, despite the flares, which helped him.

Me, I stood quietly and drank and watched.

Shnade was perched in the kitchen, on a worktop, next to a big old Belfast sink, cross-legged, rolling a cigarette. Several girls were chatting away to her; she was laughing and nodding as she rolled. But she was also on edge. I saw her chew her bottom lip.

It was Harry who was making her uneasy. He was standing beside her, arse against the kitchen units, just out of clothes-touching distance, leaning ever so slightly towards her, drinking and looking at nothing. It was like she could feel his shadow taking away the sun. He was just standing there, waiting.

No, not just waiting. More than that, more active somehow. He was hoping. Or somewhere between the two. In Spanish, there is only one word that means both, waiting and hoping, and if I could find a word for what Harry looked like he was doing, if there was a word for how I thought he was feeling, it would have meant both: waiting, and hoping.

Remember that feeling? I had it once when I thought maybe this girl I knew liked me. I thought maybe she would come to me, and for several nights I lay awake, waiting and hoping for a taxi pulling up and the clunk of a door; a taxi pulling softly away and then, after a curious pause, a key in the lock. A coat placed carefully on a chair downstairs, a cup of tea made in slightly exaggerated silence, and then a slow, fateful footfall on the stair, a quiet push on a door that is already open, a shadow against moonlight: lips and hair.

As I was thinking this, I realised that I was looking at Shnade's lips. They were slightly cracked with sun and wind. To my shock, I realised that I had been just about to propel myself from the wall and cross the kitchen floor with no other purpose than to tell her how I liked her lips. I also realised that I had been standing here unmoving for quite a long time; that I had started to nod my head in time to the beat and stroke the hair on the back of my own neck; and that strange rushes of warmth and cold were travelling up and down my neck and temples like colours rippling along a tropical fish. I wanted to smile and say *phew!*, like some childhood cartoon person. I looked over at Harry: he simply smiled vaguely at me and then let his eyes float away. But his fingers were drumming on his leg. I decided to find somewhere to sit down for a bit.

I found an ancient armchair and was about to sit down on it when I saw a picture, well, a sort of collage thing, hanging on the wall above it. I knelt up on the chair to look at it. It was an octagonal frame covered in some sort of glittery gold-shot material. Inside the frame was a circular glass, slightly convex, covering the collage: dried flowers, fragments of material of every kind, meaningless shreds of newspaper cuttings, shards of mirror, medieval angels and cherubs, repeated photographs of a goat's skull. In the centre of the whole thing was an arch-shaped section, with a renaissance madonna at the bottom, and a cheap, plastic doll, a baby with arms outstretched, in a border of gold and purple sequins, the plastic baby was lying on an oblong of mirror glass: at the top of the glass, a toy fly seemed to be moving down towards the baby, while at the bottom, a red and black lizard curled its way almost on to the baby's mirror-bed. I had no idea what the hell it was all about, but I was fascinated.

When I turned round to sit down properly on my chair, I found that Shnade was already sitting on the arm. I looked at the lizard on her arm and the lizard in the picture.

—Like it, she asked?

—Love it, I said. —What's it mean?

—Fuck knows, said she. —I just make them.

I sat down. My head was below hers now. I looked up into her eyes.

—What happened with you and Harry then?

—Nothing, she said.

—Nothing? Oh, I see: the kind of nothing that makes you not be able to sit beside him? The kind of nothing that can do the impossible and shut Harry up?

—That's good.

—What is?

—You saying that.

—Is it?

—Well, people are only scared to be straight with other people if they are scared other people might be straight with them. Fear, Ben. I think ninety-nine per

cent of human fucking evil is caused by fear. Cowardice. And being straight with people is a form of
courage. So big points to you, Ben whoever-the-fuck-
you-are. Come on, you want to meet some people?

—Um, no, not particularly. I wouldn't know what to
say to anyone. Literally. I wouldn't know what words
to use.

—So don't talk. Just smile and dance. That's what
everyone else does.

—Wrong clothes. No labels.

—True. You need some.

—No way. I'm not some fucking fashion victim.

—Sorry, Ben, you can't escape the world: wearing no
labels is the biggest label of all.

—I don't see many labels on you.

—I make the stuff myself, that's different. My own
private no-dough label. But you didn't make that shite.
You went and fucking bought it. With money. You
chose it. And all it says is you're out of the game. Like
you don't give a fuck about everyone else.

—Or that I'm just old and married?

—You want to say that?

—Have I got a choice?

—You don't look it.

—What, old?

—Married. Apart from the togs, obviously.

—You what?

—You heard. No cowardice, Ben. You could at least
lose that horrible shirt. I can find you a normal little T-
shirt, at least.

—Look, Shnade, seriously. It's not my world, OK?

—Really? I quite like it. Look at them. It's real, in a
way. Sure, everyone's off their tits, but then, who isn't?
Yeah, some of them have trust funds and some of them
have fuck all, so in one way it's shite, but for a couple of

164

years it really doesn't matter much. For a couple of years, all that matters is whether other people like you. Like some fucking dream of utopia.

—Is that why you still live in a van?

—Yep. I haven't given up hope yet, Ben. Mind you, I have been worrying about the cold a bit recently.

—About the cold? I thought we were supposed to worry about global warming.

—Ah, those bastards would promise anything at election time. No, I mean seriously. It was cold, last winter. In my van. Which is the scary fucking thing, because last winter was not cold. No colder than normal here. As cold, as wet, but no more so. Which means it must be me. Do you ever think how much of the shite we take is just because we start to feel the cold? And the wet. The wet is worse.

—Yes, wet is bad.

At this point it seemed right and proper to put my head on to her shoulder. So I did. She stroked my hair.

—But then, I said, —the thing is, as soon as you get a house, the maths gets you.

—What maths?

So then I told her about the maths, and lawnmowers and cat-shit and little fences and Volvos and how you somehow become the twat you used to laugh at and stuff, like I already explained to you. It took quite a long time, I think: Shnade just nodded and seemed to be listening.

—Sorry about that, I said, when I had finished. —I don't always talk this much.

—First time? she said.

—Mmmm, I said.

—Just remember it's only a little trip, don't try to do any real, sexy snogging, and you'll be grand. Fuck, your first time. How sweet. No, but imagine: if you knew,

165

really knew that you would never feel the cold or the wet again, or actually be hungry, what the fuck would you keep on working for?

—I love my white goods.

—That was crap.

—Sorry.

—So what are you into, Ben?

—Into?

I looked up at her eyes again. I didn't know what the hell she was talking about. And she didn't know how the hell I couldn't understand her. We stared for a moment, like lost tourists in some distant land who just mistook each other for people from home.

—Into. What are you into?

—Sorry, I . . .

—What do you like doing? What do you like? You yourself.

—What do I like?

—Earth calling Ben. What do you like doing? In your life? Hello?

—Um, fuck, um . . .

See? Like I said, I was not programmed for this. Programmed to reply to *What do you do, Ben?* yes. Or: *What car you drive, mate?* Or: *Where you going on hols this year?* and stuff. But *like?* What do I *like?* I mean, I work and live and go out and, well, do the normal stuff and all that. But what do I *like?* Me, myself?

—Um. Well. I like . . . well, watching and listening, I suppose.

—You suppose?

—No, OK, OK: I officially like watching and listening. To people.

—That what you do, then?

166

—Me? No, fuck, I mean, I work. I . . . Look, I work. Fuck. Like everyone else.

—Right.

That was all she said. And all my democratic defences melted away. I looked into her eyes, her serious eyes, and could think of nothing more to say. I was about to tell her that I worked because of my kid, but suddenly that felt like a lie too.

—Look, she said, —I got to go see some people.

—I'm fine.

—You don't mind being on your own?

—Not for a few hours. Do you?

—I think I tend to draw conclusions too fast, Ben. If I'm up, I feel I can go on for ever and neck anything that comes my way. But when I'm down it feels like for ever too. Do you understand that?

—I don't think so.

—Oh.

—Sorry, I just mean: I don't. OK, so you have a bad day and hangover and no mates about, but one day is hardly bloody eternal isolation, is it?

—Ben, I got to remember that the next time it's a rainy fucking Sunday and I'm coming down alone, which is, I add, a thing I try at all costs to avoid. If you're going to get into this stuff, remember: you can come up with anyone, but it's who you can come down with that matters. Eternal isolation. Yeah, that's good. That's when I'm really glad of Shevaun. Which is pretty sad.

—Who?

—My daughter. My daughter Shevaun. Jesus, I forgot, you don't know. Harry doesn't know. Brilliant. My night off tonight. And I intend to make the most. And she started off laughing, and waving, then came back and said: —Hey, is it the first drop for your two mates as well? Muscle-Boy and Miss Scary?

—Dunno. Um, I guess.

—Well, it's certainly perked up their love life. You'd think they only just met. Back soon.

—Their what? I shouted, but my shout was lost in the drums. I shook my head virtually. I had obviously misheard, or misunderstood, what she said, so I forgot it. Actually, I had no room in my head for thinking about Jan and The Wop, because for some reason I wanted very much to run after Shnade and tell her that I had a son. The fact that she had a daughter and I had a son seemed to me such a miraculous coincidence, a revelation of so unique and crystalline a cosmic symmetry, that it had to be communicated in all its wonder. I got up, my mind glowing bright with insight.

—Oh, Jesus, great, thank fuck, said a girl, and jumped into the chair, where she curled instantly up. I then decided that it was not a good idea to chase Shnade: not so much because it was not a good idea in principle, as because my legs were not at all keen on moving. So instead, I leaned back against the wall, next to my ex-chair, and then just kind of slid gently down it: the floor rose sweetly to receive my grateful arse.

I needed to breathe deeply all of a sudden, and to stroke my hair again: there were waves of nervy tinglings going down my scalp, as if someone was already stroking it. I put my hand up, and found that someone was.

I did not even turn round at first. I just took time to experience this new hand, and to register that it was much smaller and smoother than Shnade's hand, though it had the same number of fingers, which seemed at the time to be a most interesting discovery.

Then it appeared that this nice little fascinating hand also possessed a voice:

—Shnade's gorgeous, said the voice. —I think she's gorgeous. Isn't she fabulous? I'm fabulous. (Now there was breathing near my ear.) —I've got a ring in my clitoris hood.

—Fabulous, I said, and put my hand back to feel the speaking hand. Instead, I found a little ear. I twiddled it. I was now reclining on the floor quietly and reaching backwards over my own head, with the result that, with my eyes closed, I had no sense at all of where any of her was in relation to any of me: I was amorphic, an amoeba, an octopus. She started scratching my hair hard.

I thought about what was happening, with my last resources of rationality and of learned experience: I decided that I had cracked the mores of your modern party scene. It appeared to work like this: if you had been seen publicly hugging or stroking with someone who was part of the gang, particularly if that someone was a high-status member, as Shnade clearly was, you were henceforth considered clean and kosher and in the hugging-and-stroking frame for any of them who felt like it or whom you approached for it. Hugging, in short, and general stroking, seemed to have been Mediterraneanised, stripped of any significance other than one of vague sociability. Interesting. I thought that I would have to discuss this anthropological discovery with Harry quite soon, as soon as I felt like moving. I wondered if there were archaeological precedents for it. Harry would know. Meanwhile, since this was very pleasant and a fine relief from all that post-Protestant careering about, but on the other hand clearly all an artificial and drug-induced lie, it seemed to me that the best thing to do was enjoy it for a while, but at the same time detach myself mentally, in order to file it away in its proper place. I thought.

Except I then found that I was unable to locate the usual levers that separate mind from body. It caused me no panic. I felt like Buster Keaton, standing there with a whole town falling round my ears: mildly bemused.

—I'm Jorldeen, said the hand and the ear and the breath.

—That's nice. I'm Ben.

—That's noice too. Ben. This is Neev.

I kept my eyes lightly closed. *Neev* was a new hand that was holding my free hand.

—Hiya, Neev.

—Hiya, Ben.

So now Jorldeen, or however the hell she spells it, and Neev, ditto, were my new friends. Neev and/or Jorldeen, it transpired, also had a head, which she or they had lain on my lap without me noticing it. Finding that we had a spare waist between us as well, I put my arm round it. It was a very nice waist. I told the nearest ear so. She appeared glad to be told so, since the result was that an arm entwined with mine. Jorldeen or Neev now curled round me to talk to Neev or Jorldeen. Part of them, I thus discovered by the feel of a new pressure on my face, was specs. I did not listen to what they were saying, it was just another sampled part of the music, I could let their words become any language I wanted to; I could arrange the sounds gently to mean whatever I fancied. At one point, it is true, something or other struck me as commentworthy, an intrusion from some undeniable world of hard realism, something about someone called Sorcher (*Sorcher?*) who was having A Hard Time, apparently: *How hard a time is that*, I heard myself comment. Every now and then the conversation stopped and mutated into a wave of apparently mutual need for hugging. Hugging and stroking. It felt so deeply and quietly sexy that it never occurred to me that you could want anything more than this: any more pleasure would be too much to bear, you would simply burn out, as if at the sight of God.

But what is pleasure? Maybe it is merely the cessation of pain, and what pain is worse than doubt? I mean *doubt* doubt: doubt that we are worth anything, doubt that there is any point in it, doubt that we can ever break through the horrible, armoured-glass wall into the parallel life we sometimes see so close and colourful it makes us gasp, where we will be and act the way we know we could. That is the doubt that kills. And now, in place of doubt, there was only a primeval certainty that whatever you did was fine and correct, a sense of rightness so physical that thinking was simply abolished. There was no gap between desire and action: if you liked the look of the little hairs on someone's neck, your hand was already reaching out to touch them; if someone said they liked your chin, you had already stretched it out for them to rub.

And if we had all had fleas, we would probably have groomed them out.

Stonehenge had never been built, never mind the Parthenon and St Peter's: we were not even neolithic, we were halfway to being chimps again, we had found the passports to the happy lands that have never existed except when you are off your face, but whose possibility has haunted us since the first superchimp thought too much and saw itself spookily doubled: saw itself, and saw the possibility of being something else. Since judgement began. And now we were huddled, this tentacular me and the curious amalgam of body parts that called itself Neev & Jorldeen, in a place without judgement and ambition, the longed-for, bull-shit realm of erotic but sexless affection and gentle pleasures without consequences. I lay happily in this chemically-induced paradise, and listened to the soft noise of my brain gently stewing. It felt like rain on my head, like I was some ape lolling about with my entangled primate gang, curled around ourselves in some semi-tropical downpour at the dawn of time, looking out without desire at a new, clean world.

—I didn't know Shnade's got a kid, I said, after profound consideration.

—Do you like her? Do you love her? I do, said Jorldeen or Neev.

—Shnade has got a beautiful girl, said Neev or Jorldeen.

—Amazing. Funny Harry never said.

—Who's Harry?

—Harry's here. Somewhere. He's on TV. He had some thing with Shnade, years ago. Years and years and years ago. Maybe before you were walking.

—Ha ha. I was born in the seventies too, you know. Just.

—Ha ha ha.

—What?

—Nothing. Do you remember, say, the, I dunno, yeah, the Falklands War?

—Jesus, no, how would I?

—Did you know the gap between the Falklands War and now is bigger than the gap between Hitler and the Beatles?

—Is it?

—It is. You seem unimpressed. I like your armpits. Oh, are they *yours*?

—Well, I mean, I kinda thought Hitler and the Beatles *were* kinda round the same time.

—Hitler and the Beatles? The same time?

—Well, aren't they? You know, that funny halfway time. I mean, when some of it's still in black and white and some of it's in colour, you know? Aren't they?

—Um . . . Well, yes actually. I mean, yeah, from three hundred years in the future, yes they are. About the same time. You're right. Bloody hell.

—What's wrong?

—Nothing. She never said she had a kid.

—Who?

—Shnade.

—Jesus, course she has.

—Beautiful girl. You'd love her, Ben. Wouldn't he, Neev?

—He would. Ben'd love Shevaun. Nothing like a kid for coming down with.

—I got a kid too, I said, stunned anew at the matchless beauty of my own life and of the world.

—Wow.

—Is he beautiful? I bet he's beautiful, Ben. You're beautiful. Don't you think Neev's beautiful? Do you think I'm beautiful?

—I think you are both incredibly beautiful.

—Do you need a top-up, Ben?

—Um, sure.

—Do you want to get some more from Poscl?

—*Poscl?* Sure. In a minute, yeah?

—Cool.

Unfortunately, the sheer idiocy of that word, *cool*, was enough to just, just minutely, reopen the doors of consciousness. For an instant, I was aware of myself as myself again: as a discrete being with history and consequence again. Blast. Mentally, I snuggled back down, but I had opened one eye, literally, and with this one literal eye I noticed that DJ Skagga was lying near me. He was in what I guessed was a rather similar heap of girls to my Jorldeen/Neev clump, having left his DJ-ing to a speedy little teenager in a black cap and stupid fucking combats that made his legs look two feet long.

I had noticed before, like I said, that DJ Skagga was as old as me, quite possibly rather older. Maybe he had noticed the same thing about me, who knows? But for whatever reason, his eye seemed to be waiting to catch mine. One of his girls was lying across his lap and the other was sitting beside him. His left hand was stroking the reclining girl's lap: she had her eyes closed. So did the other girl. It looked very nice. He grinned at me. I grinned back at him. Then I thought I saw him wink. I mean *wink* wink. The way men do.

Looking back, I am not sure if he really winked or not. In fact, I tend to think he did not. But whether he winked or not, I blinked. The room snapped back into another focus. I saw that Skagga's right arm was wrapped round the other girl's waist, and his hand was in her knickers. And then I realised that I was actually stroking the arse of Neev's or Jorldeen's knickers, under her (or her) skirt.

And I knew. No, I felt. No, stronger: I believed. I knew, felt, *believed*, that I was thirty-eight and off my face on drugs with girls twenty years younger than me who were either too fucked up or too innocent, or both, to know what the hell they were doing, and that however rosy the chemicals had painted the sky, whatever I thought I was doing, I was, in fact, no, in more than just fact, in reality, I really, *really was* an old git who was enjoying the excuse to mess about with young girls in a bullshit world allegedly without judgement where messing about with young girls was fine and dandy and no one asked about the casualties so long as the next party was already booked.

I saw myself as what I was: I heard the tanks of the Taliban pulling up outside.

Harry's War on Youth

As I plunged out of the warmth and sound and happy darkness, the cold and relative quiet of the night hit me like a big wave, almost knocked me backwards. Then, to my surprise, I saw that Harry was sitting on the little garden wall in front of the house. He was directly under a street light, his baldy skull shining a pale orange. I hardly recognised him. He looked at me blankly, saw me looking at his scalp, squinted up at the lamp, then hurriedly fished a sniper's cap out of his pocket and pulled it over his head. I approached slowly.

Slowly, not because of any nervousness at talking to Harry, or any sense that this chat with Harry was any different to any other chat with Harry, but because I was at this stage experiencing my limbs as being composed of warm spaghetti, my skin as waves of cold wind across a horizonless plain of sunlit wheat, and the inside of my head as a vast, an endless icy cavern, an infinite cathedral of silent blue and white, with stalactites and frozen seas lit by occasional soundless burns of distant red and orange.

Inside the cave, my breathing came slow and in deep sighs, as if I had just recovered after a long run. I could feel every big breath run from the back of my neck to the ends of my toes. I looked up at the orange sky and tried to work out if it was actually raining or if this was just the everyday, bone-rotting, dawntime damp coming up from the Liffey. It was hard to tell. I sat down beside Harry. The stone was interesting: cold and hard.

—Hello, Harry, I said at length. —I wish I was home.

—Do you like the cap? You see, in there, right, it's all bastard candles and stuff, but what if she goes and looks out of the window, or comes to the door, and sees me radiating street light from my fucking cranium? Like a warning beacon to the whole shagging female world: here be an old git.

—Well, half the blokes in there are shaved, I pointed out at length.

—Optionally, said Harry. —Christ, I hate young people. Listen to this crap they like dancing to. Jesus. And why do they have to have it so loud? Because it has to be loud to disturb people, that's why. Because disturbing people is the whole point of it, that's why. Why do you think they have to go around in their horrible little cars *with the windows open*? So their music can disturb people. So they know we are having to listen to them.

—Harry, I think that we used to...

—Of course we did. To think of all the poor sods whose lives I made a misery with 'Oliver's fucking Army'! Of course we did. Just the same. Except it was our horrible, jangly trebles that kept people up, not our thudding basses. Choose now. But we did our best with what wattage we had. Yes, we did it too. Which is *why we know*. It's war, Ben, that's what it is. War. Fuck, I'd pass a law tomorrow that forbade any male under the age of twenty-five from owning a deck with more than ten watts per channel. I would. Little arseholes. If they want war it's time we gave it to them. Total war on youth. What's so good about fucking youth anyway? Tax the bastards to pay for universal childcare, I say. A tax on every club. A tax on every poxy bloody designer shop and retro vinyl emporium. Extra tax on every little bastard without kids. M'learned friend, what exactly is gar-*ahge* music? Is that what one's chauffeur plays? Little sods. And to think they can vote as well! No wonder we're so fucked. *DJ Skagga spins rare deep grooves!* God save us. I tell you Ben, and I stress, I stress that I'm speaking from archaeological knowledge: what is society? The word, what does it mean?

—Um . . .

—I'll tell you what it means.

—I thought you might.

—Thank you. *Society* is just our word for a successful conspiracy to stop eighteen-- to twenty-five-year-old men running the place, because if they ran the bastard place they'd fuck it up in ten minutes flat. Wherever Youth takes over, you can be sure everything will be fucked. The Bolsheviks, the Nazis, they all went on about Youth. God save us from Youth!

—Ohn, I swear to God, fuck off and stick to your own manor.

—Heavy!

It was Mr Bandanna from Shnade's van, escorting past us a little bald guy I had seen dealing pills from a canvas bag.

—Ohn, you are fucking asking for a slap, said he.

—Poscl, if you were half fast enough to give me a slap.

At this, *Ohn* or whatever it really was, began to mock *Poscl*, however he actually spells it, aka Mr Bandanna, by making a few of those funny trance-dance monkey moves, arse sticking out and legs kicking vaguely like a Thai boxer stuck in mud.

—Hey, the men? he said to Harry and me. —Need anything else before the only good head doctor round these parts says good night?

—Fuck off and die, you horrible little junkie, said Harry.

—You heard, fuck off, said Poscl, aiming a kick, at Ohn as the little guy spun away to safety, swung his canvas bag over his shoulder jauntily and sauntered away in his ridiculous trousers. —Don't listen to that little bollix, lads, he is well known the world over to ship only the absolute worst bogus shite in town. If you want sorting, I'm the man in your band, know what I mean. Jesus, at least you know who the fuck I am. Little gobshite. See yous later.

—And so we see, said Harry, when Poscl had gone in again, —that it's all nothing but business anyway. Show me the road, Ben, that leads from pills with happy smile faces to little byways in Essex where guys sit with their heads blown off by twelve-bores. So much for youth and freedom. Right, that's it. I'm burning all my stupid fucking baggy jeans tomorrow. No more big turn-ups for me.

—Better warn your producer.

—Oh, yes, well, I'll keep wearing them for that. Just to take the piss out of the little bastards.

—Harry?

—What?

—I think she's really beautiful too. If it helps.

—Ben, said Harry, —do you dream? I mean *dream* dream? Dreams never lie about people. They lie about everything else, but not people. I don't mean what the people in your dreams are doing and stuff. I mean the way you feel about them, underneath it all, the tone of music they bring with them, the emotion they drag behind them, guilt, lust, envy, fear ... the place they have in the constellation of your dreams. That's always true. And there's no point denying it. And if it's been

179

there for fifteen years, fuck, it's there for as long as you have.

—I dunno, Harry. I don't think I dream much.

—I don't think anyone does, after thirty-five. By thirty-five, we only remember.

—Yeah? I said. I really was feeling it now, coming on like the sea, waves and waves. I was having a degree of trouble controlling the vertical hold on my eyes. But it was nothing like that edge of panic I recalled from acid in the distant past.

—Do I have an audience, Ben?

—What? Yeah, yeah. By thirty-five, you were saying?

—Thank you. By thirty-five, the players of our dreams are cast: even on the rare days when we wake, blinking and lost, our alarm clocks overlaying the post-echoes of vast, dizzy spaces, we quickly identify the actors and settings of those strange, arc-lit scenes as characters from our safe past. We shake our heads, laugh knowingly at the blatant little games our brains were playing; we are already busy lining up our diaries and duties as we turn on our radios. Our city is untaken; the walls hold; and once again we negotiate coolly with the world, a sovereign power with deals to make and take.

—Go for it, Harry. Fuck.

—Thanks, Ben. I think I will. So there we are, in our fortress, in a cold, high place, and we think that after all these years we must be safe up here. Our dreams are already more like memories than real dreams, and our memories are already starting to seem like someone else's boastful stories. Except then this person comes thundering along out of our past: they enter the lost, unguarded passes, and are suddenly there in the plain before our homes, with bronze guns and scarlet banners flashing in the sun. Well, what can we do?

When we realise it is someone from the secret constellations of our dreams? Nothing. We can only throw down our rusty, useless guns, surrender our ruined gates, and hope that we may be allowed to keep, in our utter overthrow, some shred of imagined dignity. I mean, especially if we are just quiet little fuckers by nature.

—Who? I asked, this time so justifiably confused as to have been jerked partially back to life. —What, you? Harry, you're the noisiest git I know.

—Only because I'm so quiet that if I stop shouting I might disappear. Ben, fuck, you know me. Did I spend my twenties doing drugs, or listening to music in squats, or considering my ways in distant, exotic lands? Not me. Oh, no. I spent four years, *four years* of my twenties getting my fucking Ph.D. What kind of preparation is that for fabulous girls and mind-altering chemicals? And shall I tell you something else?

—I think you should.

—A Ph.D. is shit. Getting a Ph.D. is like getting your piece of false parchment that says you are an account-ant or a doctor or an architect or whatever. You think you need a huge fucking brain to get a Ph.D.? Balls. What you need is this: you need to be prepared to devote several of your prime-time twenty-something summers to sitting about being poor and lonely, in libraries, labs or seminars, reading about something no bastard else has ever been bothered to read, and doing with it basically what older men tell you to do. While everyone else is shagging and surfing. That's what you need.

—Right. So it's down to lack of practice? Well, you can make up for it now. You're rich. You're famous. You can catch up.

—Unfortunately it's nothing to do with lack of practice. It's worse than psychology. It's physiology,

Ben. No, think about it: who would do such an insane bloody thing as mortgage their one and only youth, the best years of the one life they have, in favour of some distant, alleged advantage in middle fucking age? What kind of person would do something as fundamentally mad as that? Only someone not cut out for – I mean, just *physically not born for* – surfing and shagging anyway.

—Fuck, Harry...

—So: what if what we fondly imagine to be our free will is simply the enactment of our genetic fate? What if we do not fuck up because of anything? What if some of us are fucked because we were always due to be fucked? And all we can do is put off the day of judgement for as long as possible? Just fending off the inevitable, day by day? Well?

—Well what?

—How was that? That sound good to you? I might use some of that some day.

—Harry?

—Yes?

—You are such a twat.

—Ne-ver.

—Harry?

—What?

—Do you ever *mean* anything?

—Oh dearie me. Mean? Hahaha! Ben, I fucking love you. I fucking love this quiet man!

—Harry?

—Yes?

—You've got it all, mate. You never satisfied?

—Ben, if we were designed to count our blessings we'd still be counting bastard bananas with our fucking feet.

—Right. Harry.

—Yes, Ben?

—Um, why is one of your pupils twice the size of the other one?

—That'll be the charlie.

—Oh, right. So am I like that too, then?

—Ben, Ben, fucking lovely Ben! Not unless you put it in your eyeball too.

—You put coke in your eyeball?

—No. But *I have had* coke put in my eyeball, yes.

—Won't you go blind?

—It seems not. Although Tyson said it would make me see for ever, which, if literally true, would probably be worse.

—Tyson?

—Quite. He's too old to have been christened Tyson by boxoholic parents, because Mike wasn't around then, and no one was called Tyson before Mike, which leads us to the inevitable though unlikely conclusion that Tyson is called Tyson because he positively wanted to be called Tyson. He decided that from now on he would be called Tyson.

—Which one is Tyson?

—Guess.

—The one hanging about with Shnade.

—So it seems.

—So, let me get this right, you hang around this girl blatantly, all night, and then you let her possible boyfriend, a man who has actually changed his name to Tyson, stick cocaine in your eyeball?

—Fuck, no. I insisted Shnade did it.

—Didn't Tyson mind?

—He did insist on watching. Which I find hopeful, since it suggests that he did not want me and Shnade to be alone in the loo together. He perceived me as possible competition, I feel.

—Right, I said. —I overheard her saying she didn't talk to him.

—You what?

—Shnade, Tyson. She was talking to some other girl, and laughing, and she just said, *Jesus, you don't think I talk to him?*

—Thanks, Ben.

—Yeah, she said, *Fuck, girls, with muscles like that he shouldn't have a mouth to open.*

—Ben?

—Yes, Harry?

—Why don't you just go and have a dance.

—What?

—Ben, do you think I want to hear that she only shags him? I happen to want to shag her too, Ben. What, you think I want *me* to do the talking and *him* to do the shagging? Fuck, I wish I did. How easy it would be! I wish I could gain some purely intellectual satisfaction from knowing she is talking to me while shagging him. Yes, I could be happy sitting in my wheelchair and chatting to her with my voice-synthesiser while they were shagging, I could talk her into heaven while he shagged her into ecstasy. But sadly I want to shag her too. No, I don't want to shag her. Fuck shagging. I want to make love to her for fuck's sake. I want to kiss her. I want to stroke her fucking eyebrows. I want to lie there with my dick inside her and look into her eyes so it feels that I am right up inside her head. And then move slowly. I want to . . . I want *her*! I have wanted her, her life, her body and her brain, for fifteen fucking years. And I thought, I really thought I had her safely locked away in my dreams. And now she's here again. And now she's real. And Ben, when I stand near her, it is like I am standing on the edge of a big cliff.

—That'll be the charlie.

—No, it'll be the me. You ever wish you were beautiful? I mean, so that people actually looked at you, just because looking at you made them feel good? Fuck, see this head? See this fucking great domeful of brains? If someone came up now, a guy in a black cloak out of the fog, smelling of incense and sulphur, and offered to swap it for looks, gramme by gramme . . . Oh, there go the contacts, a couple of grammes. Whoops, here comes the hair again! Help yourself, mate. Now, a bit of circumference off the head, please, swap for an inch or two on the shoulders; I can have cheekbones? Take the whole fucking right lobe . . .

—Beauty is truth? Harry, pretty people can be unhappy too, you know.

—No, I don't know. I mean, no, I'm sure you're right, Ben, I am intellectually sure you are right. But since I've never been pretty, I'll never know, will I? I will always want to have been pretty. I will always want to have been pretty and happy and popular at eighteen. If you're not, you are fucked for ever, you'll always be chasing some impossible happiness that recedes away from you faster than my fucking hairline. I will always wish that I had stayed here and gone off with Shnade when I was twenty-fucking-four.

—You what?

—You heard.

—Say it again.

Harry turned round to me. The look in his eye was the same as he had given me back in London, when I guessed we were coming here. And it was true, I had just spoken in a certain way, with a certain eagerness, a certain hardness, which surprised me.

—Well, well, said Harry. —There's keen.

—Go on, I said. —I think fifteen bloody years is long enough.

—I suppose it is, said he.

Just as he started talking, I thought that perhaps I should tell him about Shevaun. I mean, he didn't even know Shnade had a kid for Christ's sake. But for some reason I shut up; for some reason, I held that story tight and thought *not yours, Harry my old mate: you tell me about fifteen years ago. Tell me your old story. This is new. This is mine.*

The Real Day of the Mince

—Well, then, said Harry after a quick sniff to clear the coked-up passages, —there I was, twenty-four going on nineteen, dull as fuck and good as gold, digging a lake fortress site near Sligo and playing music and doing the old kiddies' stuff, you know, *Hello, children, Mr Nutty is here again, hooray!* Hand up the toy ferret's arse stuff. You know all about that. Right. Well, Shnade is there too.

—I don't think she was, like, doing anything even then. She just kind of hung about playing with the kids and making things for them out of old rubbish. She sometimes sang in the pub, but only one or two songs, most of the time she just sat in the corner with her girlfriends and smoked dope. Me, I was pissing around from dig to fair to pub, busking, shovelling, hustling: Shnade, she just sat there and smoked.

—Styx. Styx, back then, was a builder, like now. He was never about in the daytime, he used to be charging about the hills in his van all day. But he'd come to the pub about nine at night and just kind of take it over. Shnade and Styx never held hands in the pub or anything. But sometimes, in the mornings, I saw her coming out of his place.

—Fancied her? More than that, Ben, more than that. I tell you, I used to go to places just because I knew she'd be there. I started playing the music just for that: just to have a disguise to be in the same place as her. Sometimes I ended up sat near to her, or even next to her, and I could never think of anything to say to her, see, because, well, what do you say to someone when they live in another world? I mean, here they are, next to you, right? But the whole way they live is like some parallel universe. They don't *do* anything for Christ's sake. So what can you talk about? I used to just sit there and grin like an idiot when she said anything to me. Or she would show me something she'd made that day and I would take it in my hand and look at it and have nothing to say except *That's really nice*, and she'd say *Yeah*, and that would be that. Shnade is utterly ignorant, you know that? You know that Shnade knows nothing? Shnade knows as little as you can possibly know about anything. I don't mean she's thick. She's the cleverest, no, not the cleverest, the, the . . .

—Most serious, I said.

Harry looked at me again in that slightly irritating way that suggested he was surprised to find me saying anything worthwhile.

—Serious? That's good. That's right. How did you know that?

—I don't know, I said.

—Christ, you fancy her.

—Oh, that'll be the E, I said.

Harry looked at me sideways.

—Right, he said. —Serious. Yes, that's what she is. She takes things seriously. You say *Stalingrad* to Shnade and she will not have the slightest bloody idea what you are on about. I once said something about the Roman Empire to her, and she didn't have a clue about it. But it was like she didn't have all this crap getting in the way of her sightlines, so she could see right into people's heads. And she never got off hers. She was nearly always mildly stoned, but I never, ever saw her doing the kind of thing you do when you're twisted and then regret when you're sober. She was like a straight line, solid as stone, yes, serious. I think you fancy her.

—Well, since we'll be home in London before I come down off this, I guess I'll never know. I'll remember an evening of Shnade and E, and I'll never know which was which.

—Logical Ben.

—Got to be, Harry. If I wasn't . . .

—Check.

—So you were basically totally in love with her.

—Yes. Fuck. I have never ever said that. To anyone. To my fucking self.

Harry kind of laughed to himself.

—So?

—So they were funny times, Ben. The hunger strike and all that, Ireland wasn't like now, it was still poor and it was only just bloody stable, there were black flags flying everywhere you went, on telegraph poles and traffic lights, and armed cops driving about, and sweet little old ladies saying it was time for the army to take over. Strange times. Fucking prehistoric, now. And, well, Styx was into some pretty heavy stuff back then. A lot of people were. It was different then, it . . .

—Heavy? As in . . .

—As in he told me not to ask. So I can't tell you.

—Right. So you weren't . . .

—Fuck, no, I was just an idiot hanging around. Anyway, so in these strange days, right, there I was, supposed to be going off with Shnade and Styx and a few others, can't even remember their fucking names now, they aren't in the constellation, see? To Germany. To play music. And Styx, well, the couple of days before we are due to go, he's very busy and kind of nervy, not himself. There's a few strange people about the place, guys I never saw before, and, well, just this

189

funny feeling in the air, every time you go into a shop or something, like no one knows what's going on but everyone knows it's happening. Like the whole of sodding Sligo town is just waiting for us to go, and then they'll breathe out again. I thought it must be because they were fed up with the bastard diggers and crusties hanging about their town and wanted to get us out the way before the tourist season.

—Anyway, the last night before we're going to leave, it's a beautiful evening. June. And I end up sitting next to Shnade in the pub, playing, and that day I pinched a find from the site, right? Nothing valuable, but something nice: it was a Nine Men's Morris game, a sort of Elizabethan version of noughts and crosses that is, scratched on an old piece of tile. We found a dozen of them, so I thought one could walk OK. It was just: here's a piece of tile, and some English soldier was on duty with his mate on the rampart of this fort after they took it from the O'Conors, and the pair of them found this piece of burned tile and scratched this little game on it. You could even tell which of them made what scratch, the marks were different. And when they were finished, they chucked it into the ditch and wandered away and into the dark.

—So I showed it to Shnade and told her all that, and she was holding it like it was some kind of fucking magic. And I thought: Christ, for the first time ever, something I have learned, some useless little fucking fact on a list, some scrap of pointless knowledge, has actually meant something. Has moved someone. Has come afuckinglive. And when I said she could have it, there was that tiny buzz in the air, that light at the edge of things . . .

—We had a late one that night, Styx was on great form and everyone was, well, it was like they were sending us away with a party. And me and Shnade ended up standing on this bridge in Sligo, watching the sun coming up, not saying anything, not feeling bad about not saying anything. And then I asked if I could kiss her, I mean, *asked* asked, like some ten-year-old. And she laughed, and looked at me and said I was going out with so-and-so and she was with Styx, which was true; fuck, I can't even remember her name. And I shrugged, and she looked at me again, then she walked away, but when she got to the end of the bridge, she suddenly ran back and kissed me once, on the lips, one wet kiss on the lips, and ran off, laughing.

—And?

—And nothing.

—Harry.

—OK. And the police came round the next day. The Guards, I mean. It always made me want to laugh, *Guards*. I mean, that really kind of puts them in their place, doesn't it. No respect. Yeah, well, but it's not funny at six in the morning.

—I'm sitting there in front of this turf fire I lit when I got back. I can't really sleep, it's chilly in the dawn, I'm just sitting there and soaking up the warm and watching the flames and thinking about Shnade, with this massive feeling of a strange, big, new life ahead of me, and then they come looking for Styx. Why to my place? Fuck knows. Crap intelligence, maybe. But the more I think back, the more I wonder if they did it on purpose. I mean, to give us a chance to just abort it. Like I said: they were funny days.

—Abort what?

—Not a word they would have used in those days. The trip to Germany.

—What, it was . . . ?

—Hang on, hang on. So: they come round looking for

Styx. I'm standing there bollock naked, with these two plain-clothes fucking Guards standing there, IDs in hand, with just a duvet held in front of my balls, and lying, just fucking lying. I said I never heard of Styx or Shnade.

—What did they want them for?

—I never asked.

—Right. So what happened?

—I stood there with my pink arse sticking out from my duvet and gabbled in posh Brit at them. I said I had no idea who Shnade was, I only met her in the pub last night, gosh, was that Mr Styx, the one playing that nice music? I was only on holiday, I was just a normal little Brit, I was a student, I was doing archaeology, did they want to come in and have a nice cup of tea ... ? And eventually I could see this picture of me forming in their eyes: me as the prime twat of the universe. They ended up telling me to mind who I talked to in pubs because *not all Irish eyes smiled*, they said. I could see them starting to think what they were going to say to their own intelligence guys when they got back in the car. And do you know why they believed me, Ben?

—A good act?

—Because it was fucking true. At that moment, it was true. I disowned them. They were nothing to me, I ...

—Harry, Harry, what the fuck were you supposed to do? Say, *Yeah I know them and I guess I know they're dodgy and* ... I don't know. Whatever? You lied and you, well, I assume you saved everyone, since ...

—Yes, yes, yes. But it's not what you do, Ben, it's why you do it. I was scared. I was lying. Not to the Guards. To Shnade. Fuck. I wanted her, I wanted her life, and I wanted the rest as well. The normal stuff. Not serious, see, Ben. Just not fucking serious. A lightweight. A coward. I wasn't lying to save her, or Styx. I was scrabbling to save myself. And they could see that I truly, truly was terrified of the fucking police and no way would get involved in anything like that and . . .

—Harry . . .

—There's more. Right. So: as soon as the Guards have gone, I have to get hold of Styx. No mobiles, remember. Prehistoric, see? So I sneak behind these walls along to his place, and knock him up. First thing he asks, like really heavy: where's Shnade? He thought she was with me. See. I should have thought of nothing but that: *he thought she was with me, she must have said something to him, something about me, she must . . . !* But I don't. Why? Because I'm so fucking scared. I've blown it for good, I'm never going to be clean again. I'll get a criminal record, I'll go to the nick, I'll never be able to be nice and safe and normal again. Fuck! I hardly even thought about her. I just thought about getting away. About getting safe again.

—So?

Harry was stalking about now, gnawing his lip and running his hand over his head again and again.

—So, Styx tells me to get out of town for a few days and lay low till he can sort things out. Back along the walls I sneak. When I get into my place, I look out the front window and see the Guards are outside again, sitting in their bloody car, smoking fags. Listening to Boy fucking George on the radio. So I grab a rucksack, stuff it with clothes, and walk out the door. The Guards stop me, ask if they can look in the rucksack. No problem. Where am I going? *Back home*, I say. *Good idea*, say the Guards. So I take a bus heading for Dublin and get off at Boyle, and wait.

—Ah, this is where the mince comes in, right?

—Right. But it's fuck all to do with the mince. I'm there two nights, camping on my own. Fuck, Ben, fuck:

impatience, mate, impatience! There are some bastards in the world who can sit on poles for months, chewing rice and chatting to God. And me? Two days, Ben, that's all it takes. Two days alone, not knowing anything, just two sodding little days with no certainty, no security, no contact, and what am I like? Like some lost fucking dog. I lose it, Ben. Belief, I mean. I don't believe any of it any more. Me, Styx, Shnade. It's all gone. I can't hold it together. I'm turning into nothing. I try to tell myself, every five minutes, sitting on my own in the rain in my tent: she came back and kissed you, you dull fucker, after you asked her for a kiss, *asked* like a bollockless twat, she came back. And kissed you. And she'll still be there, she isn't going anywhere, she ...

—And on the third day it's grey and cold and raining, and I go into Boyle to buy mince with my last money, and as I walk along I feel like crying out of sheer ... loneliness, emptiness, I don't know. Nothingness. I sit and look at some river and think about what the fuck have I been doing, arseing around in a foreign country, trying to play some cod part in someone else's story, as crap as any German with a beard and a violin and a false bloody accent. What the fuck am I? Shnade and Styx. Look at them. Look how real they are. Me? Why the fuck would she leave him for me? Why the hell should she? What have I ever done in my life that would make anyone leave anyone for me?

—Now I know they were looking for me. I got the details wrong, see? Camped the wrong side of town, simple. Pathetic. If I had just had another two days' worth of trust. Or the guts to just go back, or ...

—But I didn't know that then. So now it's the third day, and I want to cry, and I go to get my mince, and I can't afford it until this little cunt with terminal acne takes some off again. Which you know about. And I just

suddenly feel, just ... so fucking small and far from
home. And I walk along with my wet little bag of
economy mince, going back to my lonely tent, and
realise *fuck, I'm nearly twenty-five and my CV could be
boiled down to one word: Waster.*

—Hahahaha! Do you remember? Ben? When we
thought being twenty-five was scary and old and we
better do something with ourselves quick before it was
too late? Oh fuck, ha ha ha! Ben, Ben, Ben ... Give us a
fucking hug and never mind if it's the charlie, eh?
There. Oof! Fuck.

—And that's when you went back to college.

—Yes, I subsequently devoted myself to the pursuit,
successful I am delighted to say, of a steady job,
baldness, and the occasional pile. Not cut out for it, see,
Ben: not psychology. Fuck psychology. Just pure
bloody physiology. Not strong enough to live without
... all the crap. Just can't fucking hack it without the
back-up. A quiet man, me, Ben, that's the bottom line.
A hard-working swotty little twat who once tried to
play with the hard boys and the wild girls, and ended
up legging it home to mam.

—So, what do you think? Is Ireland crap or is it crap?

—I've enjoyed it.

—Wrong answer. Anyway, fuck it, you're off your
face. It's all bollocks. Right. I'm wasted and I'm cold
and I am going to the hotel.

—I'll come too.

—No, stay. You're fine. Don't fucking lie. You'd
rather talk to Shnade. If you snog her I'll kill you. Good
excuse to get rid of the one man who can shop me for
cheque-book fraud, eh Ben?

—Harry, she's out of my league.

—See, I knew it was love. Anyway, I'd rather be on
my tod for a bit, sorry, but ...

I knew it was bad then, because Harry never wants to be on his own; he's always the one who keeps the party going. Like the tarts and rent boys, I guess. But tonight I could see he meant it. He had that strange air, that indefinable something about him that he had never really had. Like he was carrying his own big story around inside him, and it was enough to get him anywhere.

So who was I to tell him his story was, well, not wrong exactly, but somewhat outdated? *My old friend*, I could have said, *I'd rather come with you and, by the way, I know something about Shnade that you really should know before you get too far off on this little trip down Memory Lane.* But who does that? Not me, not you, not anyone this side of the River fucking Euphrates. Nope. We just let it run, and I just watched him go.

Archaeologically speaking, says Harry, we were not meant to say goodbye. The vast majority of all the people who ever lived, up until our very own grandparents' time, says Harry, lived out their big or little lives, with whatever festivals and tragedies came their way, among the people they knew and loved and hated. A journey to the next ring-fort or walled city was once a lifetime, says Harry, and even then almost always undertaken as a gang of petitioners, traders, pilgrims or warriors. The worst punishment to the Anglo-Saxons was exile: it was, quite literally, regarded as worse than death, because it meant you were doomed to die among strangers. And even now, deep in our language, in the same language we chat away about bytes and webs in, what do we do when we die? We pass away. We leave. We go.

Maybe he is right. Maybe there is too much premature going away in this world. Maybe each time we say goodbye we really do die a little, and each time we die a little we grow scars and scabs that toughen up our skin, until we can say goodbye and die a little and hardly notice the thickening of our nerves, the erosion of our feeling lives.

Harry was nearly out of sight now anyway. Funny. You do not often watch someone you know so well for that long without them waving, or winking, or otherwise making it clear that they know you are there, watching. Harry thought I had already gone, he had already left me, left Shnade, left the party for good, as far as he was concerned. I wondered what he was thinking.

I thought about him asking her to kiss him, fifteen years ago.

And then I found myself thinking about being with Harry, years ago, in the Pyramids of Bedfordshire.

The Pyramids of Bedfordshire

It was about ten years ago, after Harry got respectable but before he got his telly slots. Harry was digging up some old stuff or other in Bedfordshire, and as it happened, I had to go to a funeral nearby, 'twixt Bed-Pan line and the M1, in that rather thankless part of the world that lies at the limit of bearable commutability: where the equation of house prices, travelling time and job availability only just stacks up.

It was a weird funeral, because it was my first cousin's. He was the same age as me, almost exactly. And it wasn't a car crash or a bike wreck or AIDS or an OD or a show-off party stunt gone wrong or any of the other things which we expect to hear when a young man dies these days. It was just disease. I forget which: some horrible disease or other, for which there was still no more cure than they had a thousand years ago. In other words, he died of Death. I hardly knew him as an adult, we hardly met more than once a year when we were kids, even; but I remember one summer when we spent a week, aged nine or ten, being able to reduce each other to howls of utterly inexplicable, hysterical, pre-pubescent giggling simply by saying the phrase: *Wormwood Scrubs*. And now he was dead of Death.

I spent the night before the funeral with Harry; I arrived on his excavation in the early evening. Archaeologically speaking, Harry told me, looking me in the eye carefully but unconsciously sucking in his cheek like he had a bad molar or something, to lose a first cousin through Death pure and simple at my age was nothing extraordinary. Not for most of the people who have ever died, and maybe not even today for eight-tenths of the world's nearly-thirty-year-olds.

—After all, he said, —why do you think we grow wisdom teeth? Because in lovely fucking green Nature, that's all you'd have left by the time they grow. Look at this one here (he vaguely indicated a skull that was lying about half excavated: you could see this horrible great smooth round hole in the jaw, and the amazingly white root of an ancient tooth showing through). — Cause of Death almost certainly dental abscess. A lot of them are. I mean, look at us: knocking on thirty. Shit, we should already be wondering why we haven't got any grandchildren yet.

—You first with the sprogging then, Harry.

—No fucking fear. Let me knock this on the head and we'll go to the pub. The sprogs can wait. Thank fuck for medical science, eh? We are pretty well bound to make sixty however hard we . . . Sorry, fuck, Ben, I wasn't thinking.

—It's OK, Harry.

—Yeah, right, OK, just let me . . .

And Harry hopped off across his trenches and trowelled surfaces to check everything was cleaned up in case it rained at night.

It was a wonderful summer evening, with long shadows on the red, excavated earth. A job experience skinhead was sitting with his feet dangling down into the biggest trench, idly watching the light that the setting sun made through a big multicoloured golfing umbrella that he was holding up. His face glowed with an absurd happiness.

—See that, said Harry, pointing to the layers that were clearly visible in the trench. —Archaeologically speaking, peaceful and slow change is bollocks. If it happened like that, where would I get my layers from? Look: see that line? Burning. More burning here, a serious disruption layer, more burning there, and we haven't even got to the Iron Age yet. What you reckon, Ben: maybe it's the same for us, eh? I mean, in our lives? Here, come and see this, this is the best, this is as good as it gets.

It was a late Stone Age grave of two small children, placed head-to-head in foetal crouches. One skull had partially collapsed, and they were left in such a position that one appeared for all the world to be whispering to the other. I swear to you that I saw hardened archaeologists standing lost in thought at the sight of them. The site photographer and Harry had got all excited about what a great image it would be for poster, or even the cover for a coffee-table book called *The Secrets of the Dead* (looking back, I realise that this was quite possibly the first time Harry had ever thought about the popular angle on archaeology). As Harry flicked the last dirt from the little bones, I sat beside him and watched the little skinhead turning his brolly and lighting himself delightedly, and stared out across the fields, into the setting sun, at the pyramids of Bedfordshire.

I invited my hackles to rise at the sight of the great, lost, lonely buildings with their vast, black mouths open. They simply radiated a sense of awesome space. In the stillness, the awareness of them on the horizon seemed to call up the ghosts from the earth.

The pyramids of Bedfordshire stood there, and still stand there, in their inexplicable, functionless immensity, without meaning or purpose to those around them, yet apparently guarded by a superstitious inviolability from the encroaching residential developments, bypasses and industrial estates. It is as if they were relics of some mighty civilisation, now utterly lost yet still revered in half-understood memory. Which is, perhaps, exactly what they really are: because what I call the *pyramids* – sorry, but that is how I first thought of them, and that is all they can ever be called to me – are actually the airship sheds at Cardington, where once, in the last days of British certainty and Empire (the last years before European civilisation bore Auschwitz, too), the R101 hung swaying in its cavernous lair. Pyramids is what they looked like that summer evening; pyramids, or Assyrian tombs.

Harry and I got blasted in the pub and I slept with one of his digging girls, whose name and features I can no longer even remember. Next day, before the funeral, he and I went to the airship sheds. It took us longer than I had imagined to get there, and the view from the south turned out to be hidden, so by the time the road signs actually started to indicate RAF CARDINGTON, I was getting pissed off, as well as irritated by the growing fear that I might be late for the funeral after all. Pissed off, that is until the two endless sheds started to rear up and fill the windscreen, slowly and inevitably.

I don't know if these two sheds are actually the biggest free-standing structures in the world or whatever, but as you drive down the unnatural canyon between them, they certainly feel like it. And when you swing round (needlessly fast, of course) past the end of the shed, keep swinging through 180 degrees, and go in the little garage-door-sized entrance in the back, you are sure of it: as you leave the daylight and enter the darkness, the interior shoots away in all directions.

Imagine the inside of Paddington Station, except utterly empty and three or four times as high, lit with shafts of light from the colossal side windows and from bright holes in the unsafe, net-hung roof. When you clap, or toot the horn, you get echoes; but you also get the sound floating endlessly above your head, refusing to resolve itself away. With a little effort, you can imagine the huge, silver ship hanging at airborne anchor in the limitless emptiness. Looking up at the almost invisible heights for too long gives you upward vertigo. I remembered reading some book at college where the guy describes a cathedral as *so large that it seemed to exist at the very border of that which mankind can bear*. That big.

The strangest thing was walking away from Harry's car, and walking and walking and just walking, and then turning around and seeing your best mate, in his car, far away and surrounded by nothingness, yet still in the same room as you, the same human, enclosed, finite space, waving to you. How often do you see that? Never. It was like being a ghost, it made me hurry back towards Harry, laughing with unease. As I echoed my way back, the huge, silent hall began to feel like the waiting room of eternity.

But we were young and dull still, still fully behaired and still half bulletproof with Youth. So we drowned out the uncomfortable silence, and filled the endless room with a car-culture flourish: Harry floored her, and we raced straight at the massive, closed airship-get-out doors at the far end. It was long enough to get a fair whack up, even in a ghastly old Morris Marina TC, which is what Harry had back then. Harry braked late, and we squealed round and drove back up, hooting as we left (as requested by an eccentric sign at the door).

We charged out into the open world again: space flew away all around us; and we stared up and wondered by what logic the high, uncaring blue sky could feel so much closer and more friendly than the man-made dark behind you.

And then it was time to go to the funeral service in a very fine little old church, with carved angels looking down from the roof: time to bury my cousin.

(It was a good funeral. There was crying and singing in the church, a big procession to the grave, and then drinking and laughter afterwards, while a string quartet played solemn but major-key Mozart. This is as it should be at every good funeral. The C. of E. did its best to ruin things, of course. The only good thing the C. of E. ever had was the finest language in the world, words that knocked the Catholics for six, words that really did seem to intimate light in the vastness that surrounds us the moment we shut the fuck up and think for five minutes. Those words have been traded in for sixties tat, and now the banal mouthings just get in the way of any true feeling. How can you mourn decently when your ears are stopped with the wretched, off-peak platitudes that today pass for the rites of this final passage? But today even the C. of E. was powerless. The church was filled with prosperous young men from the City: blond, hardly balding men more used, as my cousin's best friend put it, to thinking little further than the *Telegraph* sports pages. But they had now felt the breath of the cold places decades earlier than the actuaries had led them to expect. And because they had truly felt it in the church, they were able to laugh and drink without false shame in the hall. A good funeral.)

As I drove back home, alone, I saw the airship sheds again, black on the horizon, sharp against the sheer, cobalt silk of the last summer light. I thought of seeing Harry in them again. And I remembered another thing: that next to each of those late Stone Age burials, Harry's diggers had found a little pit, containing a smashed pot full of roasted hazelnuts. You could still see they were hazelnuts straight away; some of them even rattled after five thousand years. (Later, Harry had one of these pots, as I said, restored as part of his stupid opening sequence. In one show, he rattled them in a piss-take of some old advert for coffee beans.) I thought of those little pots and of standing there on Harry's digging site again. In that evening light, with the shadows growing deep in the eye sockets of the skulls and the airship sheds standing vastly on the edge of your vision, you did not need to use your imagination much to know that this had been a place of ceremonies and weeping. And I did not need clever Harry to tell me why those hazelnuts were there. I knew what they were all right: just a little snack for your loved ones to take with them, something for the road as they walked off away and passed into the great, dark spaces.

A Confession

Now, here in Dublin, I watched Harry walking away from me. And so now, I have naturally to pause and make a confession. The thing, the fairly obvious thing, is that from here on in, *I will not always know exactly what I am talking about.* Up till then, we had not been out of each other's sight all evening, and so what happened to one of us happened, at least in terms of time and space, to all of us. Easy. But now the ways started to part.

So now, in some of what is to come, you will have to trust my guesses as to what was going on. I have my sources, naturally, and would not say anything I knew to be wrong, and will admit it when I am not sure. I know roughly what happened, and I know Harry well enough, and the other people involved, to put the rest of it together. As for what was going on in Harry's head whenever, I can only report what he said, or make pure guesses.

Especially since, as it turned out, there was, how shall I put it, some degree of reasonable bloody doubt, to put it mildly, in Harry's own head about what was going on in Harry's head. Round and round we go.

As soon as you start looking any closer, as soon as you wrinkle your hominid brow and start to worry about just what the fuck people are up to exactly and why, forget it: wild guesses are all we have. So we have to, simply *have to*, assume that our wild guesses are in some way informed; that we share enough humanity or what you will to be roughly comprehensible to one another.

So: I assume, *I insist on assuming*, that in some way, at some level, Harry saw the world like I do, and hence acted roughly as I would have acted, or at least as I could imagine myself acting if I had been Harry. Which means to me that even where I have no direct evidence from what he said or Shnade said he said or whatever, I can hold it together. Or at least, keep it roughly on the road.

Right then: it is possible that after he left the party, Harry went strolling calmly home alone through the Dublin night, feeling himself to be that sovereign being of all our dreams, coolly aware of his reality, his futurity and his inalienable right to walk the earth. He may, conceivably, have been laughing at the thought of meeting Shnade after all these years, *well, well, well,* and chuckling at his having been so thoroughly gob-smacked, despite all his fame and money, by bumping into a somewhat ageing crusty who lived in a van and who he had never even really kissed. He could, I suppose, have been considering in an entertained and detached manner the comical folly of taking class As at his age, in that company, midweek.

But I doubt it.

Sorry, but I doubt these light-hearted possibilities.

No, when I think of that night, of what must have been, what *I think* must have been going through Harry's head as he walked home, it is more like a firestorm.

I don't know, like I said, but I can see it. It rings true to me, and that is all I can offer. If I did not think this, I would stop right here, and write Harry off, and when people come to my door, as they still occasionally do,

206

like I said, and ask why the hell it all happened, I would just say: *Look, I don't know, he was my friend but one way or another he was fucked, OK? Bye.* Which would be little consolation as I sit here and watch the Peckham evening fall, and wish he was coming up the path.

Like I said: we don't choose the places or the times or the people or the cheap tunes that haunt us for as long as we have, and Harry, for no logical reason, is stuck in my dreams for keeps. I don't dream *about* Harry as such, he is not the fulcrum of my unconscious mind at all, but he's often there, one way or another, just kind of kicking about the place.

And then again, I do quite often think of him consciously too. I mean, it would be such a laugh if he walked in right now, and looked into my house, and I could see his face when he saw what's going on here! I can imagine just what he'd say, he'd fling up his arms as if addressing some god or other, and say:

Actually, no, I don't know what he'd say. Not really, not enough to persuade myself. That's the trouble. You can remember everything someone ever said to you, you can mix in the real sound of their voice in your head, but you will never be able to hear what they would have said about something they will never see. They, this human, who, like all of us, can never be sampled and pinned down because we are not fixed, we are changeable and incalculable, are simply not there any more. They are gone. Silent.

That's the trouble with people being dead.

Surprisingly Small Hands

But let's not rush on to death. Death is a patient man: he will not mind waiting a little while longer, he can nurse his pint happily enough, he knows we will all get there in the end, after all, carrying our poor little pots of hazelnuts and our snipped-off balls of bright red wool. No, let's go back for now to all we have: the hub of life, the noise, the music, the lights and the people. The party.

I was cold now outside the house, and Harry was almost out of sight down the long, straight road. I picked him out one last time as he passed under a street light. Then I turned, and went back into the party, suddenly grateful for the heat and sound. But then I remembered about Neev and Jorldeen, and why I had come out here in the first place. Maybe Harry was right? Maybe none of it mattered, maybe I should just tell all my warning systems to switch off, and just do whatever happened? Or maybe I should be at home, in Peckham, in my quiet bed, with my wife asleep beside me and my kid oblivious in his cot?

A friend of mine once had a nervous breakdown. When I asked him, later, what it had been like, he furrowed his brow with an honest but hopeless effort to describe it, then brightened up and explained:

—You just can't choose anything. You can't think of any reason why one thing should be done before another, or why doing *this* is more important than doing *that*. So you just do nothing. I mean, you just sit there, until the quiet worry about what you are going to do next becomes a noise like thunder in your head. Then, as far as I can tell you, you fall off your office chair and start crying, and when they ask what the matter is, you simply don't know.

Well, that was how I was starting to feel. I could not face going back to where I had been before, but I could also not face the thought of wandering in the cold and the rain, back to my little hotel room, where (as I guessed) I would lie sleepless and haunted for hours. I just wanted to go home. Except when I thought of my house, and my bedroom, and my little garden and all, it was all in black and white, something that was already firmly history.

My breath was now rushing quickly in my ears. I turned round on the spot several times, slowly, lost. I made myself consider real problems: Jan and The Wop. They did not know Harry had gone home. They did not know the way home. I had the map. Good. That was better. Now I had a mission, and hence some rational, explicable reason to move. I had to find them, clearly, to make sure that they got back to the hotel OK. Yes. I had to be responsible. That was better.

Thank fuck for structures, eh?

I checked the rooms of the house one by one until I was drawn up towards the final landing of the tall, old building and the last, steep, little flight of narrow stairs, towards the attic room.

Away from the music here, people were cuddling and snogging and talking bollocks quietly into each other's stroky ears, utterly lost to the world. As I trod through this primordial human minefield, various eyes rolled briefly up at me, eyes as lost as any smackhead's eyes, yet set in smiling faces, connected to limbs that

209

could still move, and tongues that could still talk and laugh. *Shit*, I thought: I imagined for a happy moment that I was twenty again, that Harry and me and Jan and The Wop were twenty again, and that all these whacked-out faces were people I vaguely knew and vaguely liked and vaguely knew me and vaguely liked me. Maybe that was Jorldeen down there? I teetered on the stairs a minute, and felt again the vast gravitational pull of human longing for other humans. I recalled the days of my own brief heroin experiments, right back when the eighties were new, and with a rush of knowledge, I thought: *Right. Well, if it's this good every time, and it comes in a nice, clean, easy pill for a tenner a shot, what the fuck kind of twenty-year-old is ever going to say no to it? What the hell can anyone do except try to help make sure that the kids understand the dosages and don't end up necking stuff that's cut to shit with crap?*

Which wise thoughts carried me into the attic room where, among other folks, I saw Jan, this tall, skinny, brainy, and difficult girl, and The Wop, my narcissistic mate, engaged in mutual worship of one of Jan's little breasts that peeped out from under her spangly top.

I stood and watched them. I had never seen Jan looking so relaxed: tired, yes; very, very tired, years of tiredness; but now utterly calm. She helped The Wop's hands (*he has surprisingly small hands*, I thought, then realised that I had always known this, so why should it be *surprisingly*?) to stroke lightly across her nipple. Her other hand was rubbing over and over his muscly belly. He was lost, lost at last, in wonder at a woman's beauty.

So then I decided to go: now going home alone to my little room seemed much less sad than being here and not doing this kind of thing. I could feel the waves of drug starting to recede, and my cold armour reforming where warm skin had been. I shifted my weight so I could turn without falling over any of the stroking folk. At this, Jan looked up and saw me. She smiled instinctively first, then blinked. Slowly, without any great fuss, like someone getting out of bed unwillingly to go to work, she took The Wop's hand away, pulled down her shirt, and frowned. With that one frown, all her little lines returned. The Wop yawned blearily, actually yawned, and said:

—What? not aggressively, quite factually.

—Harry's just gone off in a strop, I said. —And he left me the map, and I'm off, and I thought I'd better get you. So . . .

—Shit, said Jan, having in the meantime returned to fully-functioning *Homo sapiens* status and realising what she had just been doing and with whom.

—Great, said The Wop, blustering transparently. —If there's one thing more fucking pathetic than walking off in a strop from people you know you will see again anyway, one day, it's walking away in a strop from people you know you're going to see on a plane in four hours. King-size wristjob!

Jan moved his arm from off her shoulder and stood carefully up.

—Right then, I suppose we'd better come with you.

—Look, I said, —I'm sorry, I didn't . . .

—Thank God you did, said Jan, and brisked past me, attempting to laugh.

—Fuck, blew The Wop, shaking his head straight.

I led them out of the room, so we could all go Indian file and avoid eye contact for a happy moment or two. I fished out the map from the hotel as we went, to give something definite to do. But at the bottom of the second, body-filled flight of stairs, approaching the music again now, Shnade was waiting.

Now there was no doubt about it. She was beautiful.

—Where's Harry? said Shnade. *Said*, as in yelled in my ear. I felt her big, unplucked eyebrows on my cheek.

—Gone, I screamed back.

—Gone?

—To the hotel.

She dragged me out of the room and down the corridor to the chill-out room, where the quieter music meant that conversation, and thus human interaction at some higher level than *Hey, cool combats!*, was vaguely possible.

—Fucking Harry, she shook her head. —Can you tell me, Ben: what the fuck is the point of coming all this way and not staying for the last two hours? He's half off his head, he's not going to sleep now, so what's the fucking point?

—I don't think there is one. I think he just ran away again.

—What d'you mean?

—He told me about running away from Galway or wherever it was.

—Excuse me, said Jan, and shoved past us with little respect. The Wop followed her.

—I'll catch you up, I said. I handed over the little map to Jan without looking up. Without looking away from Shnade's eyes, I mean.

I should have spotted it right then, I suppose: because I know, as in more useless knowledge, as in objectively, that the danger moment is the moment you find yourself thinking someone is lonely. That's what stalkers do. And here was Shnade, in a pulsing sea of her friends, on her utterly home ground, and for just one moment I, this wandering idiot off his face hundreds of miles from wife and child and home, saw her looking at nothing and I thought: *Fuck, she is so lonely.*

—Running away? Did he say *running away*? she asked.

—No. More or less.

—Well, it looks like it works for him, doesn't it? she said. —Bigshot Harry.

I watched her eyes: they were gazing inward at some interior world, some big sea of lost possibilities. Sad? Perhaps. But certainly not sentimental: *solemn*, maybe. The kind of solemn that is so far from the backslapping chirpiness we have learned to call *happiness* that we may easily mistake it for sadness, though it has no more to do with *sad* than a Happy Meal has to do with happy. A simple, solemn recognition of some lost, some wasted potential for human warmth. I wanted to kiss her eyes. *Want* is too small a word.

—What works for you? I asked blatantly. It just came out. She looked at me as if for the first time. She waved her arm vaguely around, indicating the party; the life; her world.

—What, getting off your face the whole time?

—Who said I was off my face the whole time?

—No one.

—So I look like I'm off my face the whole time?

—No, I ... well, yes.

—Nice. Well, you know, yes, actually, there are relatively few days of the week when I am not off my tits, or coming down, or planning the next one. Yes, I guess I hop from chemical boulder to chemical boulder through the river of life. And yes, I'm getting bored with it. Yes, I really want to find the warm grass on the other side and just lie down for a bit. But the thing is, Ben, that's horseshite. There isn't any other side to get to. All this balancing from stone to stone in the big, fast river isn't what we do to reach Life; the balancing from stone to stone is what Life is. So we may as well keep hopping on, stone to stone and hand to hand, because if we look down at the water too long, we're going to get dizzy. Well, you're flying.

—How do you know?

—You can't take your eyes off my lips.

—Sorry.

—No, it's nice. Everyone loves a first-timer. It reminds us of our own innocence. Before we knew it was just the drugs and it would wear off tomorrow. Enjoy it, and make sure you have company for the comedown. Better catch up with your lads now. Take care, Ben. And say bye to Harry.

I do not know what I would have done next. I think I might have tried to kiss her anyway. I'm glad I didn't, in a way. I mean, I will always remember how much I wanted to, and I think perhaps we remember what we *desired*, more than what we *did*: the treasures we store up for our old, cold, lonely years are not the memories of our triumphs, but of our fierce young longings. Well, relatively young.

And anyway, what could I do or say? What kind of fucked-up world is it where we have to pretend not to like the people we like in order to make them like us? Where you have to stay cool towards people who blow you away? Where we all dream wildly of love at first sight and all know that we could never admit it if it ever happened because everyone, including the object of our first-sight love, would think we were sad

nutters? Well, how the hell can you treat a world like
that as anything but an excuse for a laugh? So I smiled
at her, and sort of felt myself start laughing.

Well, it felt like a sort of laughing.

Except then we heard shouting, and I guess we both
heard that it was Harry doing it. We looked round:
down the road, just visible to us, Harry had left Jan and
The Wop and was now racing on, towards the house,
back towards us. Jan grabbed The Wop, who seemed to
be protesting, and dragged him on with her. Now
Harry arrived.

He stood before us, panting and shining with power.
—Come on, he yelled, and dragged me and Shnade
bodily back into the house. Inside, he blasted past
feebly-protesting Yoof (*Hey, wow, like fuck, shit, man,
chill willya, whathefuckya . . . ?*) scattering bottles of water
and half-empty cans of lukewarm beer, pulled the jacks
clean from the decks of the chill-out room, slapped the
protesting little substitute music man gently to the
floor, stood on DJ Skagga's face as he tried to extricate
himself from his woozy groupies in order to protect his
far more vital hardware, and started shouting orders
like some Old Testament prophet who has just snorted
vodka and speed after hearing the latest menacing
bulletin from the Lord.

The cops were coming, said Harry; the *Guards*, rather.
And any little twat in combats and trainers who didn't
want mum and dad to wake up and find him or her
nicked should clear off now and take his or her drugs
with him. Or her.

No one failed to hear Harry, or understand, or obey.
Really, you should have seen him. Irony be fucked:
Harry was standing there in the lights and the smoke,

surrounded by comatose, whacked-out folk, arms outstretched above the huddling, cuddling clumps of semi-
humanity like some medieval angel trumpeting his
gleeful way into Hell. When he finished, the room was
silent as a dead recording studio.

—Harry? said Shnade, her voice bursting into the
echoless space. —What the fuck happened?

The Sound Death Makes

Harry let her question float, and swung his gaze easily from her to encompass the rest of the room: faces were filling the doorways; the main music had been killed too now. He was not looking at Shnade any more. And yet I got the strangest feeling: that it was all for *her*, that it was her he was *not-looking* at.

—Just clean the place up, and if they come, *when* they come, we were just a bunch of Brits on holiday. Just clear anything dodgy out. Here's the story: you bumped into us, we came here, we left. I had to tell them we'd been somewhere and it just kind of slipped out. And we drank beer. Understand?

They understood all right. Harry was just plain glowing with the backlit certainty of a man who is in sole possession of a bloody cracking story, who has the Big News of the night in the palm of his hand, who is damn sure that he will get bought drinks for as long as he can spin it out, and has a good idea that his status in the tribe has just been radically, and permanently, upped. He was The Man. And he was fucking loving it.

Harry now turned to Shnade. And now this man, who had been hanging about near her all evening like some moonstruck ploughboy, who had felt the merest rush of air from her passing as if it was an express train whistling heedlessly by him, simply marched up to her and took her by the strong, brown, be-lizarded shoulders and dragged her off.

I followed, without even thinking whether it was

weird or not to do so, or whether Harry wanted me to
or not. To be honest, I don't even think he knew
whether I was there or not. As I followed, I got this
strange buzz of connection, and for a second, I thought
I could feel what Harry was feeling, which was: ahead,
a red mist, a flickering electric haze, a fog, darkness. All
around, inside him, the crackle of internal wires. And
behind him, unseen, but felt with every radar he had,
Shnade, watching. Nothing else: just her.

—OK, said Harry, outside the house again, —so there I
am, right? Off my tits and wondering what the fuck I
am playing at, going home to my poxy little cardboard
hotel room, utterly certain that my emotional life is a
pile of hopeless shit and wreckage, my physical body is
a heap of rotting scrap, and my only possible future is
loneliness and despair, right?
  (Good old Harry. Such a twat.)
  —Harry . . . said Shnade.
  —All right, all right. So I'm just wandering down the
street towards the Liffey, thinking about fuck knows
what. Then next thing I know, this fucking big van
spins out of some little lane in front of me and hangs a
righter, and as it's crossing my path, this guy is fucking
chasing it, right? Twenty feet in front of me. The guy's
holding some piece of scaffolding or whatever, and
wellying the shit out of the side of the van. He's
shouting and screaming, *cunts cunts cunts* or whatever,
bang bang bang. And then the Transit stops dead, OK: so
the guy, he's running, he's got momentum with this big
piece of whatever in his hand, he ends up a few foot in
front of it, yeah? And then guess what? What does the
driver do? Fuck, he just spins the wheel and floors it.
Just turns and squashes him. You ever hear a ribcage
going? Nor me. Do you know what it sounds like? Nor

me. But I know that's what it is. It is the sound Death makes, when he treads on the half-dry twigs out there, in the dark, beyond the light of our pathetic little campfires.

—For Christ's sake, I said, —are you serious?

—In a minute, Ben my man, I'll take you to see. OK?

—Harry, so just what the fuck has this got to do with my party?

—OK, look, so there I am: me *here*, the dead bloke *there*, I knew he was dead, you just know, he's either dead or very badly fucked up, and the van's *there*. He's stopped it about fifteen yards past me. And then he starts to reverse the fucking thing, right? As in, towards me. Who has witnessed the whole bastard works. And so I think: hold on, not a good idea to hang around; (a) the dead guy needs an ambulance, and (b) there is no fucker in sight, and I need to get out of here. And so I leg it, and when I see a box, I call the ambulance, and when I tell them what's happened, they ask for my name, and like a cunt I give it to them without thinking, and say I'm a Brit, and next thing I know, course, I'm through to the cops and they already know my name now, and fuck . . . I don't know, Shnade, before I know it they know where I'm staying, I'm in some kind of fucking shock, shit, I just seen this bastard getting squashed and, anyway, look, I got to meet them back where it happened, and they're bound to ask where I was before, I'm the only fucking witness, so I'll have to tell them. It's too late now, I can't say I don't fucking know where I was or else what they going to think? That I'm off my tits, is what. And next thing they'll fucking blood-test me and hey: bang goes the career. So we hold it together, right? Like I did that time in Galway, right? Remember? Nice respectable Shnade who said good night to her nice respectable mate Harry about two a.m. and went to her nice normal bed. Without a hundred fucked-up little twats lying about the place dribbling MDMA into the carpet. Yeah?

—Fuck, said Shnade.

—Look, said Harry, —we've got to get back to the hotel.

—I'll stay and help clear up, I said.

—No, no, no, said Harry, —we're respectable Brits on a city break, we don't split up like that. They might want to check stuff with you anyway.

—Why should they? I argued.

—Because it's a bastard murder and I'm the only bloody witness, you dull fucker. Don't you understand? This is going to get into the press and everything. Shit, I wish I'd never talked to the fucking cops, but I did, you just *do*, and it's too late now. We are nice, normal, respectable Brits, and we just happened to be in the wrong place.

I looked up and, to my astonishment, Harry was grinning at Shnade. *Grinning*, the twat.

—Got to rush, he said. He stepped up to her, swift but cool. —Maybe catch you tomorrow at Styx's, he said.

—I thought you were going back this morning?

—Well, by the time they take the statement and all . . .

Then Harry kissed her once, for just one second, on the lips; and turned and left, leaving me blatantly to follow in his wake. I could only admire the sheer ruthlessness with which he treated me. I looked back at Shnade. She was looking at Harry's back with the weirdest mixture of suspicion and resentment. She didn't even know I was standing there. So I decided to leave while my pride could still put my invisibility down to her confusion and shock; before my rank as a walk-on player in all this became utterly undeniable, even to me.

Lying Through his Teeth

Outside, Harry was already jogging away; as I caught up, we kicked a bit harder and hit a loping run. The drugs started to bubble again as my blood pumped harder: this time not as a fuzzy warmth, but as pale fire in my temples. We were flying.

—Shit, Harry, you know the way home? I laughed, not caring a fuck if he knew or not.

—Jump that bin, Ben?

—OK.

So we did, and neither of us fell over either. Young again!

—Ben, I tell you, it's bloody scary. I haven't been in this bastard city for fifteen years, and even when I lived here, I only came to this district a couple of times. But shit, I remember it all. I remember it all! Can you remember my phone number?

—You what?

—Tell me my phone number.

So I did. Then Harry rapped back with mine as we raced through the rain and the night.

—Good, said Harry. —That means we're still locked on. It means our phone numbers mean more to us than numbers: they're still hieroglyphs of us. That's why we don't need phone books. Let's burn our phone books, Ben! Fuck me, Ben: when do we stop making memories?

Good timing, actually, for Harry to ask that question,

because the next thing that happened was so memorable that I have no difficulty, none whatever, in conjuring it up again for myself right now, right here in Peckham. I may not know, even now, exactly why it all bloody happened, but I can tell you what I saw all right. I may be a boring bastard, but I am a fine witness, at least.

I don't mean the police cars and the ambulance. It is not the police cars and the ambulance I remember. They were there: two police cars already arrived, an ambulance squealing up, and various cops and paramedics. A straggle of people: maybe ten or twelve, hands in pockets, smoking. I remember nothing of them. I mean, my supposed memories of them are as light-polluted as our supposed ideas of Beauty: when I try to remember what exactly the police cars and the ambulance looked like, all I get are second-hand bursts from the telly and the flicks: blue, Yank-style lights (they even think of *themselves* like they're in a film, for Christ's sake) and dark figures telling everyone to back off quite unnecessarily.

It's not the dead guy I remember either, for the good reason, perhaps, that I could not see him. I could see the ambulance guys lifting some ominously heavy weight; I remember an arm flopping down and hanging like a pendulum till someone tucked it back with illogical concern. So much for the bloke. What I really remember, I mean, the stuff I don't have to try to remember, the stuff that can and does just jump right out at me of its own accord, still, any time of day and night when it feels like it, is: us.

Us: Jan and The Wop being ushered away from the

223

body by a big cop in a mac, who was asking in a loud, Ulster voice if the gentleman from England who called the ambulance was still about: Harry going forward and giving his name to the cop, who nodded and shook Harry's hand; the two of them chatting, faces lit by the police car lights, the cop indicating one of the cop cars and Harry nodding and pointing to us.

Jan and The Wop, she covered in blood up to her elbows, saying, in the strangest voice I ever heard: *Someone had to try to help him. There was no ambulance when we got here, we* ... (she looked down at her bloodied hands with a slight, distant surprise). *I took his tongue out of his mouth,* she concluded simply, as if she had just described an everyday action which required no further explanation.

She looked over my shoulder at Harry, who was coming back to join us, and I remember half realising right then that what Jan had just said was aimed at Harry. Harry, I don't remember his exact words, but Harry said roughly that *Yeah, it was all very well, Jan, but at the time, it had seemed pretty bloody sensible to run for the ambulance.* The Wop backed him up: *Well,* said he, *I mean, yeah, cos the blokes in the van are possibly weighing up the odds on one squashed bloke and one live witness as against two squashed blokes. Potentially nasty news.*

I remember the silence then, as I handed round the cigs (Jan took one in a hand still red with blood). Maybe because I remember that it made me remember something else (maybe as we get older we only remember things that make us remember other memories; maybe there is nothing new left, nothing that we can experience without it reminding us of something else?). It was like trying to keep myself together against all the evidence of my senses, the way I once tried, years ago, twenty years for Christ's sake, to keep it tight when I was driving home with acid still flying about in my head, with cars that weren't there shooting in from the sides of my eyes and Southwark Bridge stretching and bucking impossibly ahead of me: you know, when all you can do is tell yourself that your senses are lying, that *this cannot be happening*, and try to navigate on pure critical reason. Except this time it was the other way around: this couldn't, logically, be happening to me, to a respectable thirty-eight-year-old guy, and I was having to tell myself that *actually, it was*: this time, my reasoned judgement of what could possibly happen was having to yield to my senses.

—Well, said Harry quietly, —I've got to go give a statement now. They'll take us back to the hotel any minute. We'd better agree on what we all did earlier.

—Shit, I said, —will they let us get the plane home?

—Well, I can't see me getting home today.

—Right, I mean, yeah, you'll have to give a full statement. After all, you saw the whole thing.

—Yeah, nodded Harry. —Why not stay? We can go to the session at lunchtime.

Out of the corner of my eye, I saw Jan's and The Wop's hands quietly link, bloodied and wordlessly complicit. I found myself thinking that a day off work, at last, would be a bloody nice thing. Like Harry said: who was going to argue? Everybody would say how horrible it had been for us. To my surprise, I remembered that Styx had indeed invited us to his pub tomorrow, and that Shnade was going to be there too. In all the madness I found I could recall this fact very plainly: I found, too, that it made my heart beat faster again. I had never felt less like sleep in my life.

—Yeah, I said, —maybe. But what if they ask why you were on your own? I mean, why weren't we there? We'd better get it right.

—Well, Jan and The Wop were otherwise engaged, I suspect.

—Fuck off, said Jan.

—What was I doing?

—Oh well, I left early because you were talking to some girl and I got jealous and decided to go home.

—OK. Who was I talking to?

—Shnade.

I looked up quickly, but Harry had meant nothing by it. It had not occurred to him that I had really thought anything about Shnade. He had taken the piss out of me for fancying her, but he never really thought...

—*Fuck Harry*, I thought.

I looked back at where the body had been. They had already chalked a white line where this person had been lying when he suddenly entered that endless tunnel, and became as historical as the dinosaurs. Now you see me, now you don't. I wondered if he had felt it. I wondered if they had developed specially waterproof chalk for drawing round bodies in the rain with. It seemed probable.

Fuck Harry, anyway.

Something was gnawing at the edge of my brain; something that worried me. I looked again, expecting to see blood in the dark puddles, but there was none, or at least, none that I remember. There were several dozen pills though, I remember them: pink and white and cream-coloured pills, being gathered off the wet road by the cops. I saw one of the pills, a brownish one, maybe it had been white before it got wet, disintegrate into soggy mush as a cop tried to pick it up: he looked

226

at his fingers with ancient, instinctive, hunter-gatherer disgust as it squished between them: as if whatever it was was far worse as damp squash than as hard chemicals. One of the cops picked up a sodden canvas shoulder bag, and peered carefully inside.

I looked at the bag again.

I had seen it before.

—Harry, I said. —Look, I, um, how far away did you say you were?

—Hmmm? said Harry.

Harry looked up as he lit up. I saw the flare of the match echo in his eye with a fire far wilder than even the charlie could have sparked.

—How close were you, Harry?

—What the hell you on about, Ben?

I looked into his eyes and the trapdoor gave way. That's what I remember most. I recall, I can still feel it now, here at home, a trapdoor flexing under my feet on a wet Dublin street.

I knew right then that Harry had not run from the scene because he was scared, and he had not been put through to the cops before he could say no, when he only meant to call the ambulance. He was lying through his teeth. My friend, my oldest friend, had not been thinking, as he ran, about the bloke lying in the road. The sight of Death had bounced clean off Harry. All Harry had been thinking was that *now, after all, he had an excuse*. He was covered. Now he could run back to Shnade's, with something to say that would knock her dead. A story from the wild side. Big bad Harry returns. The twenty years I had known Harry reeled past at an impossible speed, and for a terrifying instant I believed in Fate again, and thought, with one of those blasts of druggie clarity, when the curtains of all our bullshit rip back: *Of course! How could we have been so blind? He fucking loves it. For fifteen years he's been lying through his teeth, to us, to the world, to himself. This is it. Dark and drugs and fading shots of IRA gunmen, the music and the night-time and the rain. And Shnade. This is where his dreams are set. The rest has all been one great heap of bullshit. This is where Harry has been going every night since he ran away. The past. This is his fucking home.*

—What? said Harry again.

—Harry, I said, —I mean, look, yeah, it must have been quick, and, but . . .

But Harry had already turned away, and was waving with media-seasoned familiarity to the big cop in the mac, a sergeant as I now saw, who was striding towards us, gloved finger pointing at Harry in friendly interrogation.

—Would it be Dr Mac-Donald? said he.

—It would. Is, indeed, smiled Harry toughly.

—A bad business, Dr Mac-Donald.

—It is. Is he . . . ?

—Aye. Another one gone home to his mammy.

—Sorry? said Harry.

—That's who the wee fellow wanted. They always do, Dr Mac-Donald, d'ye see? Not their sweethearts and not their wives. Always their mothers. Well, if you're ready so?

—Fine, said Harry, and he followed the cop off to the car before I had a chance to talk to him again. He was already at the car when he turned back to us. —Come on then, boys.

Oh fuck, I thought.

Inclusive Lying Time

—Jesus, said the detective sergeant, as we drove back towards the hotel, with Harry up front beside him, and us three in the back, —no way to end a party night in Dublin, is it? Promise you won't go spreading it about, or the Tourist Board'll go ape. Quite a way from the hotel, too. Right in the badlands. How the hell d'you end up there?

The sergeant, Sergeant Gallagher he was called, a Donegal man as he told us, was probably no older than us, but with hair that was already more white than sandy. His sharp, weather-beaten or maybe drink-beaten face was set in a look of vague indignation, that Ulster face we have all seen so often on telly in the last twenty years, a cross-denominational set of the features that seems ready at any time to start denouncing something or someone. His lips hardly moved to let his deep sounds escape: a lip-reader would have had a hard time of it with Sergeant Gallagher. But his eyes were of the most incredible blue I have ever seen: a sea-going, western blue, outragedly bright, yet pale, as if powered from inside with a private light.

Myself, I had a normal upbringing of that good, decent, scared little lower-middle-class sort, where the main lesson in life is to hoard your money and feelings against some rainy day that will (of course) only ever come too late. In this scheme of things, the police are guardian angels with just a tint of menace; saviours who you would do well to keep in with; friendly seniors in the rough playground of life, who would keep the tough council-estate lads in check but were liable to exact homage. In short, while it would never occur to me to go and lob bricks at the police, I have the Little Man's fundamental, instinctive wariness of too much contact with them. Especially when I know that my best mate is possibly digging himself deeper into the shit with every word; especially when the cop he is talking to sounds like every Derry madman you have ever heard.

—Ah, we were at this pub in the country, said Harry, easily. —Styx Fitzpatrick's out in Dunboyne.

—Styx Fitzpatrick's? Styx Fitzpatrick's . . . Ach aye, of course. Know it well. Gas man. Well, you know the Ould Country a bit so?

—I used to work here years ago. Always wanted to come back.

—Bad timing!

—Tell me about it.

—So, ye's were out there, were ye's? Very nice. The city's awful bad these days. I tell ye's, lads, there are places I wouldn't go, not a mile from here, without eight strong men, four dogs and a brace of riot vans. I swear to God. So, what? Ye's were boozing away and then ye's just kinda . . . ?

—Oh, you know the way, said Harry, cool as you like and more Irish than you could possibly desire, his lilting come-all-ye brogue standing out with insane authenticity against the sergeant's Northern gravel. — They were chucking everybody out and we met these girls . . .

—Ah, now! chuckled the sergeant.

—And we came back to some party.

—No luck with the lassies?

—Ben was luckier than me, the bastard.

—Howye, Ben, said the detective, in the mirror.

—Hi, I said.

Very, very blue eyes.

—Well, chattered Harry, —we had to leave anyroad. We're supposed to catch the flight back this morning.

—Of course. Well, you should get on it yet.

—Let's hope so.

—Now, listen, would ye, and stop me if I'm utterly bloody arsewise on this: but would you be that Harry Mac-Donald off the telly? The historical fellow?

—I would.

—Well, holy God. Yeah, I watched that programme many's the time, with my kids. Jesus, I hardly knew ye with that big bald head on ye. When did that happen so?

And thus we, or rather Harry and Sergeant Gallagher of the Guards, rapped merrily and Celtificatingly away until we reached the grotty hotel.

—Jesus, not much of a place for a media man, said the sergeant.

—This particular trip isn't tax-deductible, smiled Harry.

—Canny fellow yourself. Looks clean enough though.

Clean. That was about all you could say about it: a clean hotel that Harry had booked over the phone. Clean, and beige.

In the tiny bar another, younger plain-clothes man was waiting, chatting to a hapless barman. This new cop was a big, metropolitan lump of a man; a hulk of urban Dublin battery-flesh so white and sunless it shone almost green where his too-short blazer revealed a good six inches of his fat, crossed forearms. His face had nothing in the way of cheekbones or chin: it was a great, soft, prematurely balding egg in the middle of which sat one of those sets of small, slack-jawed features: quintessentially poor-white city features, the sort of sugar-fed face that was bred to be ready to meet our daily barrage of modern shocks and setbacks with mild astonishment or fatalistic disbelief.

We made our polite introductions and the three of us were told very nicely that since we had seen nothing of the murder itself (they were already calling it a *murder*, I noted) we could get a few hours in before the flight, and make our depositions by post.

I could not keep still. I was amazed the cops, the Guards, didn't notice it; every moment I was expecting the blue-eyed bastard to stick me with his Semtex gaze and just say: *Sorry there, sir, did ye have something to add?*

The fact kept whizzing round my head: *Harry had not even noticed who it was being killed.* But if he was that close, how the hell could he not have noticed? Maybe Harry was worse off his head than I thought. But if he was so off his head, how come he was so confident about the rest of what had happened? How could he be so calm about talking to the cops? He wouldn't just lie, surely . . . ?

But who the hell was I to talk? I was hardly bloody straight and sober either. And how many of the twats in combats and trainers in Dublin carry canvas bags? Maybe I was just getting comedown paranoia? How the fuck was I to know, I had never come down from this stuff before for Christ's sake, I hadn't come down from anything worse than a couple of stiff vodkas too many since Harry's last bloody False Birthday, I . . .

—What you reckon, Bensta? Harry going to stay tomorrow?

—I think so.

—Right. Well . . .

—I suppose no one would deny we had a good reason, said Jan.

—No, I agreed. —I mean, Harry said it'll be in the press and everything.

—Two hours' kip! Nightmare! Just on health grounds alone, we should . . . so, shall we . . . ?

And in a second, all of us were pacing around outside this crap hotel, at more or less exactly equal distances from each other, and lying into our mobiles to various answerphones across the sea in London. We were all highly aware of each other as we strode and fibbed.

Have you ever wondered what proportion of mobile phone traffic is lies? I mean not counting the stuff that is plain dodgy? Scan us, scan the satellites with me now and see what we can hear, buzzing and ticking around the world: lies. Lies to lovers, lies to partners, lies to old friends we don't want to mix with new friends, lies to colleagues about missed trains, lies about deals and wheels and meals, lies to our old parents about why we can't come up this weekend and lies to our little kids about how we can't make storytime tonight. Watch us striding outside bars, baking our brains with microwave lies; see our body language conniving brilliantly in our alleged unfreedom as we invent these plaintive, imprisoned lives for ourselves. And all because we do not dare to simply say that we are doing it *because we want to.*

How many inclusive minutes of lying-time a month do *you* get?

(I read, after those bombs in London, that you are on

233

camera fifty per cent of the time you are in W1. But what if it was one hundred per cent? What if everyone knew that they were definitely being filmed all the time, everywhere? Shit, we would all have to stop lying, out of the sheer, amoral fear that we would be found out. We would have to be honest. We would have to stand outside our bars and say: *Actually, I can't make the flicks with you because I just want to get pissed with the boys and not have to think about where this thing is going;* or *Actually, you better ask Daddy to give you your story tonight because I want to get drunk with this guy I met who doesn't bore me to death with his penny-pinching whingeing;* or *Sorry, Mum, can't make it this weekend because there's loads of things I'd rather do.* The world would suddenly become a very pure, and very scary, place. Scary, because after all, why do we lie? Out of fear. Lying is what we do to stop looking the world in the face. You think they can't make a videophone that we could carry about like a mobile? Of course they could. But would *you* buy one? What, and let people *see* you lying? No demand, no product.)

Each of us finished lying to our bosses' and partners' and kids' answerphones about how *Look, hi, it's four a.m., Dublin, um, Harry saw this murder, um, some bloke got squashed with a Transit, yeah, Harry was right there, the police, the Guards, are still with him, and we've all got to talk to them and, look, we're all shagged, and, you know, probably a bit shocked too, just wanted to let you know soon as poss., can't see us getting the morning flight, um, look, call you later, yeah? Bye. Byee.* Then we stood and looked at one another in the gentle rain.

Jan was biting her lip again; she looked almost resentful, as if she had been bounced; The Wop seemed

234

suddenly tired. I wanted to talk it through, but who could I talk to? Jan and The Wop were starring in their own private drama: Jan stood there, arms folded; The Wop ran his hands through his hair, just outside intimate distance. They looked like a pair of teenage lovers going up on a ski lift, ski-less, towards some quiet, high place, flushed and silent, so aware of each other's every motion that the air crackles between them.

I watched them: amazing, I thought, that's all we are: incredibly sensitive machines for relating to other humans. Look what we can do with other people. How many sets of radar have we got? And no wonder we scratch ourselves bloody when we are not getting enough of each other, when all this amazing potential is locked in a little plasterboard box with easy-to-clean surfaces and an entryphone. No wonder we batter ourselves senseless against the bars of our cages.

Except no one built them but us.

What was going on between Jan and The Wop was this, and I knew it as clearly as they did, which is to say, vaguely, but clearly: they did not really want to be left on their own. The moment I was not here, they would be faced with the consequences of their actions. As long as we stayed in our little False Birthday gang, we could maintain that myth called Us that freed us from all judgement; as soon as we admitted that we each had our own private lives, and responsibilities, and conse- quences, the game would be up. But now Harry was gone, and when I went back into the hotel, Jan and The Wop would be real again, people again, a man and a woman who knew damn well what was going to happen next, but did not want to admit that it was now pretty much inevitable. We all like to keep our illusions of free will.

I could not bring myself to leave them blatantly to

their fate by going back inside, to bed, but I was buggered if I was going to stand there all night long. So I said I was going to take a quick walk. They just nodded.

I walked over to a funny little park with sculptures in it, and as soon as I was out of their sight, I sat down on a bench and felt the tremulous chemical shivering in my blood again, though now fading slightly away. I waited. I felt myself slipping away. I drew myself up again and went back out of the park: Jan and The Wop were gone.

I left it just long enough to ensure that there was no way I would meet Jan sneaking into The Wop's room (for some reason I was quite sure that it would be her who went to his room, not the other way around). The whole business between them had seemed quite harmless to me, but with the drugs now wearing off, I was also aware that it was, in fact, an earthquake from which we would never recover. It had that strange taste of an ending about it. But I was cold now, very cold, and there was a rather unpleasant, slightly disquieting buzzing up and down my arms and in my jaw, like when they made you hold wires at school, to show you the effects of low-powered electricity. I felt the first little snouting twinge of panic that it might be my heart: *sad old git dies of Ecstasy in pathetic attempt to stay young.*

I made it to my room and lay down. I felt tired now. I lay still, and drifted about; I thought I was almost there; if only I had remembered to turn the lamp off, I could sleep; I would have to get up and turn it off. I forced myself to open my eyes and roll off the bed.

Then I found that it was dark anyway; the lamp was already off, and what I had thought was the glow of the lamp coming through my closed eyelids was the chemically fired LCDs inside my head. For a very nasty instant I was quite certain that I was never, ever going to sleep again.

I lay and tried to do the circular breathing I had not done for years. I tried to keep utterly still and calm. I told myself that hundreds of thousands of Yoof do this shit every Friday, and very few of them actually drop dead of it. No chance. I flipped through an alien Irish newspaper and read meaningless accounts of what people I had never heard of had said about things I knew nothing about in a parliament whose name I could not even pronounce. I thought about the canvas bag. Already, I was less and less sure.

I rolled out of bed again, and surveyed my thankless little room. I swore that if we ever did this fucking False Birthday crap again, we would go for a Holiday Inn at least. I turned on the telly, but before I could even find any Eurocrap to watch, someone was battering on the wall for me to shut up. I could hear them flump back down on the bed. Pipes squeaked; a lav flushed somewhere close by.

Clean, that was about all you could say. Clean plasterboard.

Then I realised that I could hear voices; that I had been vaguely hearing voices for some minutes. I almost panicked again until I realised that they were real voices, not some drug-induced psychosis. It was Harry and the two cops, coming right through the cheap walls of my room. Something banged against the wall by my head; it felt like they were in the room with me. A table? Someone scraped a chair across a carpet, and sat down.

Like a spy, I silently turned over, knelt up and put my ear to the wall.

—Right, said Sergeant Gallagher, his bass rumble

cutting easily through the plasterboard. —Let's go for it so, Dr Mac-Donald.

I held my breath and listened.

A Statement of Fact

The fat cop was speaking with artificial clarity, in a horrible Dublin twang:

—My name is Harry James Murray MacDonald.

What? I thought. Then I realised that he must be reading from a statement.

> — I am a lecturer at University College London, in the Department of Archaeological and Cultural Studies. I am also a TV presenter. My normal residence is at 201 Eltham Villas, Tooting, London, UK. On 16 February I attended a private party given in a house on Ardagh Road, Dublin 1. I do not know the name of the host, nor do I recall the precise address. I was only in Dublin for the one night to celebrate a traditional date among my group of friends. I had been out in Dunboyne, at a public house called Styx Fitzpatrick's, where I availed . . .

—Donal, wait, better put availed *myself* of an invitation, said the sergeant. —That's the way the Brits say it.
—Is it?
—Isn't that right, Dr Mac-Donald?
—Yes, actually.
—Right so. *Availed myself* of an invitation given to

come to a party in a public house. In Styx Fitzpatrick's. Gas name, eh? Now, go on, Dr Mac-Donald. How much did we agree you had taken?

—Um, six to eight pints, I think we said.

—Or five to seven.

—Or five to seven, yes.

—No whiskey or anything?

—No whiskey, no. No shorts at all.

—Shame it wasn't just four, mused the sergeant. — No? Oh well, still and all, you remembered the licence plate, didn't he, Donal? And that's recorded on the phone message, too right it is, real time and uncut, so no clever bastard can suggest we coached anyone. God bless technology! Carry on so, boys.

Once again the fat cop's voice took over. It sounded like he was reading with exaggerated care, to an idiot. I pictured Harry slumping in his chair, desperate to be left alone.

> —During the course of the evening I con-
> sumed five to seven pints of beer. At approxi-
> mately two a.m. I decided to leave the party
> as I was feeling somewhat tired. I left alone. I
> proceeded in what I believed to be the
> direction of the Quays, hoping to find a cab to
> my hotel. I intended to get some sleep before
> my return flight to the Mainland.

—Fuck, I don't believe I wrote that. The *Mainland*!

—Jesus, Donal, you'll get slagged for this.

—Can I change it?

—You cannot. Anyway, he's Brit. That's what they say, Donal. Them and you. The Mainland. Well said, *Constable* Fallon.

—Jesus, Sergeant, leave off, will you?

—Get on with it. Dr Mac-Donald seems to be fading somewhat. Would you like more coffee there, Dr Mac-Donald?

—Sorry, what? Eh? Oh, no, no, no, I was just . . .

—Grand so. Go on, Donal.

— . . . to the Mainland. I do not know Dublin and so found myself somewhat lost. I believe it was in the area known as the Smithfield. After some time I found myself in Capel Street. I noted the time on several clocks in the window of the Unwanted Gifts Exchange. It was two twenty a.m. I continued down Capel Street and was near to the Quays when I became aware of a white Transit van or similar. It appeared to be pulling out of a yard or cul-de-sac on the left-hand side of the road, seen from the north. I do not recall the van passing me or executing a U-turn. I am sure it was pulling out from a yard or cul-de-sac. I do not recall the name of the shop next to this yard or cul-de-sac . . .

—Whoops, hold it there boys. Now, Dr Mac-Donald, you're still fine with this, aren't you? We want no mistake about this one.

—Yes, yes, yes, said Harry. —Whatever.

—We'll get the bastard yet so.

— . . . for definite but I believe it was O'Conor. As the van drew into the street in the northbound carriageway, I became aware of a man carrying a large object. It appeared to be an object of wood or metal. I was approximately thirty feet away at this time. I was on

241

the opposite side of the road to the cul-de-sac or yard, still walking towards the Quays. The man appeared to be following the van out from the yard or cul-de-sac already mentioned. It seemed to me that an altercation had already taken place, because the man was shouting at the occupants of the van. I did not hear exactly what he was saying, but it included the terms 'ya fucking bollix' and 'I'll crease you, you cunt'. This man then struck the side of the van several times with the object. The van then executed a sort of S-shaped manoeuvre in the road, and struck the man. The man attempted to avoid the van, but failed. He made a motion rather like ...

—Hold on, Donal. Like what, Dr Mac-Donald? I mean, how would you explain this to a hostile barrister?

—Christ, I don't know, like, like, oh, God, look: I'll show you. Like this.

At this point, I heard a sort of quick-step scuffling sound.

—Hmm. Would you say that was like a full-back with some tricky winger coming at him, Donal?

—To the life, Sergeant.

—Very fine, Dr Mac-Donald. You should take to the stage some day!

—Can I sit down now?

—Course you can. Donal?

... rather like a soccer defender attempting to block the progress of a rival winger. Notwithstanding his efforts, however, the van struck the man in the region of the right thigh and he fell. The van stopped. It then reversed a small distance, about two yards, and then proceeded to drive over him. I am certain that it was a deliberate manoeuvre. There is no doubt in my mind on this point. The front offside wheel of the van passed over the man's chest or abdomen. I heard what I take to have been the sound of his ribs breaking inwards. He made no noise and did not move again. It was clear to me that he was very seriously injured. The van then straightened out and proceeded slowly northwards. By this time, I was almost level with the struck man. The van was thus passing me slowly, going in the opposite direction, northwards. I recorded the licence plate number of the van to memory. It was 546 UZI. I recall this partly because it is unusual in the UK, my home country, for number plates to call automatic weapons to mind. I would point out that I was not too far under the influence of alcohol to recall this number later, when telephoning for assistance, with no written aid of any kind.

—Great. That's very good. That'll shut them up. Lovely.

— I then became aware that the van had stopped. The man continued to lie still and make no sound. I became aware of the occupant or occupants of the van. I could not make him or her or them out clearly, because the glass in the windows was darkened. But it seemed to me that he or she or they was or were observing me. The van began to reverse

243

again, in the direction of the motionless man, which was towards the Quays. This meant it was also following me. Being alone and in a foreign country and in a district unknown to me, and being convinced, as I was, that the incident between the Transit van and the motionless man had not been an accident, I elected to run and call the police rather than attempt first aid. I have no training in first aid and was not keen to involve myself in any discussion or similar with the possible occupant or occupants of the Transit van concerning the events I had witnessed. I proceeded to run towards the Quays as fast as possible. The van now proceeded at speed in a northerly direction. I called 999 from a Telecom Eireann box located outside the Wig and Pen public house. I then returned to the scene of the incident to await the arrival of the emergency services. I did not see the white Transit van again. I was in control of my faculties throughout the episode.

—Dead on so! Well, Dr Mac-Donald? No trouble putting your name to that then?
—None.
—OK, Donal?
—Grand, Sergeant.
—Well then, if you'd just put a paw-mark here, Dr Mac-Donald. All fine and dandy so. Right. I'd say we'll let you get some sleep, then, Dr Mac-Donald; you look like you could use it. Don't blame you. Tell you what: as a mark of our gratitude to a responsible and civic-minded citizen of a semi-foreign country, why don't we send a discreet ould car round to bring you out to the

airport? Ah, no, don't mention it. Sure, it's the least we can do. The car'll be here at seven so. No, no, really. Safe home now. We'll be in touch, no fear. And remember: not a word to the Tourist Board!

I heard the door go. I tried to imagine Harry, sitting there alone. Then, as the policemen passed my door, I quite distinctly heard the sergeant say:

—Donal, I really think we have the bastard cold this time.

And for a crazed moment, I had to stop myself thinking they meant Harry.

The Greatest Sin

Afterwards, I lay there on the small hotel bed, feeling the horrible plastic undersheet crinkle and crackle, wondering if they put it there in case their guests pissed themselves or in case their guests died. Then I decided not to think about guests dying and, with some effort, recalled from my distant youth what it had been like on acid, and how the one thing you could *not* do was think about how you had to score some sleep sometime, and eventually managed to go with it enough to kind of snorkel about just below consciousness.

At one stage I was holding Shnade's hand; just holding her strong hand. I could feel the pressure of her fingers quite distinctly. Then I found I actually had my arm cocked backwards and my hand was underneath my head, numb from the weight.

Sometime afterwards, this timeless drug-time was thankfully ended by the alarm telling me that in that weird, lost realm called sanity, I would have to get up now if I wanted to catch the plane. It seemed such an incredible thing to have to do. Soon, in the world of theoretical reality, I would be looking down again on clouds. Most unlikely.

Then I heard Harry's lav flushing, and before I knew it, this definite evidence that he too was awake had sent me bounding out of bed as if it were a fire alarm I had just been waiting for. It was not so much that I wanted to see Harry as that I needed to see someone or other. For all my brave talk to Shnade last night, I was suddenly feeling that being alone for another five minutes would be unbearable. Making a mental note never to take E again, even in the unlikely event of my being offered it ever again, I opened the door and went in. Harry was lying on the bed.

—Fuck, he said.

I wanted to ask him what he had really been thinking when he saw the murder. I needed to talk to him about the canvas bag, just to set my mind at rest, and find out how the hell he had not recognised Ohn. But instead, I fell into that strange canyon between what we intend to say and what actually gets out. You know, like when you lie awake all night working out exactly what you are going to say in the meeting at work tomorrow: it will, you are sure, be important and grounded and well-worked out and hit home and all that. And then daylight comes along and evens everything out again, and when it comes to it, you just let the old flow of good old normality carry you on. Not out of cowardice or anything as strong as that: out of sheer leaden gravity, and out of the question which, I sometimes think, is the question we all ask every day, these days, whether we know it or not: *Why bother? Who gives a fuck?*

True. Who gave a fuck if Harry saw it was Ohn or not? It had been dark, after all. It had happened quickly, Harry was off his head, he ... well, Ohn was dead one way or another. And who the fuck was Ohn to me anyway? Some mate of Shnade's. And there again, who the fuck was Shnade to me? A girl I had never met before, a girl I would never see again, just some dream that still spooked about inside Harry's fucked-up head.

—Yeah, me too, I said.

—Ben: why do we get up just because this little pile of plastic and quartz says we have to?

—Um, because we lost touch with the Old Ways?

—Bollocks. Christ I hate hippies. They go around whingeing on about Gaia and Stonehenge, and they seem to have no notion that Stonehenge is just a fucking great alarm clock, built by priests and kings, or priest-kings, most likely, to make the rest of the poor, scared, ignorant Stone Age sods do what they wanted, when they wanted. Fuck, I'm wasted. Did Jan and The Wop shag, do you think?

—I think probably. Harry?

—What?

—You know when you saw the guy getting squashed?

—Yeah. Well?

—Was it Ohn?

—Who?

—Ohn. The little dealer. The one who . . . Harry? You all right?

—Christ, said Harry, and he froze, absolutely still, hands halfway to his head, white. His gaze shot away from me, back inside his own head. I knew right then that Harry was reeling back wildly through his footage, and that I was right.

Then the phone rang. It rang and rang.

—Fuck, said Harry, still locked solid, —I didn't even see . . .

—Yes, thank you! I said angrily into the phone, unable to stand the ringing any more, assuming it was a wake-up call and blaming whoever was making it for the unbearable rise in the volume of telephone ringers, today.

—Ben?

—Shnade?

—Is Harry there?

—Yeah.

—Ben?

—Yeah?

—I need to talk to Harry, Ben.

—Harry's fucked, I said, without thinking about it. — I just told him it was that bloke Ohn that got killed. It was, wasn't it?

—Shut up, Ben, and put the sharp eyes to bed, willya? Give me Harry.

I passed the phone to Harry, who took it like an ancient philosopher might take a poisoned drink, or a bold, brave spy might accept his last fag before the firing squad: like he did not want to do it, but knew that from now on *what he would have liked to happen*, and *what was going to happen* were entirely different things.

Shnade was brief. Harry put down the phone and stood up like a man on autopilot.

—She's outside, round the corner. I got to go down.

I don't know why I went as well, and I don't know why Harry didn't stop me. It didn't seem to occur to either of us. We just went. We were joined now, more than ever: we both knew without saying anything that somehow this had become both our stories, and whatever happened next would one day belong to both our pasts. We went down in the lift together, as if in a dream.

Shnade was not in the foyer, but instinctively we proceeded out of the front door. She was standing in the little sculpture garden, in what I now learned was called Parnell Square, looking nervous and cold in the rain. She waved us to follow her but stay back.

She sloped up round the corner of the big, Gothic, Presbyterian church and disappeared. We snuck after her, already taking on the role of hunted fugitives without knowing why.

—Harry, I said, —is there anything I should know?

—No, shit, you know fucking more than me.

—I don't understand, I said. —They threw that Ohn out of the party, he didn't look like some mate of theirs, so . . .

Then Shnade's van was suddenly before us; she was getting in and waving us into the back. The big back door was open just a crack, and it looked very dark inside. She waved again, more urgently.

—Remember you said about that stuff that happened to you in Galway fifteen years ago, with Shnade? I asked. I was thinking about the long-lost gunmen in sideys and shades. Suddenly, they did not seem so harmless.

—Yeah, said Harry.

—Harry, are you quite sure this is OK?

—Get in before some fucking cop sees you, hissed Shnade.

—Thing is, Ben, said Harry, —I am just so fucking tired I don't care much. So don't go by me. I'm getting in, but never trust the judgement of a tired man, Ben: tiredness is the greatest sin. No, not *sin*: curse. Up to you, Ben; I just want somewhere to sleep. Like the horses. Remember? In New York?

And he headed towards the door, and the dark inside.

Remember? Of course I remembered. That was what the yellow lamps at Shnade's party had reminded me of.

—Yes, I said, as Harry climbed up into the darkness of the van, —I remember.

Where the Horses Sleep in New York

It's simple: we went to New York, like I said (remember?), when Harry got his first serious cheque from his telly work. We had to see the capital of the twentieth century before the new millennium, said Harry.

—Watch now, boys, he said, as we came out of the big tunnel from JFK and saw Manhattan for the first time. —We're all like King Kong, see? We've all seen this place in our dreams. We know it before we ever get there. It kind of reminds us of home. Or makes us long for home. *Hiraeth*, we call it.

And all we did was what everyone does in New York: climb high buildings and ride in yellow cars and eat big food and drink cocktails in nifty bars and photograph each other standing about in the steam coming up from the manholes or whatever they call them. And then, just before we had to grab a cab back to the airport, it was about four a.m. and it was cold, it was snowing, and we ended up, Christ knows how, down in SoHo, outside this big old brick building with a massive, hundred-year-old wooden door. Everything looks medieval in the snow at night, and this door looked to me like it led to a big, dark cathedral. There was a little window hole in the door, and a light inside. We couldn't resist it: we peeped through the grille, like it was either a speakeasy or a confessional, and inside we could see this fat cop, looking just like every fat Yank cop in every film that was ever made, sitting reading some sports paper by the light of a bendy lamp, with his fat legs crossed and his gun in his holster and his cap back on his head. And all around him, these horses, stalls and stalls of them, receding away from us, beautiful horses sleeping in the shadows given off from soft yellow lamps clamped low on the wooden frames.

—You ever just want to wake up in clean sheets and hear birds and smell bacon cooking and lie there and just . . . be quietly happy? Harry whispered. —You ever dream that one day you would wake up and know exactly why you were here and what the bastard fuck it was all about, and what you would be doing at seventy? Well? Sorry, forget it: welcome to the third millennium. The horses get somewhere to sleep, even in New York, but for us, boys, the ride goes on for, well, for as long as we got. Maybe we just took the wrong exit sometime a couple of thousand years ago. Or maybe we should have stuck around 1800. Or maybe we were fucked ever since we came down from the trees. Ah well: it won't last for ever.

Then we all just watched and watched and got covered in snow, and came home.

Back in Dublin, I followed Harry into the darkness of the van.

We Know Nothing

— How the hell was I to know? pleaded Harry, as Styx Fitzpatrick rammed him up against the thin, drumming wall of Shnade's van.

—Fuck me, Harry fucking MacDonald, I sometimes wonder did you ever come inside a woman in your fucking stupid life?! Do you always slip your fucking little dick out at the last moment? Or do you just kiss and run away the whole time so you never even have to show them how small it is? Fuck! I should have known. Fifteen fucking years ago, and you were just the same: sit there singing along with everyone else, proud to know the big bad boys in the 'RA, and as soon as things go sticky ... You think you can piss about with everything? You ...? Or is it the lot of you? Brits? Fuck me, if there is one thing we poor bloody Paddies should have learned, it is never to trust a British fucking leftie liberal bastard. You're all the same, you are, aren't you? It must be in the fucking blood. You go on your demos and blow up pylons in Wales and ... and you actually believe, deep down, that you'll get a nice fucking job on the telly out of it, and a house in Notting Hill, and end up taking tea with Tony fucking Benn and everyone loving you because you were such a bold fucking rebel! You think it's all some kinda student joke, and it'll all get sorted for you because you're Brits. And the minute you smell anything like real danger, the moment it stops being *Ballyfuckingkissangel*, you run to the Guards and sing like fucking nightingales.

—I only called the ambulance for fuck's sake, gurgled Harry.

—Have you any idea what the fuck you have done? screamed Styx.

—No! screamed Harry. —Of course I fucking haven't, or I wouldn't have done it! Why didn't you stop the van and tell me it was you, for Christ's sake?

—How the fuck was I to know you'd go and put a stupid fucking black cap on? You ran before I could see it was you for sure.

—Of course I fucking ran! I didn't know it was you!

—If I'd seen your big bald fucking head . . .

—Well, how the hell was I supposed to know you're a sodding drug dealer? You always told me you hated drugs, you always said the IRA would top any drug dealer round your manor, you . . .

—It's true, said Shnade. —Styxy, remember how long he's been away.

—He doesn't even know about Shevaun, I said.

—Who? What? said Harry.

—See? I said.

—My kid, said Shnade.

—Your what? gaped Harry.

—See? I said again.

—Christ, said Harry.

—OK, OfuckingK, roared Styx, and let Harry down, clearly in no mood to be told the obvious by anyone but himself. —I thought you got the hint when I said I was still keeping my powder dry. Fuck. Ah shit, I guess I forgot how long you were away. Times change, Harry. A man's got to make a living, and contacts is contacts and guns is guns and dark little alleys will always be useful. Fuck, I didn't say I was proud of it, I said . . . I just said, times fucking change. When we were eighteen, I would have laid you a hundred to one we'd be sitting here by now in a united fucking Ireland, Prods and Catholics all happy together, all forgotten. Well so. And now you've gone and hung me out to dry and we have to think what the fuck to do about it.

Styx, of course: it had been Styx. Ohn had been treading on Bandanna Man's patch, and Bandanna Man worked for Styx, so he called in his ex-Provo padroni, and Styx drove into town in his Transit to have a hard little word with Ohn. But Ohn was so stupid, or so young and dull and convinced that anyone over thirty is a tosser, that he tried to mix it with Styx . . .

—So you squashed him? I asked carelessly.

—I didn't fucking squash him! Deliberately, I mean. He chucked that fucking piece of wood at my windscreen, and I just threw my hands up like this, without thinking, and I squashed him like that. It was a fucking accident, Harry.

—But . . . Harry's ability to speak was breaking down seriously.

—Harry, I said, —think about it. You didn't even recognise Ohn.

—See? said Shnade. —So how can you be sure? How could you tell them you were sure?

—But I . . .

—Fuck me, Harry, why the Jesus did you go and tell them all that?

—Because I thought . . . I thought it was true. That's what happened. That's what I saw. I don't understand. OK, so you want me to lie and say . . .

—Who said anything about lie? roared Styx. —Just tell the fucking truth.

—But I did! shouted Harry suddenly. —Why the hell would I have lied?

—You didn't lie, I said quietly. —But maybe you wanted an excuse. You wanted a story, not just an event. You told them what you saw, but maybe what you saw didn't happen quite like that. Not quite.

—But if I don't know what the truth is, how can I . . . If I don't know what the fuck I'm even seeing, how can I ever . . . Fuck, if I don't even know what the truth is, I can't even bloody lie!

—Ben, said Styx, quietly. —Good man yourself, now tell him he has to believe me. You know the score. Look me in the eye and then tell Harry . . .

So I looked into Styx's eyes. And I knew nothing. Nothing at all. I knew that this was a strong, dangerous man, and I knew that he had very good reasons for wanting me to believe him. All of which I had known before I looked him in the eye. All this eyeball stuff is cowboy bollocks. We can never tell anything from another person's eyes. Another person's eyes are just mirrors, reflecting what we want to see: the people who said they were hypnotised by Hitler's eyes were actually drugged by their own need to be told what to do next. And if we want to see love, we will find it where there is really only a friendly regard. Know? We know nothing.

—I wasn't there, I said, —so I don't know.

—Jesus! snapped Styx, and for a moment I thought I did see something in his eyes: something about dark alleys and sawn-offs.

—We could always stop worrying about the truth, said Shnade, quietly.

—What? said all of us males.

—Lads, said Shnade, —do you think there's some guy up there handing out end-of-term prizes for the truth? Do you? Congratulations, young fuck-up muggins, your life has been a pile of shite, a long haul without a taste of happiness, but Holy God, weren't you always the fine boy for the truth! Here, have a coconut. Fuck, lads, do you want to know what the truth is? Come on, Harry, you're the bigshot archaeologist, spit it out. The truth is bones and dust. The truth is six feet under with a decent wake if you're lucky. The truth, lads, as far as I can gather, is that we are sitting on a shagging little ball of shite at the edge of a solar system which is in some third-rate galaxy at the end of one spiral arm of one cosmos in one corner of the big bad fucking universe. The truth is that nothing matters a flying fuck.

—It fucking matters to me, growled Styx. —Because if he tells them . . .

—Styxy.

—What?

—Shut up, willya.

—OK so.

—Right. Now, given all that shite, what do we do? I tell you what. How's about turning it on its head: *so who gives a fuck about whether it's true or not?* Now, Harry, I don't know if you saw what you said you saw and if not why not and whatever the fuck else was going on in your head. I like you, I always liked you, and I never liked you because you told the truth. I liked you because you were a laugh and I liked you because you courted me like you were a girl yourself and I never knew why the fuck you just upped and left like that the day after I kissed you, when any eejit could tell that what I meant was: *not now, but soon.* And I don't know if Styx is telling the fucking truth either, and I don't care about that either because I like him too: he courted me like a fucking bullock, and I liked that too, and we had a good time for a long time and then we stopped having a good time and we made each other's lives shite for a short time, then we stopped that too, and so now we're old mates and he sorts me very fairly thank you with Shevaun, and . . .

—What? gulped Harry.

—Well, whose the fuck do you think she is? growled Styx, regressing to his Iron Age persona in defence of his gene-pool.

—So to be honest, lads, I don't give a priest's dick about which of you is telling the truth. All I care is what happens. That's all that matters. What happens. The result. The rest is just wank-off fucking undergraduate games for, for, for . . .

— . . . for stupid little gits with their pants sticking out of their trousers? I suggested.

—Excellent, said Shnade.

—That's mine, said Harry.

—No it's not.

—Oh.

—Like yours; but mine. So what happens, Shnade? Harry and Styx watched her. So did I.

—Well, said Shnade, —it's obvious. Harry retracts his statement. He says sorry, lads, I have to come clean, I was off my tits and I now have my doubts and I can't put my name to that shite in the cold light of day. And then the Guards don't get Styx, who could, I remind you, have just had Harry stiffed this morning instead of talking it through like an amicable man. But didn't. And then Harry goes home and fuck all happens to him.

—Because he's a fucking Brit and the Guards can't touch him over there, added Styx.

—A famous, funny, nice, well-loved Brit, nodded Shnade.

—Right, said Harry. —So I just . . .

—Um, sorry, I said.

—What? said everyone.

—Not quite, I said. —It's not quite that easy.

—The Guards can't touch him, said Styx.

—So it's you they've wanted to nail for years?

—Since the fucking hunger strikes, nodded Styx.

—Right, I said. —And Harry told them he was at your place?

—Well, yes, I didn't fucking know . . . said Harry.

—OK, OK. So: the police, the Guards, know there's some connection between Harry and Styx. And now he sees you, he *thinks* he sees you kill someone, he tells them so and then takes it back.

—Well, I suppose . . . burbled Harry.

I don't know where it came from. I felt perfectly at ease, quite outside the problem, wholly without involvement. I was some kind of lawyer, nothing more.

—No, they won't just let you retract. Sorry, they won't. You know they won't just let him do that.

—He's a Brit, said Styx again, but with dawning uncertainty.

—A famous Brit, repeated Shnade, but already half guessing what was coming.

Harry was still sitting on the floor. He had lit a fag, and was looking at us as we discussed him. He looked like some exhausted serf, or a prisoner of war who cannot march any further, gazing up at us, quite unable to understand the language in which we, his masters, were deciding his fate: utterly beyond comprehension or caring.

—That's the trouble, I said.

—How come? said Shnade.

—They don't have to touch him. They only have to test him on some kind of suspicion. They've got plenty of circumstantial for that. And then they find his blood's full of drugs. So what do they do? They just let it out to the press: TV PERSONALITY IN DRUGS MURDER RIDDLE. Harry's fucked. No more telly career.

—He's right, said Harry, quite matter-of-fact. — They'd love an excuse to dump me now I'm bald. Well, at least we know where we stand then: I stick with my story, you go down. I change it, I'm fucked.

—I'm not going down, Harry, said Styx. I mean *said*, just *said* said. Not muttered, not murmured, not growled, not grated, not whispered. Just *said*. Just a statement. —It's not going to happen. Too old for that. And nothing to go down for, know what I mean? Fuck, Harry, I'd have done twenty years happily enough, when we were young, for the Cause. But I'm old now, Harry, and the Cause has turned into blowing up kids in marketplaces and shooting retired peelers off the backs of their fucking tractors. Thanks to you blind fuckers. But fuck that. This is the thing: I'm asking you as a friend, Harry MacDonald, an old friend, a man who I was glad to see last night, and who was glad to see me. If you're my friend, act like it, and I swear to fuck I'll never forget it. And I'm not even going to say the other bit, Harry, because I shouldn't have to, and I don't have to, and you . . .

—Don't fucking threaten me, snapped Harry, surprisingly hard.

—Yeah, shut the fuck up, said Shnade.

—All right, fuck! growled Styx. —Sorry. Fuck.

The van was very, very quiet. Harry especially. He was sucking at the back of his mouth, like he had a big loose tooth, and looking at his fingers as if he had never seen them before. Rain started to beat softly on the thin roof and the tinny walls. Styx took out a cigar and extracted a big brass lighter. I looked at Shnade's tattoo and, quite absurdly, found myself starting to drop off into a sweet, dreamlike daze.

Styx struck the lighter. It made a loud, metal clack. A bit like a gun being cocked, I suppose.

Well, maybe a bit like a gun being cocked if you were outside and listening with a microphone and recording everything we'd been saying.

Which was, I suppose, why the Guards outside decided it was time to chuck the tear-gas in, drag us out and kick the shit out of Styx and Shnade while covering them with machine pistols.

Safe Home

—Subversive bastards, said our blue-eyed sergeant of the Guards as he shoved us into the waiting car. And no, the word *Guards* didn't make us want to laugh any more. —Well, Dr Mac-Donald, said he, turning from up front, where he sat comfortably next to the fat constable, who was driving us to the airport at a stately, undeviating cruise, —you are a silly wee boy for a man of the world and no mistake. Jesus, did you really think we'd swallow that guff about *six to eight pints*, and you sitting there hanging, with one pupil like a pin and one like a fucking football?

—It was too, laughed the constable.

—Ach, I swear that hoor's melt Fitzpatrick is right about one thing and no more: you Brits take the sheer shagging biscuit. You really do think we're all a bunch of eejit culchies, don't you? Tut tut, Dr Mac-Donald, and you a fellow Celt and all. Well so, lucky for you we were about, by the sound, eh? Plenty of bogs in County Meath, had we not been on the ball. You should choose your friends more carefully, Dr Mac-Donald. Like your man said: this isn't *BallybloodyK*.

—And not *Waking Ned*, neither, said the constable.

—It is not, agreed the sergeant. —But don't you go telling that to the tourist board!

I looked secretly at Harry. His face was slack and dead. I tried to find some sign of thought beneath this pale, blank mask, but could discover none. Then I found that, maybe unable to bear the sight of a friend's face robbed

262

of all meaning, I was superimposing things on to him, as if his face were merely a screen.

I saw Harry, younger, fifteen years younger, the last time he had met up with the Guards; Harry in his own story, which was now mine too, standing at a door in Galway (I have never been to Galway, but I saw it all right: *to me*, it was Galway), faced with two big plain-clothes Guards, pink and blushing and very, very Brit-looking, holding a somewhat unwashed duvet in front of his balls and stammering away about how he only met this Styx Fitzpatrick and this Shnade in the pub, and had no idea where they were and what they did and . . .

—Ah well, no need for any fuss with the press, and tests, and all that shite now, eh, Dr Mac-Donald? Best so. A nice clean statement and no worries: sound as a trout. And don't you go worrying yourself, Dr Mac-Donald, that kind of lowlife has no reach these days, if you see what I mean. Once Fitzpatrick is under wraps his whole dirty little gang will melt away, like the foggy dew itself. No contacts over the water. No reach, do you see? Ah, you can sleep quite safe. Airport up ahead, boys. Your friends are there already: we had to wake that little pair of lovebirds up ourselves. Jesus, I'd say they'd have missed the flight quite happily, too, wouldn't you say, Donal?

—Happy as a nest of rabbits, nodded the big constable.

—Sure and why not? Here now, Dr Mac-Donald, you've a new series coming up on the ould telly, I hear. That's great news so it is. And a nice wee coffee-table book to go along with it, they say? Fair play to you: that'll rake it in all right, I'd say, eh? Tell you what, I might be after you for a signed copy when we get to the trial, eh? The kids'd be delighted! Now, let's be getting you safe home, shall we?

Harry said nothing. I knew why. He had come back to the scene of his youthful cop-out, a cop-out that had haunted him for fifteen years, and instead of laying the ghosts to rest, he had woken them up from the cold ground and brought them back to life, not as safe, secure, sentimental memories, but as real, live, danger-ous people. And he'd fucked it up again. And this time, he would not get a second chance. His face made me dizzy: he looked like he was already dead.

Soon, we would be looking down on clouds again.

The Big Four-Oh

A year later, and it was Harry's fortieth Official False Birthday. The big bad 4-O from which there is no return. I mean, fuck, thirty-something is one thing, thirty-nine or thirty-one, at least the first bit is the same, but *forty*? So there we were, in the cab again, steaming through wet, cold London again.

—Fuck, said The Wop, —the thing about thirty-odd was if you meet some creamy bird, say she's twenty-six or whatever, right? Well, thirty-something could still be her big brother. Nice, exciting big brother. But forty is Dad, and no one wants to shag someone who could be their dad unless they are so fucked-up by whatever went on with their actual dad that someone who could be their dad wouldn't want to shag them, innit?

The Wop: what a git.

—And what kind of possible dad wants to shag people who could be his daughters, Wop? demanded Jan.

—A male one, Mate, said The Wop.

—Pathetic, said Jan. —And you don't think we possible mums want to shag young guys with flat chests and little goatees and big, fuck-me-please-Mum eyes? Wrong again, Wop.

She still calls him *Wop*, even though they have been a number ever since Dublin. It's a bit like the way old posh women used to call their husbands by their surnames. In those days, the women got nicknames; and, indeed, The Wop unites his blokeish tendencies and his evolutionary ravings by calling her *Mate*, as if that's her name. Other people have even started to do so too: they get called *Hi Wop, Hiya Mate* most places now. Endearing, in a ghastly sort of way.

Sometimes, I get this hallucinogenic thought they really might end up, her in a shawl and he in a black suit with trousers tied up with string, sitting on their rocking chairs on a little patio in Acton, shelling sunflower seeds and rocking slowly as the meaningless traffic thunders past them to nowhere: Wop and Mate. Not much, perhaps, to show for all their big dreams of changing the world, just fifteen years ago: but what else is anyone supposed to do? If we could stay as strong and filled with hope as we were at twenty-one for just half-a-dozen pathetic little decades, maybe we really could build utopia. But what do we get? We get born into a world with Mick Jagger on the front of the papers and we get bald and old in a world with Mick Jagger still on the front of the papers. And that's our lot. We get tired, give in, lie down. And meanwhile time pelts along. I was alive, just, when Churchill was alive; and Churchill met the last survivor of Waterloo. So I could, in theory, have heard about Waterloo at just one remove. The world turns, and Mick Jagger sings on. You stop at the top of the hill to catch your breath, turn round to see the wonderful, widescreen view for just a sec; and when you set off again, you find your legs have gone. And then the temptation of Normal is hard to resist: what else have we got to hang on to?

They are the perfect couple, though. The Wop simply cannot conceive what it must be like to be able to afford to systematically bring yourself down twenty times a day. That's the way he sees it, the only way he *can* see it. Whereas Jan can clearly never even imagine that anyone who can look at himself in the mirror every few minutes and think *Coo, tasty pecs*, or whatever The Wop thinks, can be anything less than rock-solid in their self. Each thinks that the other must have unlimitable reserves of pure self-confidence. They are, in short, perfectly designed to make each other seem like superpeople to each other, instead of the mere human twats that they (of course) really are. Which is a pretty good definition of love, maybe.

Cynically, of course, you might also say that they were both probably the right age to have a last big go-for-it romance. As I recall, when you are both too young, the grandest, wildest affair is silently under-mined by you both knowing, in your secret heads, that this is, in fact and honest truth, unlikely to be the last time you feel like this; and as I suspect, when you are both too old, the most modest passion may be inflated by you both fearing quietly that it might be.

But who knows? Maybe attraction really is a pleas-antly complex social thing, not just a question of primate gazes and pheromones? Maybe those who meet on Saga holidays truly do not have to blank out the wrinkles and sags because they simply do not see them? Maybe the process by which I for one simply do not fancy eighteen-year-old girls any more goes on and on? Let's hope so: let's hope it is all about something else. Soulmates, for Christ's sake.

After all, everyone (well, everyone except those guys who built the big, first-generation bungalows in Ire-land) knows that a matching pair of, say, stone eagles, is not two stone eagles the same and just turned around. A matching pair is two exact opposites, two stone eagles that could never, ever fill the same space however many ways you spun them, except in some impossible inside-out universe. Matter and anti-matter.

So if you start off with someone thinking how wonderfully like you this new person is, all that can possibly happen as you spend more time with them is that it turns out to be bullshit, because no one is like anyone, full stop. Whereas if you find that among the things that turn you on about someone is just *how* other they are, just how bizarre and incomprehensible their whole world is, well, you are on to a winner, because that is the way it's going to stay. The more you know them the stranger they will be. So the lesson of The Wop and Jan (aka Mate) is this: if you are ever tempted to write *So-and-so seeks similar* in your real or metaphorical Personal Ad, forget it. What you should write is: *Hopelessly fucked-up idiot of type x seeks hopelessly fucked-up idiot of type −x for inexplicable soul-mating.*

Talking of Ireland, that was where we were heading. *We* being me, Jan and The Wop.

Harry lives there now, you see.

I suppose it was for Shnade he did it, in the end.

What happened on that day, on his thirty-ninth False Birthday that long year ago, was this:

As we approached the check-in at the airport, escorted by the blue-eyed sergeant and the bulky constable, Harry was very quiet. For some time now, he had been sucking his cheek like he had a busted molar.

Without any apparent decision, with no display at all, Harry plonked his bags down in the middle of Dublin Airport. He did not do it like someone who is dumping all their useless stuff because they have just realised they are about to annihilate their life; he did it like someone who expects to come back and pick up their valuable bags pretty soon, though maybe not right away.

—Just a sec, said Harry to me.

I watched him go, as I assumed, to the lav. The sergeant hesitated for a moment, and looked at the constable. Harry turned on his heel and looked at us: he was already quite a long way off, and for a second I was back in the airship sheds, watching him walk backwards away from me, a small figure in vast space. I made a meaningless, instinctive move towards him.

Then he ran. Just ran.

Good old Harry, such a twat.

I mean, he could have just called his lawyer. He could have waited till we got back to Britland, called his lawyer and said his piece. But instead, here he was, in Dublin Airport, running up to the armed anti-terror cops like some loony, shouting that he had been placed under undue pressure by the Guards, that he had given false witness, that he had been off his head on charlie and that he claimed the protection of his Holiness the Pope, his honour the Teashock (or however the hell you pronounce it) and Tony fucking Blair. The whole airport turned blearily towards him.

—Fuck! screamed the sergeant as he raced towards Harry; the whole airport jumped.

By now the armed cops had taken Harry powerfully by the arms (having bloody nearly machine-gunned him in their first, hair-trigger surprise).

I started to move towards him. To my shock, my moral shock rather than physical shock, the fat-bastard Guard laid me out with one big whack to the side of the head.

—Major wristjob, moaned The Wop.

—No, said Jan quietly, taking The Wop's hand (as it turned out) definitively, —he's doing it like this because it's the only way Harry can do things. He has

269

to make an idiot of himself because if he thinks about stuff he'll never do it. I saw him do a bungee jump once, and he was just like that. It's what he does best. It's the only bloody thing he does, come to think of it.

So that was that.

Harry retracted his statement. And when the Guards tried to play their tape of us in the back of Shnade's van to prove that Styx had confessed to the crime and had threatened Harry, which they were sure he had, that being what they so much wanted to hear, they found that he had, in fact, done neither. As you may recall.

So Styx walked.

As I had correctly guessed, the Guards made up some reason to involve Harry, tested him, found charlie up his nose and E in his blood, and stitched him up good and proper with the press.

Pathetic, really: Harry had been paid major bucks for three years to hint naughtily about sex and drugs and crime on prime-time telly, but as soon as he actually touched the stuff, he was out on his ear.

I think, and Harry thinks, that maybe they were waiting for him to fuck up anyway, because they immediately drafted in some rent-boy type, a flop-haired clone twat dressed in the usual crap, to present *Among The Dead, Live*. They did so with such indecent speed that they really must have had him up their sleeves (or trouser legs) beforehand. No more pretence: the new Young Presenter just stood there and looked pretty and gabbled and mugged to camera. Harry was philosophical.

—Well, fuck, Ben, there was a market niche and I took it while it was there. I caught the half-hearted tail-end of *The Ascent of Man* and *Life on Earth*, and I made some hay. The twats in combats can have it now. Their world, not mine, I am pleased to say.

Harry's nice liberal university did not, of course, chuck him out just because of this. Perish the thought. They just had a normal Academic Development Board meeting where they stressed through their beards that now Harry was relieved of the pressure of his outside interests, he would naturally be expected to contribute fully to the department's research profile and administrative load in a way which had been generously overlooked in the past. Oh yes, and now that new coffee-table tie-in book he had promised them would not be coming out, and hence not splashing the uni's nice new expensive logo everywhere, and now he could no longer deliver an abnormal amount of nice posh female applicants to the college, he had bloody well better get back to the British Library, book his seat long-term and buckle down to another boring academic book sharpish, or else he could expect by implication the crappiest teaching and the worst admin jobs, in spades, the ex-flash bastard.

—And they said it with no pleasure at all, said Harry.

I wish I had been there when Harry sat quietly for a moment, sucking his cheek, then stood up, laughed, told them that actually he'd fibbed about his age to get their stupid bloody bursary all those years ago, that he'd been lying in one way or another ever since then, and that his one consolation for having wasted fifteen years of his life in lies and evasions was the certainty that every bastard in this room was lying just as much, in one way or another, and would still be lying to themselves and their lovers and their friends when they were lying on their bloody deathbeds. Oh, and that for the avoidance of doubt they could go fuck themselves and their job, starting immediately.

—Great story, Harry, I said. —Is it true?

—Broadly.

—You mean not?

—I mean, Ben, that if it was true it wouldn't be a shagging story, would it?

And look, I'm not saying Sarah left Harry just because he lost his jobs. I told you, I like her. But shit, we are all human, and if you have pretty nearly decided that it is about time to sever ye olde ties anyway, well, it gets rather easier to actually *do* it when your other half suddenly transforms from highly-paid media whore into unemployable twat overnight. It kind of backs up your judgement, if you see what I mean.

In short, Harry MacDonald, twat supreme and God's walking joke on earth, finally blew it bigtime. And now we were all going to see him in Dublin, which is where he now lived, playing music.

Harry had managed to escape from his lawyers with enough dosh for a quite nice little flat nearish the centre, and Styx had set him up with a few gigs and some useful goodwill. None of us had seen him since he left Britland.

—See, said Harry, the last time we met for a drink, in the Museum Tavern (where else?), —I am off into a new bloody life, like it or not, and if I'm going to do that, I have to do it for real. No safety belts. So no offence, boys, but see you next birthday, yeah?

We arrived at Dublin mildly charlied up again (Jan had sorted it this year), but hardly sucking diesel. The conversation in the Museum Tavern, in the cab, on the plane, had been desultory: we had all been in that horrible mode when you are all trying to pretend that you are not waiting for the Main Event. But we made it to the pub where Harry was allegedly to be found without being forced to admit our own superfluity to each other.

We walked into the pub and looked around. It was decorated entirely in Catholic tat from old farmhouses and chapels: sweet madonnas with babies, saints in various stages of torture and agony, nuns in different guises of erotic adoration, plastic candles and holy-water dispensers, improving texts inviting the Sacred Heart or whatever to protect the undersigned members of the O'whatever family. The clientele consisted of a load of German tourists and a fat middle-aged Irishman, his back to me, in a T-shirt, with his hair plastered back in a ghastly ponytail, a big red beard, and love handles clearly bulging out from his jeans. Beside him, an old guitar stood propped up, capo strapped on, primed to play, and a bowrong or whatever the fuck it is called, which had, written on it, the words: *Annraoi Mac Domhnaill*.

—Well, the fat Irishman was saying to the barman, — I don't know if he's big bollix, but he's some kind of bollix all right.

—Too true, said the barman. —Howyes, lads, what can I get you?

—Um, Guinness please. Lager, Wop? What you want, Mate? OK. Um, we're looking for ... Fuck me: Harry!

—Ah well, said Harry later, as we sat around a table by the turf fire, —the thing is, boys, you'd be surprised at how far fat and jolly goes, even these days. And it's so much easier to keep up.

—Well, said Jan, —fat you can do, I can see that. But *jolly*? You?

—Aha, but that's where my plan is working. See, I spent three years of my twenties, when I should have been doing this stuff with Shnade and trusting to love and the future, on my backside, seriously studying, getting fucking ridiculously overeducated and tight-arsed. Too many fucking brain cells created or lit up or whatever. So now, my theory is that it should take about the same amount of serious drinking to shut them up again. And it's working. I am delighted to say that I am already pretty hazy on the differences between Assyrian and Sumerian culture of the fifth millennium BC. Already, I genuinely cannot tell the difference between Mozart and late Haydn. Yes, in a couple of years I should have reached the average knowledge of an intelligent autowhatsit, you know, someone who educated themselves . . .

—Autodidact, I said.

—See, it's working.

—Very good.

—Thanks. An autodidactic small farmer from Sligo, which I might add is actually quite a high level by pig-headed Saxon standards: high enough for any reasonable man.

—What's this Irish shit? asked The Wop, brutally.

—It is, dear Wop, a political decision, like everything else in this big, new, wandering world. Some become bikers, some become Goths, some become clones of LA Yanks, some rediscover their ma's forgotten Jewishness and learn Hebrew, and some ape their social betters all their lives. Some, lest we forget, pump up their bodies. Me, I choose this. I feel it suits me. What else am I supposed to say? Authentic? Of course it's fucking not. What is? You should see my occasional girlfriend, she'll be singing later maybe: German as German, Gretchen by name, speaks better Gaelic than ninety-nine out of a hundred Irishmen, and goes down quicker than the *Titanic* on whoever is the wildest and most Gaelic-seeming man in the pub. Which, I might add, is frequently me.

—Sounds like a fucked-up nightmare.

—Fucked up? Yes, I suppose she is. Compared to a vision of perfect authenticity and self-conviction, I suppose she is. Who isn't? Authentic? Authentic is for failed Jesuits who want to gnaw their own lives away, politicians who want to declare wars, and poets who want grants. Fuck authentic.

—So where's Shnade? I asked.

—Up to her tits in boiling lead, I hope.

—Still love, then.

—Of course. The phrase *eternal love* is utterly fucking thick and redundant, because if it is really *love*, it is always bastard eternal. Shnade is wherever she is. Shnade is not with me, except when I dream. Hard but true. I thought she would be, at first, of course. Like an eejit, I thought the world was still run by some good old boy up in the sky, watching what we do, ticking our work, and arranging the correct and proper payback for all the effort we put in. I have Gretchen instead. Love it may not be, but there we are.

—I'd like to see Shnade.

—You will too, later, I'd say. And Styx. They've found, and I use the word *found* advisedly, this great new madonna somewhere, they're delivering it for Michael.

—They're together again?

—No, fuck. But she's fed up with her van in winter.

—She said.

—Bad timing, really: there's me getting fed up with the quiet life just when Shnade's getting sick of her van. See? Well, it should have been fifteen years ago, and it wasn't so ... Still, you don't need many of those things to fill up your dreams for the duration, do you, and what more can anyone ask? It's a bloody short life, isn't it?

—Too short to waste it on some fucking 'mare-ish act, growled The Wop, genuinely angry.

—Act? laughed Harry.

—All this fucking Catholic jollity stuff.

—In Spanish, I said, —they have no word for *serious* except *depressed*. I mean, it's the same word, *serio*: serious, and depressed.

—Exactly, cried Harry. —Good old Ben! Only teenagers want the truth, Wop. The truth is that as soon as you stop and think about it, on your own, it's all bloody skulls and bones. So I don't think about it. Simple.

—So you're running scared?

—If you define the seeking of human company as running. You poor little Proddie, Wop. I am very rarely alone, yes. But archaeologically speaking, that can scarcely be called unusual: people weren't. Ever, really. We're not made for it. Give me good company: God and the Truth can go fuck themselves. Which, I believe, is more or less a vulgar fucking paraphrase of the philosopher Hume. Damn and bastardry, I still remember that stuff after all: time for another, must be.

—Harry MacDonald cops definitively out, laughed The Wop nastily. —Ne-ews! Then he got up and stalked off to the loo, his jacket bulging with his worked-out shoulders and his righteous scorn.

—What about the book? I asked. —What about archaeology?

—Ah, archaeology! I am more inclined to let the dead rest, these days, Ben. What the fuck difference does it make whether we know what Stonehenge was for or not? Even if we could, which we can't? How the hell is all that knowing going to help us here and now, Ben? On my life. What, fuck, you think if we really found out and pinned it down and knew for sure, it'd help us sort our heads out? Lists, man, nothing but bloody lists. Unless it shows us something that really matters, and changes us. And the only thing I can think of that archaeology shows us is that whatever we build and worship now will one day be a few incomprehensible ruins sticking out of the hills, with sheep and young lovers shagging on top of them. Did you know that as a matter of archaeological fact, we have got through 99.86 per cent of the time since we came down from the trees without anything recognisable as civilisation? See? I still remember those bastard lists.

—So, said Jan, quietly, —you've given up wanting to know? So if this was Nazi Germany and you were a German, you'd just drink up, get fat, and go along with it? Not bother to know?

—Well, it isn't; and they most of them did.

—Not all of them.

—Ah, Jan, have I ever, ever, in all the years we've known each other, pretended to be a hero? Look, I'm not saying that *no one* has the guts or the madness or whatever it is you need if you are going to sit in your dark room and wrestle with God and work it all out. Just not me. And historically speaking, the ones who tried it don't actually have a very good track record. St Paul? Lenin? Luther? Nietzsche? Hitler? God save us from the seekers of sodding salvation. And I'll cover the drinks. Michael: same again over here when you're ready!

—But don't the police, I mean the Guards, hassle you? I asked. Harry looked at me, surprised.

—Of course they do. They'd love to nail me. I do have to be rather circumspect about my class As.

—Christ, you're into that as well? snapped Jan.

I looked at her covertly and realised that all through their years of on-off affairs, Jan had secretly wanted Harry to be better than he was. She was now, at last, truly regretting every time she had shagged him. Hell hath no fury like a person whose expectations of another are not fulfilled. I looked at Harry too, and saw that he knew he was unlikely ever to see her again. Twenty years of circling each other, dead and wasted. He let the knowledge of this hit the water in the bottom of his well. He blinked, and took up his new pint. The Wop returned from his piss, to be greeted by Jan with a look of vast relief, as if she had feared for a moment that Harry was all she had.

—Ah, well. Yes, I am into that too. Ben, I see our bubbles have parted. Look, how shall I put it: to the people I hang out with these days, well, getting hassled by the Guards is just part of the average CV, see? It just shows you're in. Do you know, I think it's that generation thing again: we old seventies lefty Brits still believe, somewhere deep down, in the State. We're still scared of them because we don't really think we can sort it without them. They never really thought like that over here: historically speaking, all law is English law as far as some of them are concerned. So yeah, they hassle me; and no, I don't care. And yeah, I get shitfaced about once every five days on more than just the black stuff. I assure you that as long as you can be certain of having a few quiet pints with a few nice people for the couple of days afterwards, it seems to do no harm. But then, so long as you can be certain of that, what else do you want? Apart from undying love, obviously, which doesn't seem to be on the menu. But there we are: I had my chance, which is about as fair as it gets.

—So this is it, Harry? asked Jan, looking round the bar.

—It's somewhere.

—You happy?

—Well, there's a question. No, fuck, it's the only one that matters. A radiant and permanent sodding happiness? That would be nice. But it looks like I've blown that, so I thought I'd better just disappear for a while and sit down for a bit and work out a few things I actually like doing, and do them more often, with more people, before it's too bloody late. And, well, me, I like getting mildly off my tits and singing four days a week, and seriously off my tits in between. Always have done, always will. So now I sing, and drink, and occasionally go for it somewhat. What else am I supposed to say, Jan? That I expect an angel to come walking in and sort it all out for me at any moment? Do you?

—I expect to look after my kid, snarled Jan, breaking the last taboo, uncovering the one thing none of us had yet dared mention. —Pretty handy for you, this new life.

—If you think avoiding your child is a handy thing.

—Ha fucking ha. Well? So Hannah just doesn't exist for you?

—Vice versa, actually. I think of Hannah every day. And I see her every week.

—What? Where?

—London, of course.

—You never said.

—You never asked.

—You never call, I said. It felt almost like a lover's betrayal.

—Ben, I go there to see Hannah, that's all. In the house I pay for, with the au pair I pay for. And when I do, she seems vaguely to recognise me. Which is no doubt for the best. For her, I mean. Fuck, boys, grow up: do you really think the sight of me, at present, like this, here, is likely to instill in a child a profound sense of the pleasure, wonder and warmth of human existence?

—Too right, said The Wop.

—I usually am, said Harry. —Fuck, if only being right got us anywhere, eh? And well, maybe when Hannah's older, if she ever really needs a dad, which, archaeologically speaking, is open to question, I'll be a bit more sorted.

—More sorted? So this isn't it, Harry? I said. You think one day you'll . . . ?

—Harry, said Michael the barman, —they're here.

We all looked round, out of the window, and saw Styx's van, the white Transit, pulling up. Styx got out, then so did Shnade. Her hair was bright red this time, with little plastic butterflies holding it in a dozen tiny bunches. They both waved at us, as if we were people who they saw every few days or so and were always genuinely glad to see, without us being the kind of friends they would actually go much out of their way to be with. Then they went to the back of the van, pantomiming the fact that they had something worth looking at inside. We proceeded to the door to watch the show.

It was a cheaply beautiful plaster madonna and child, almost as tall as Shnade herself. She hid behind it, grimaced, waved again, and this time held out a little red something in her hand.

—Howyes all? Present, Harry, she said.

Harry hopped across the road to help Styx carry the madonna and take his present.

I watched the three of them across the road. They were joshing about something, I caught the lilt of Irish from all three of them, but not the words. And suddenly it was as if the road was a mile wide, and I was looking through binoculars at them: two guys who had given up on their youth and hopes, and a thirty-something crusty woman who got by in some way or other. Three strange people who lived daily lives of which I knew nothing at all, messing about with a knocked-off piece of cheap carving. They seemed to slow down, to almost freeze.

I thought of them sixteen years ago, in my imaginary Galway again, and wondered what they had been like when they had it all in front of them. I wondered what I had been like then, too. When does it stop all being in front of us, and swing round silently into the rear-view mirror? My own life drifted away from me, like smoke after fireworks. The pint in my hand was cold. I felt like a ghost already.

—Oh, fucking brill, said Harry, and waved the little red something that Shnade had given him. —Look at this, Ben, man, you'll love this one!

Well, I was thinking as I smiled at Harry, *so what? It's going to be a good night after all. A bloody good night, I feel. And what else did we come for? Some revelation? Some big sign in the sky to show us where to go? Good old Harry, such a twat.*

I smiled, and raised my glass; my pint slid down expectantly.

The car hit Harry as he trotted happily across the road, waving his little present at me.

Christ knows how fast the little cunt was going, or what he was on: there was a big crunch and Harry flew clean over the roof of the car. He bounced. We ran. Styx and Shnade dropped the madonna: it shattered into colourful plaster-dust. When we got to Harry he was lying with an expression of enormous, almost comical surprise on his face.

—Fuck, he choked. Then he looked at Shnade, and laughed once, and coughed softly, and died. Just died. We knew he died. You don't have to know; you just *know*.

Funny, Death: one second you are here, part of now, part of tomorrow, as much in the inexplicable mix of things as anyone alive. Then you get hit by some little twat in a Corsa and you are just as dead as some poor Stone Age sod whose little pot of hazelnuts has been lying uneaten by his head for five thousand winters. The moment you step away from under the blue sky and into the big, dark building, you are gone with the Zeppelins.

Meanwhile, although Harry was clearly gone, the thing in ex-Harry's hand was still there. I took it out to look, without thinking why.

It was a cheap plastic red wallet, about the handy size of a credit card. Inside was a seriously bad little print of St Anthony, a tiny circle of white cloth with a dot on it, purporting to be a relic of Padre Pio, and a fold-out card which said, in every language I could think of and several I couldn't: *I am a Catholic, please call a priest.*

At which I thought the only good thing you can ever think about the way a friend dies: *Well, he would have liked that; I hope he had time to know it; I think maybe he did.*

Serious Stuff

And maybe this: that it might teach us something before it is too late.

I think, despite everything, that there might be a logic to it, which always means a potential lesson, though only in the shape of a warning. Our friends' disasters are not signposts for us, of course, only lighthouses: they cannot tell us which way to go, because only we can decide that, free and lost as we are (and as we would want to be if we were not). But they can show us where the rocks are that will rip the guts from our little boat if we keep on the way we are. And what Harry showed me, I mean showed – not told – did, demonstrated, lived, is this: that it is our belief in salvation that fucks us up.

I do not mean *salvation* as in holy clouds and angels. The salvation I mean is sneakier and more cunning, and we believe in it so implicitly that we are not even aware of our blind, ridiculous faith. Our religion is: Life, Liberty and the pursuit of a second chance. We spend our days in mere rehearsal for the time, the great day, when we will iron it all out and start to *really* live. The day when our PEPs mature, our careers pay off and our mortgages are redeemed. The great, bright moment when all our daily evasions, compromises and dissatisfactions will all be rewarded and transfigured.

No wonder we are all so obsessed with surviving a very long time: we need to make sure we have enough time to keep on putting it off.

There is a famous story, sort of a legend, by Kafka,

that I remember from college. We used to argue about it, the way you do when you are nineteen, Harry and The Wop and Jan and me. You may know it. If not, try it: it's the one about the guy who goes to The Door To The Law and expects to just stroll on in, but they won't let him through, so he sits and waits, and at the end, when he's too weak to move, this bastard great scary doorkeeper says: *This door was only meant for you, and so now I'm going to close it.*

Harry always argued that it was all something to do with capitalism and oppression and alienation or whatever (fuck knows what, all that stuff seems so old now it is not even old, just plain forgotten). Jan always said it was something to do with male fantasies about getting through doors, i.e. fannies (ditto). The Wop always said it was about a wristy bloke who didn't have the bottle to make the leap to his destiny (of course).

I never understood it at all. But now, with these forty winters under my widening belt, I think we were all missing the point. The legend starts with the guy already at The Door To The Law, but we never asked *why he came there in the first place.* You see, I think that, like in all the best stories, what really matters happened before the curtain ever went up: the guy was fucked the moment he left his village; the moment his little, normal life suddenly seemed pale and grey compared to the golden lights of his imagined Eden; the moment he longed for salvation.

So I now tell myself, as I stand here alone by my window, with the little hazelnut pot I sneakily lifted from Harry's office standing on the window ledge beside me, that there is no quiet, enduring, timeless, immutable happiness. We long for it, we dream for it, we tell big, tall stories about it, but if it was ever there, well, we lost it when we started thinking, which was a long, long time ago. The only heaven we are going to get is for a few hours, chemically assisted and hard on landing.

The reason I am now here, alone in Peckham, is because of what happened after Harry's funeral.

It was on the third day of Harry's wake in Ireland, and we were all hanging. We were being driven on only by duty, the desire to have a good story to tell in the future, and a losing gambler's unwillingness to walk out into the cold, grey world. Shnade was going out to Styx's back room to score some more charlie on my behalf, when she suddenly stopped for no reason, and looked back at me. We had been on the batter for three days together: us and the world and his wife, without anything of great note passing between us, except maybe a little jangling in the air when I said I was going to stay on after Jan and The Wop went home on day two. And now she looked over her shoulder at me like she had briefly forgotten what I looked like, and just wanted to check up.

Then she frowned, just looked at me carefully, changed direction and went out of the back door, to the car park. I did not need to be told to follow.

I was well behind her: as I walked down the corridor she had already gone out and the door to the car park was shutting. I remember standing in the dark for a tiny second, my heart thumping with the certainty that whatever happened next was going to blow my life apart: that just by following her out, I had given up everything I had for lost. I stopped for a moment and thought of Anna and little Hugh. And then I swallowed, and went out through the door.

I came blinking into the daylight. Across the car park, Shnade was already almost at her van. I thought of Harry in the airship shed. Our two sets of feet scrunched on the gravel, unnaturally loud, out of sync, far apart. She opened the big back doors of her van and sat on the floor, feet dangling. I walked up and sat beside her.

After a while of smoking and doing nothing, we held hands and cried without ever turning to face each other. Then she leaned her head on my shoulder. A shoulder to cry on. I had never thought how literal that was. It made me feel timeless: like ever since our half-chimp ancestors first discovered sadness and loss and yearning, people like us have been crying on the shoulders of people like us, like this, at times like these.

When we kissed, our tears and snot mixed.

Then we clawed desperately at each other: we wrestled ourselves into her van, as if trying to make absolutely sure that each other still existed, and we both came almost before I was inside her. Safe sex? We never even thought about it. It was nothing to do with safety. It was a pure, hard, fuck against Death. We were not people, not individuals, just tiny particles of that impossible thing called Life, helpless, hopeless animals haunted by the monstrous certainty of mortality, doing the only thing we could do, the only thing we can ever do: spitting in the face of eternity, biting and scratching, fucking and crying.

We held each other for a long time. My face was stuck to her shoulder with sweat and snot and tears. But then the miracle happened: as we became ourselves again, I began to stroke her thick, black eyebrows. I stretched the skin gently from the sides of her eyes, and she passed her hand slowly over my unshaved cheeks, and we started to make love, this time for Life. For life: *for living*, and *for ever*. For ever for me, at least, and I knew it then: as I came to come, I felt like my cock was right up inside her head. I held her face as I came inside her, looking into her eyes, and I saw her eyes reflect back at me what I must have been shining into her, or she into me, or both: the burning fire of joy, and the terror of the loss of joy.

I knew right then that, however old we get and however far apart we drift, she will always be beautiful, this beautiful, that beautiful, to me.

Time be fucked.

We lay and smoked cigarettes and talked for a long time then, about little bits and pieces of our past. We talked about lots of things, but not about Harry. It was not that we were avoiding talking about Harry, it was just that Harry did not come up. Harry had gone down. Harry was dead and buried.

—I think I might make a trip to England, she said afterwards, when we were smoking with our feet dangling again, smiling like teenagers.

—Might? I said. —Might, if what?

—If nothing. We use the word differently, Ben. As in I *might* have another pint. Meaning I will, unless anyone objects very strongly.

—I can't think of anyone who would.

—Fine. To be honest, it's tough being a crusty over here: the real tinkers don't like it. The Quinns are giving me a fucking hard time of it the last few weeks.

—Hold on, I said, and went around the building, out of her sight and earshot, and called Anna.

It was the easiest call I ever made because there was no possible choice of words, no possible softening of the truth, no possible way back. No point in lying, even on a mobile. As soon as she answered I just said:

—Listen, Anna, I've just fucked with an Irish girl and I am completely fucked up by her. I'm sorry.

And curiously, her reply was very simple too:

—Right, she said. And then, after a long pause. — Fuck. Well, c'est la vie, I suppose. Better go to my lawyer.

—Yes, I said. —Whatever. I'd like to share looking after Hugh.

—I should bloody hope so. Well, I hope you enjoy it.

I went back and told Shnade I had to go away and would be back in a couple of days. She said she'd probably be around. I went away without saying anything to anyone.

And then I had to do it all. I had to watch Anna cry her eyes out in front of me, not like she was crying for me, or us, but just because of the way things are. She said, through her choking tears:

—All I ever wanted was a little place and a nice guy and a few kids, you know?

And there was nothing I could say, because what else should anyone want? If quiet love is not enough, surely we are fucked beyond saving? But what is *wanting* to do with it?

So I said nothing and did nothing. I just stood there. Then I had to watch her drive away in her Morris Minor, while Hugh watched his Disney video, and then I had to go back in and be with him and play games while she stayed with a friend for a couple of days and I found somewhere else to live. I tried to make it seem like an exciting adventure for Hugh. I read him carefully-chosen kids' books called *Emily Moves House* and stuff, and listened to him explaining that the lion off the *Teletubbies* sometimes tried to eat him when he disappeared and went away into his dreams. I said it was just a cardboard lion with wheels. Not in his dream, he said.

When he was asleep, I walked about my now vaguely hostile ex-home, and wondered why the fuck I had just destroyed my life. I caught myself thinking insanely that I could make it all better again with Anna. As if everything was still repairable if I just made the call; as if I was guaranteed a second chance; as if the world was secretly arranged for my own little personal benefit, and nothing else really counted.

I lay awake in panic, trying to tell myself that it was the comedown and knowing damn well that it was not. It was the terror of emptiness, the horror of the cold truth, the knowledge that you really can fuck it all up beyond repair.

I thought about calling Shnade, but a last vestige of sanity and self-respect (maybe they are the same thing, really?) told me that even if I could physically call her, which I couldn't, because she didn't have a phone, there was no way I could call her.

One evening, I was trying to sort through the pile of clothes that seemed, along with a few, a very few, records and books, to represent the entire sum of archaeological evidence that someone called Ben had ever actually existed on earth. I unrumpled a pair of jeans and, as I held them up, a shower of fine white sand ran down on to the carpet. It must have got there the last time Anna and I had been on a beach, together.

I watched the sand trickle away, and felt ice in my guts. So what was my future? Forty and fucked. What could I do? Go for a small-minded deal with someone vaguely acceptable, a reasonable match? End up as a lonely old man, weighed down with thin, blue carrier bags, staring in disbelief at the impossible smiles of the beautiful young girls on the top shelf?

It was Harry who got me through those nights.

I lay and thought of my dead friend in his tent in Boyle, Co. Roscommon, a lost generation ago, sometime in the last millennium now, packaged archaeologically away with William the Conqueror, sitting alone with his mince and his dread. I talked at night, aged forty, to Harry aged twenty-four:

—You do look better with the hair, Harry, I said.

—So did Rameses the bastard Second, and no one asked him either. What you doing here, old Ben, alive among the bloody dead?

—I'm fucked, Harry.

—Possibly, Bennyboy, quite possibly. Archaeologically speaking, who isn't? There again, and I stress I speak from personal fucking experience, I think Death may be overrated, seen from anything but a simply private perspective. I mean, fuck, think about it, Ben: the Somme and Auschwitz and Hiroshima and Vietnam and . . . and what happens? Does the world stop? Does it fuck. It hardly takes a bastard breather. A quick suck on the orange, a hard word from the coach, and what have we got? Two minutes' silence? Nope. Dull little fucks in combats and daps, surfing and shagging and thinking up new ways to get shitfaced, that's what we got. And fair play to them. Death? Tell us another one.

—Harry?

—Yeah?

—Would you just shut up for two minutes?

—I have limitless time to shut up in, lovelyboy, so you better say something worth shutting up for now.

—I'm in love with Shnade.

—That'll do. Well, fuck me.

—I've left Anna.

—Well, that is the usual and correct consequence of being in love with someone else.

—You reckon she'll still be there? I mean, for me?

—Fuck knows. If she's there she's there and if she's not she's not, it doesn't make a bastard bit of difference, does it? Well? Does she rule the constellations of your dreams, Bennyboy?

—I think so.

—Bad answer.

—Yes.

—Then walk as if she was with you, brother, and see it as if she was there.

—But what if she isn't?

—Then she isn't. But everything else is bollocks and lies. And look what the fuck that got me, Ben: piles, a shite fucking TV show and a bastard early bath. You got to stick it out and go for it, lovelyboy. You'll probably be fucked if you do, but if you don't you'll be fucked anyway. And not bloody probably, but for shagging sure. Logical Ben, remember? Dig in, Bennyboy, take your hits: and when you see the chance, spread the bastard ball wide and fast.

Good old Harry.

After three days, Anna came back and I went. When I left the house, my supposed home, I could carry all my stuff in bin bags again, in a cab, as if I was twenty again. I called Styx Fitzpatrick, who said he had not seen Shnade but could get a message to her.

—And fuck knows what she's planning, but if she goes to fucking Britland she brings Shevaun back here to see me at least once a month or I come over and bring her home. I swear to fuck. So what's the message?

The message was that I would be on that little wrought-iron bridge across the Liffey all afternoon and all evening the next day. I could not think of any other landmark where she could not possibly miss me in some tragic confusion.

I stood on the bridge from one till three, trying to make sure that whenever Shnade turned up she would find me looking confident, calm and profound. By three, I had not only run out of cigarettes: I had also realised, with mounting sweat, that I was going to have to go for a pee soon. Very soon.

Fear struck me. I scanned round and round Dublin, leaping from side to side of the bridge, switching my gaze from left to right bank of the Liffey, straining my eyes, wishing madly for binoculars, trying desperately to assure myself that Shnade was nowhere in sight among the milling crowds of people. Cool no more: the passers-by on the little bridge, almost all of them tourists, by now clearly suspected that I was, in fact, some very minimalist sort of street-theatre actor doing his turn as The Lost Nutter Of The Halfpenny Bridge. Or maybe just a lost nutter, for real. I groaned and gnashed my teeth as I realised that in my idiocy I had deliberately chosen somewhere where it was possible for Shnade to see I was *not* there ages before I could see her. If she had decided, or just happened, to come up the Quays, either way, while I was pissing, she could easily see a me-less bridge and, by the time I returned, she could be already back out of my sight again, for ever.

See? I was not worried any longer about her seeing me, judging me from a safe concealment and deciding not to make herself known. I was too far gone for that. It was just the fragility of the world that terrified me: not the possibility of some deep tragedy, but the threat of an utterly meaningless, purely accidental, farcical disaster.

—Fuck you, Harry, I muttered to myself. —I can't just wait here. It's not cowardice, or fear, or pathetic impatience, it's my fucking bladder. And if she misses me now . . .

—So piss down your leg, laughed Harry.

Then I realised it was me laughing, and that I had quite possibly been speaking out loud to myself.

I ran for the south Quays, for one of the pubs in Temple Bar. It was Beach Party Nite again that evening, I noted. As I pissed, I tried not to think of myself still standing alone on the bridge in three hours' time, while Beach Party Nite kicked in.

I came belting out of the pub again, fingers still struggling with fly-buttons, trying desperately to calculate whether I had been away long enough for Shnade to have, meanwhile, arrived, looked about, and gone. I stormed up to the crest of the bridge, shoving aside tourists, eyes locked on the far side of the river, sweeping.

We ran right into each other. We had to switch our eyes back from infinity to see our faces.

—Shnade!

—Ben, I thought you were fucking running off . . .

—No, fuck, no . . .

—I was watching you, I was just about . . .

—Thank fuck!

—Then you started twitching about and ran off.

—I needed a pee.

—A pee?

—I needed a pee.

—Jesus, and there's me thinking it was the wildness of love.

—It is.

—Stop.

—What?

—So. You sorted?

—Or fucked.

—Depending on what?

—Well. Um. On you.

—That's heavy.

—Right.

—Hey, I said *heavy*, not *bad*. What's so good about lightweight? But salvation is not on offer, Ben.

—I didn't think it was. I just thought maybe you . . .

—But then, she said, as if I had not even spoken, and as if it would be better for me not to say anything more right now, —what kind of Proddie fuck ever thought being alone was good for anyone? I mean, sure, you have to be able to do it now and then, but as a career? Fuck that. So. Where were we?

—In your van.

—Nice one.

—Thank you.

—But don't evade the question again. Ever.

—OK.

—Why you here, Ben?

—Because . . .

—Ben. I advise you seriously to say it with a smile. I laughed.

*

Shnade didn't have any packing to do, because it was all in her van anyway. We drove to Britland next day. We slept the night in a layby near Snowdon, having had a few pints in a pub where everyone spoke Welsh. No wonder the Germans don't stop there: just *too* damn authentic. The wind rocked the van all night long; it was like being in a boat at sea.

But Not Sentimental

Shnade has been with me most of the time, through the winter. Now the spring is here, though, and she is already thinking of her festivals and long visits to Ireland and stuff.

I never want to go to Ireland again, and I have not been to a festival for fifteen years, so I'm not going to start again now. Anyway, it is her thing, not mine, and I know it would be death to us if I tried to do something just because she does it. So she will go away, and I will be left here, alone. Waiting and hoping. Like I said, I was always pretty good at waiting; but I am scared about how I am going to cope with the hoping.

She has been and gone to Ireland a few times already, with Shevaun, to see Styx, and each time so far she has come back. The fact is that whatever she does, I will be here, and she knows it. How the hell could I ever go away? You can't get away from your dreams. I have no bargaining power, no possible negotiating position, no threat. Sometimes, I feel like the straight man in a stand-up routine, or the drummer in a band, you know: the one everyone thinks could be anyone. The lucky fucker who has had an undeserved break and will be forgotten in a day as soon as the lead girl decides to go solo.

But equality be fucked too: since when was love anything to do with equality and deals? A lucky fucker, that's me, that's fine by me. I remember Harry once said that only we modern Western twats thought it was a vague kind of insult to say that someone was just plain lucky. Everyone else in the history of the world, and most people today, would say it was a pretty damn good thing to have said about you.

Quite. Every time we are together, I find myself looking at Shnade and thinking, every few minutes: *Jesus Christ on a bike, I am so fucking lucky.* So fucking lucky it hurts. If she does go away and not come back I will just stop, as in full.

But when she is gone, and while I believe she will come back, I never feel like one of the men who has not had sex for too long, even though I actually have much less sex with Shnade than I used to with Anna.

Maybe it is not sex they are missing in all the pubs in the country; maybe they only think it is.

She's pregnant now. She tells me the baby is certainly mine: like every man in the history of the world, I have to believe her, or not, and so I do. Not that this means anything about whether she would go away or not. Her having my kid, or a kid I choose to assume is mine, is no reason for me to believe that she will not leave me. Kids are nothing to Shnade.

I don't mean that badly. I just mean that as far as Shnade is concerned, kids are things that you kind of lash on to yourself and drag about with you while you keep on doing whatever you were doing anyway. Shnade thinks that anyone who doesn't do something they really, really want to, like go to a festival or dump a man, because of having a kid, is seriously fucked-up and will, one day, load it all back on the poor kid. So getting Shnade knocked up, if indeed it was me, is no security at all. On the contrary, it's going to screw my life up even more, if she stays. I mean, I already have little Hugh to worry about, plus all the complications and minefields now that me and Anna have split, and also Shevaun, Shnade's little girl.

(I am still not exactly sure how it's spelled, *Sceabaughmn* or something for all I know, and nor is Shevaun, because she is eight and cannot read or write at all, having spent her whole life in vans and tents. She is also prone to use the phrase *you fucking bollocks* – well, *ya focking bollix*, she actually says – rather more often than most eight-year-olds of my acquaintance.)

Sometimes, I look at Shevaun and wonder, Dear God, logically, just what the hell will become of her? But then I remember that I know very well what will become of her: nothing will become of her, or of any of us.

See? That sneaky belief again, that false logic. *Become of us?* What? As if we were all, one day, going to add up our lists one more time and suddenly find that all our useless facts and knowledge had miraculously added up to the square root of infinity? That we will, one glorious day, burst out of our tomb-like Executive Units, scatter our white grave-goods to the four winds and emerge from our cocoons of work and debts and lies as new creatures of a strange, bright beauty?

A tad unlikely.

No: here is the real logic, not the ridiculous logic of salvation through mortgages, but the simple logic of reality: Shevaun, like all of us, will have her various fiestas and tragedies, and all we can hope for is that she, and all of us, gets more of the parties than of the grief. And then one day, she too will become nothing, like all of us.

So much for logic.

Meanwhile, she is alive, like the rest of us, and hence something to behold which logic cannot grasp. She is amazing at getting on with people, she is little Hugh's number one heroine and she can just lie down and sleep anywhere, under any circumstances, which is a good preparation for a certain kind of life, just as being computer-literate at four (like Hugh) is a good preparation for another kind of life.

Because the truth is that all that stuff I used to believe about Heroes Of The Modern Age and self-sacrifice of parents is all bollocks. Kids don't need all this. Kids are built to get through anything. *To keep babies warm and dry?* Did I really say that? Dearie me, what a toss. Babies can live for six days under collapsed tower blocks for Christ's sake. Shnade is right. Kids are tough cookies: all this sentimental guff is just excuses for our own control freakery and cowardice and careerism, and one day we will be asking our kids for payback for all our alleged sacrifices.

And guess what they will say?

No, just give them people who are getting on with it.

People. That is what I have more of now. Sometimes too much. Shnade needed to sign on from somewhere and so I took out a huge mortgage (again) on a little house in Peckham, and she signs on as my lodger. And not only her. She persuaded me to redesignate my little living room as a theoretical bedroom and take four other crusties in as sign-on lodgers too. My personal space is more or less non-existent nowadays.

On the other hand, what is personal space except something to rattle about in?

It helps in one way. If I were living alone, I think I would find it far harder to hold my job down (a bizarre phrase, when you think about it. What, like your job might escape if you don't hold it down? Or jump up and bite your face off?). The chaos in my house is so

bad that I find it easy to treat my paid work as some
stupid hobby which I have chosen more or less at
random, in order to get out of the house and spend
some time with vague and undemanding acquaintances
of a similar bent who like putting on stupid uniform-
like clothes to do this hobby in. Like bowling or
something.

In the week, I pick my way through the crusties who
festoon my house; I wash and get into my stupid hobby
get-up (i.e. my suit) and head off through my unknow-
ing estate, feeling like some spy on the world of my
own former normality; then I sit on the train and read
the paper and think: *Tee hee, little do they know I am now
a crusty secret agent and have five of them signing on from
my place and getting your tax money for us, ha ha ha!*

The best thing is that I have no qualms at all about
the thing all my workmates, especially the ones my age,
have very big qualms about, which is: Being Overtaken
By Younger Blokes. Not me.

I no longer envy Youth.

I don't mean I despise youth or anything like that. I
mean I no longer even think about it much, to be
honest. Maybe this is because I have found a sort of
freedom, a weird sort for sure, but a sort of freedom
which stops me envying that alleged Freedom we
associate, as Harry explained way back then in Styx's
pub, with Youth.

Now I am kind of free myself, I look at people
without even thinking about how old they are. Instead,
I think about whether they are nice, interesting people
or not.

And what's so weird about that? Shit, what other
civilisation in the history of the world has ever thought
that people who are young must have anything in

common with each other, and nothing in common with people older than them, just because they are young?

Actually, Young Folk don't think like that anyway, as far as I can see, however much admen try to persuade them to in order to simplify their marketing strategies. I mean, look at my crusties, for example: if half a dozen twenty-year-old crusty women are sitting down in some horrible pub, their dreadlocks hanging into their cider and ash, they won't even notice if a gang of bad-shirted townyboys their own age comes strutting in, bottles of crap beer in hand. But if a forty-year-old crusty they have never seen before comes trundling up, they'll instinctively make room for him at their table and ask what's up in the world of crustydom. To them, what matters is not how *old* you are, but how *crusty* you are. They have even constructed, I have noticed, a certain weird version of Respect for Elders and Tradition, like most civilisations: I have several times watched with disbelief as the young crusties sit on my floor, nodding with dopey attention while the old ones sit on my sofa and relate again the great tales of Crusty History: *Ah, maaaaan, you shoulda been with us at the Poll Tax do, fuck, oh, shit, just to see the Bill get a proper bloody pasting for once, man, ohhh, it was gorgeous, yeah, and the Stonehenge Free Festivals, fuuuuuuck ...*

Amazing. A place for the old, even; a campfire for all.

Some of the crusties who hang about in my place are just gits in rags, sure, in the same way that most of my workmates are just gits in suits. But that is to do with gittery, not with age. Some of the crusties are wise, and it no longer strikes me as at all unusual that someone much younger than me biologically can put me straight. I mean, why not? If some young bloke or girl has been to places I have never even heard of and done stuff I have never even thought of, and experienced things I have never even dreamed of, well, of course they will be much more worldly-wise than me (assuming they have not become a Casualty, that is. It does happen. But then, every way of life has its walking wounded, and many is the neat suit that only just holds together its owner's crumbling life). You can collect your pension knowing nothing worth speaking of, or you can have been in hell and heaven by twenty. Like the man said: *It ain't the age and it ain't the mileage neither, it's the kind of roads you done.* Morally speaking, I would put myself at about twenty-three. A shame this has happened to coincide with a somewhat creaking, forty-year-old bod, but there you are: better late than never. Much.

And morally speaking, my crusties are very traditional folk. I don't mean nicking stuff and fiddling the dole and dealing and crap, I mean *actual* morality: any crusty who tries to two-time another one is going to get told, and pretty damn quick, that if she or he doesn't come clean to him or her, someone else will make the call for them. And not just morally: the men mainly do stuff with tools, decks and oil, and the women mainly do stuff with material, hair and herbs. Yes, of course, you can say that they are all sad fucks who are trying to get off the bus of the future, but on the other hand that is perhaps not a very bad thing to say about someone, compared to what you could say, should you wish, about the mindless fucks who throng the endless out-of-town shopping malls of a weekend.

Strange times, and no guidebook.

In the midst of all this chaos, I am, I confess, generally to be found slightly stoned. I have discovered, to my surprise, that this agrees with me very much. But then why shouldn't it? After all, every lovable Mediterranean peasant has a glass of plonk with his second breakfast, another couple at lunchtime and another couple at dinner, and they live longer than we poor Northern sods despite the ghastly fags they all smoke as well.

Mediterranean, yes, that is what I feel like.

So long as Shnade is here; so long as I believe she will soon come back.

I depend on her entirely. I admit it. Not on her doing anything for me or to me. Just on her being there, just on her demonstrating her own existence. Here is an example of what I mean:

One of my so-called neighbours shopped us all to the social security recently, but luckily for us his wife (for some unknown reason) tipped us off while returning from Tesco. I like to think that her mind was made up by seeing me in my suit trying ineffectually to stop Shevaun peeing in the street, but you never know. So anyway, Shnade organised everything: the four crusties tidied their stuff into rooms and their food into separate shelves and I moved out completely into her van for six weeks, which, according to Shnade, who has quickly made herself into a fine authority on the British social security system, was the time we needed to make sure the Snoopers would have come and gone. There is, after all, no law that says you cannot be the owner of a house and live in a van, and rent the house out to four crusties. Not yet, anyway.

The crusties had a hard time keeping up the pretence of being settled, I think, but for me, those six weeks were about the happiest time of my life. I woke up in Shnade's van each morning, got into my work/hobby gear, went to work on a different tube, train or bus every day, came home, found Shnade, or at least some message from Shnade as to where she would be, went to some pub I had never been to, then went to sleep in her van, with her. I saw more of London in those six weeks than in the rest of my life put together. During this time, I arranged to have Hugh only at weekends, but for whole weekends. Anna did not like it much, but however much she hates Shnade, as well she might, she was not going to take it out on Hugh, and she can see he loves Shnade and her van. And shit, six child-free weekends in a row is six child-free weekends in a row: Anna took advantage of this rare social opportunity to meet and get to know a very nice Dutch lawyer with a kid of his own. She seems happy, which makes me happy too.

But here's the point: the social security did indeed send an investigator, who required me to meet him. I sat in my kitchen, with the crusties tactfully out mending their vans and stuff, and, cup of tea in hand and suit still on body as evidence of working respect-ability, told him that I just wanted to pay off my mortgage ASAP because I had lost everything once already through my divorce and was not convinced I could keep my job for ever, what with economic conditions the way they are and all that.

This had the twin advantages of appealing to his sense of normal human motivation and being true. As I talked to him, I thought of Harry sixteen years ago, in Sligo, convincing the Guards that he was just a scared Brit. Words are strange allies: as I spouted this crap, I started to believe it as well. It really did have the alarming ring of logical truth. I am sure he left me with a picture of a sad and desperate man who was being taken for a ride by lowlife crusties, but was doing no actual wrong.

By the time he left, I wondered if that was what I indeed was. A dark moment.

Then I told Shnade about what I had said and how it had gone down, and she just laughed and said:

—Brilliant! and kissed me, so then I decided I was a brilliant liar who was pulling the wool over the eyes of the forces of the State.

And which was true? Either.

The exact same story can be despair if you are alone in a bedsit and a great laugh if you are in love in a van: the supposed facts of the past rearrange themselves like quick-change artistes, depending on the lighting state of now.

A lucky fucker, me. The only question is how long my luck will last. I hope for ever. And sometimes I dare to think it might be true. The other week, right, Shnade and I were chatting with two of the crusties about Harry, and eternity and suchlike. Shnade said that although she is a girl, and hence will live longer than me, and although I am a few years older than her, her life has seen so much more battering about and general wear and tear than mine that we will probably hit sixty-five about as fucked-up as each other. So then we should become smackheads.

You think she's joking? You think Shnade is an airhead? Nope. Shnade, remember, is a very serious person indeed about things that are serious, it's just that the things she thinks are serious are not those that most people think are serious. Keeping your payments up and your nose clean and your story straight and your eye on the mileometer are not serious things to Shnade. Making sure you don't have a horrible time for the last few years of your life is a different matter. Of course, smack is for the birds right now: who wants to waste their time smacked off their face while the party is still going on? Not me and not Shnade. But but but. When the bod is finally turning back to dust, when it is all getting a bit too much and hurts in places you didn't know you had, what could be more logical than smack? She said we should start freezing the odd gramme seriously when we are about fifty, to make sure we have enough. She proposed we start by chasing it, and only move on to needles when things get very bad. And that we always keep enough handy in case one of us, or preferably both of us simultaneously, decides that today is a good day for the Golden Shot.

I loved that moment. Not because of the smack, you understand, but because, for the very first time, I heard Shnade say something which meant, no, which just kind of quietly implied, that inasmuch as Shnade ever makes any plans at all, she is making them in the vague and general assumption that I will be around.

Which is enough for me, because that is where I will be: around and waiting and hoping. Where the hell else would I go?

Serious, see? Not weighty, not sentimental, but serious as fuck.

She's *Sinead*, actually, of course, by the way. But not to me.

Meanwhile, my life, as you will have gathered, is full of problems. Not troubles, problems. I have things to sort, like anyone else, but these are not Troubles, not things I lose sleep over. Not, in short, the sort of things I used to spend so much time worrying over, all those things which take up so much of our bloody time and are all really only displacement activities for love.

I would not care if I never went shopping again, or if every fucking stupid restaurant in London closed down tomorrow, or if anyone dents my motor, or if my carpets get beer knocked on them, or if I get stuck in a jam. Or if someone puts ash in Harry's old pot of hazelnuts. I mean, so it's five thousand years old. Big deal. Who wants to carbon-date it? Not me. And it is certainly not for sale.

Good old Harry, such a twat.

So anyway, today I am alone in Peckham, waiting and hoping as usual.

Hugh is with Anna, Shnade has taken Shevaun to some festival or other with all the other crusties, and I have got back from work, knackered. I'm seeing Jan and The Wop tomorrow. We don't see each other much at all now: with Harry gone, the ties are fading, and I have great difficulty persuading them that my life is not a wristy nightmare (Wop) or a regular crapfest of self-delusion (Jan). But the difficulty of persuading them is not the thing: the sure indication that one day soon will be the last time we meet is that I don't even want to persuade them.

Why should I? I do not want to persuade anyone about anything. I am the last to argue that my life is some Hippy Heaven. Of course it's fucking not. It's complicated and noisy and hysterical and messy, occasionally downright unhygienic and always just plain bloody knackering. I am tired all the time, to be honest. And maybe I am a deluded toss. Quite possibly. And yes, on nights like these, I look with disbelief around my own house, and my own life, and long for salvation. For absolute order. For crisp linen sheets, fresh towels and the smell of bacon cooking in the bright morning.

And peace. And certainty.

I already know what will happen here tonight, when Shnade is away at her festival, because it has happened

308

before. I shall be standing still here at three in the morning, looking out of my lonely bedroom window like some mad sentry who has been left too long alone out here on night patrol, and has no way of knowing when, if ever, he will be relieved, and by whom, and cannot even remember who sent him out here, and who he is watching out for, and why.

I shall fly in my head over London by night, and see us all, the despairingly lonely and the unfulfilledly hitched, trying to sleep, pretending to each other that we are asleep, haunted by a dream of Eden.

And then, yes, I shall wish, Christ, I know that tonight I shall stand here and ache and wish, wish, wish that Shnade would be here now, and never leave me, and hold me tight for ever in her strong brown arms, as big as she is in my dreams, and take me away from all this mercilessly passing time.

But she will not be here. I shall be alone, and I know that I shall find myself longing to see the Taliban coming backlit over the hill, riding on tanks that shine with the bright certainty of truth, hung about with righteousness and bullets. Some security or other. Something to hold on to. Something to own.

It is starting already: the longing for salvation.

But I have been here before, and now I tell myself: stop. Yes, I am tired and my life is a mess and it's all a bit bloody much really sometimes and it can't go on like this and it will end in tears . . . but then what *can* it go on like, and how else is it supposed to end? It's not like we actually have a choice. I mean, who asked to be born with a dream planted impossibly in their heart? Not me. But that's the way it is, and it will go on the way it is, whether we like it or not, and we will die without getting there, however much we cry at night, because there is nowhere to get to. Like Shnade said on that first night: the balancing from stone to stone is all we have; that, and the people whose hands we are holding.

So maybe the only way to live is to embrace all this mess and chaos now, so that when we get old, as we will, we are so damn knackered, just simply, physically, fucked by living, that all we can think is: *Christ almighty, that was hard bloody work! Any chance of a rest now?* and then let go hands, kiss goodbye and slide gently, gratefully into the fast, dark river. Maybe that really is what we were put here to do: graft hard, occasionally party, and be glad of some quiet at the end of it. Maybe. I don't know. But, like I said, what good was *knowing* ever? I only make guesses.

And my last guess is that we might as well enjoy it for what it is while we can, because it's all we've got and, well, like Harry used to say as his happily, crappily ironic sign-off, as he strolled out of shot and away, merrily tossing the skull of some prehistoric king over his shoulder, you know, the way he used to say that stuff, the way everyone used to love him saying that stuff before that day he learned that irony is balls, your dreams are for keeps, and happiness is serious stuff:

Bye for now, and get one in for me, whatever you're on, because, hey boys, we'll all be dead long enough.